Close to Death

Susan Handley

Published by Sunningdale Books

This book is a work of fiction and any resemblance to actual persons, living or
dead, is purely coincidental.

1.

Sitting at the large island in their expansive kitchen, Karl and Fern Marshall breakfasted together, as they did every day. Karl swiped the screen of his phone, catching up on the news in between bites of toast, while Fern stared at her plate, at the two slices of toast growing cold. They used to talk over breakfast. Not these days. What was there to chat about? She had nothing to say; at least nothing her husband would want to hear. She rose from her stool and carried her plate over to the bin. Karl lowered his phone and looked over; a dark eyebrow hooked enquiringly.

'I'm not hungry,' she said in reply to the unasked question as the untouched toast slid from the plate.

'It won't hurt you to lose a few pounds. That skirt's looking a bit on the tight side.'

She ran a hand across her stomach. Although still an enviable size eight, there was no denying her curves had become curvier of late.

'Shit!' Karl said, glancing at his Omega. 'I'm going to be late.' He pocketed his phone, took a last swig of coffee and rushed out of the room.

Fern walked over to his vacated stool, pushing it under the counter as she reached for his dirty dishes. The cup slipped from her grasp and clattered noisily over the white quartz surface, sending coffee splashing over the floor, where it puddled on the bone-coloured porcelain tiles. She rushed to wipe up the mess, cursing her recent spate of clumsiness. A minute later, she crossed the hallway to the utility room, a soiled cloth balled up in her hands. She gave a start when the door opened unexpectedly and Karl stepped out. Behind him, on the counter a basket of dry washing lay in an untidy jumble.

'Couldn't find my running shorts,' he said, hurrying towards the stairs.

'They're in your drawer. I put them away yesterday,' she called after him.

To the backdrop of footsteps thumping overhead, Fern entered the small room. She pressed the door closed behind her then quickly turned and grabbed her rucksack from its hook on the wall. Setting it down, she reached inside. Her fingers snaked past the familiar forms of the bag's contents; past her purse, a packet of tissues, a balled up waterproof jacket and a lip salve, down to the bottom of the bag and through a small slit in the lining to the phone secreted within. She paused and tilted her head towards the ceiling, listening hard. All was quiet. She pulled the mobile out, checked for messages — there were none — and returned it to its hiding place. By the time Karl returned, ready for his customary goodbye kiss, she was back in the kitchen, sitting languidly at the breakfast bar, hugging a fresh mug of coffee.

2.

DI Alex York was working at his desk when the call came in. The control room supervisor did most of the talking. York listened, making a note of the salient points. Putting the phone down, he rose from his seat and looked through the glass wall of his office out to the maze of desks in the room beyond where the serious crime team were hard at work. He homed in on DC Cat McKenzie's desk. Her chair was empty, though the bag hooked over its back suggested she hadn't gone far. A second later, he spotted her crossing the room, steam rising from the drink in her hand.

She saw him looking. Lifting her mug, she mouthed, 'Want one?'

He shook his head and beckoned for her to join him in his office.

'Take a seat.' He gestured towards the chair on the opposite side of his desk.

'What's up?'

'A case has come in. A missing woman. Possible assault.'

'*Possible* assault?'

'Apparently she phoned her husband, sounding like she was in the throes of a violent assault. He raced home, convinced he was going to find her seriously hurt... or worse, only when he got there, there was no sign of her and no evidence of any disturbance.'

'Sounds interesting. You got the details?'

He passed her a slip of paper.

'Take Darren with you. It'll be a good case for him to cut his teeth on.'

'I don't understand why we're going,' DC Darren Crawley said, gripping the sides of his seat as McKenzie navigated around a tight bend. They were fifteen minutes into the half-hour journey. The town's choked streets had given way to kinked and curved country lanes that unfolded in front of them like a ribbon. 'I mean, there's no evidence of any crime, so why don't we just pass it to the misper unit to deal with, like any other missing persons case?'

'You seem to be forgetting the phone call,' she said.

He offered no further challenge and the rest of the time was spent in silence. Soon, they turned onto a quiet, narrow lane flanked with fields and pockets of woodland. McKenzie scanned the signs hanging from posts that punctuated the verge. Oakdene was the third property along. She slowed the car and turned onto a wide stone-chipped driveway, tyres crunching noisily as they made their way towards a large Georgian-styled property fashioned from brick the colour of honey. A dark blue Range Rover sat in front of a triple bay garage; a high-end sports model, all squat and muscly, with fancy alloys and low-profile tyres.

She brought the car to a stop alongside a marked patrol car. A uniformed officer, a thin, pale-faced man, was pacing nearby, talking on his radio. He ended the call and waited as McKenzie and Crawley climbed out.

After brief introductions, McKenzie let her gaze roam, taking in the house, the garage and the car. Mr and Mrs Marshall were clearly well-off but enough to warrant kidnapping? She nodded in the direction of the house.

'I take it you've checked the place over?'

'Inside and out,' Melrose replied. 'Place is as neat as a pin.'

'Whose is the Range Rover?'

'The husband's. Hers is in the garage. Engine's cold.'

'What about the home phone... is there an answering machine?'

'There is, but there are no messages. We also tried the woman's mobile. It went straight through to voicemail. I left a message.'

'How's Mr Marshall?'

'He's quite agitated. Keeps insisting we do something. But I told him, we can't just organise a search party on the back of a single phone call. I've left my partner in the house with him, making him a cup of tea.'

McKenzie nodded.

'Okay. Well, I think we can take it from here, thanks.'

She started to walk towards the house, then after a few steps, stopped.

'Is that a camera?' she asked the PC, pointing to a white cylinder sticking out from under the eaves.

'Yes. Sorry, I should have said. There's also one on the garage roof and another around the back. We had a quick look at the footage from around the time the attack supposedly took place but there's no sign of anyone arriving or leaving. Wherever Mrs Marshall was when she called her husband, she wasn't here.'

Leaving PC Melrose outside, McKenzie and Crawley headed indoors. Passing through a long hallway they made their way to the kitchen: a large open space that looked more like a laboratory than the heart of the home. White quartz worktops and glossy white cabinetry reflected the light from a constellation of overhead LEDs. A display of black-framed photographs adorned the wall to their left.

In sharp relief to the white surroundings, a dark-haired man wearing a charcoal suit and black roll-neck was standing, staring out of the window, nursing a white coffee cup. He had a classically handsome look about him — strong jaw, straight nose. He looked at them expectantly with dark eyes that peered out under long lashes.

McKenzie acknowledged him with a nod.

'Good afternoon, Mr Marshall. I'm Detective Constable McKenzie and this is Detective Constable Crawley.'

'Finally, someone's taking it seriously.' He started across the floor and handed Crawley a slip of paper. 'My wife's mobile number. You'll need it to find out where she was when she called me.'

Crawley slipped the paper in his pocket.

'We'll get straight on to it sir.'

'All in good time,' McKenzie said, turning to the female PC standing at the central island and said, 'Your partner updated us on our way in, so you're free to head off now.'

'I hope your wife turns up soon, Mr Marshall,' the PC said before leaving.

Marshall turned to McKenzie.

'Don't you need them to help search the area or do house-to-house enquiries? That is what you do when people go missing, isn't it?'

'The first thing we need to do is to make sure we've got all the facts. Why don't you start by telling us what makes you think your wife is in danger?'

'I've already gone through all of that with those other two. We're just wasting time.'

McKenzie maintained a steady stare.

'Okay, fine.' Karl Marshall pushed his fingers through his hair. 'It was just after four. I was chairing a meeting in my office when my mobile rang. I was annoyed with myself at having forgotten to put it on silent — I wasn't expecting any calls — and was about to decline it when I noticed Fern's name on the display. It's not like her to call me at work so, thinking there must be problem, I answered it. There was a...' He cleared his throat. '... a scream. She started screaming. I tried to get her to tell me what was going on, but she just kept screaming.' He put his hands to his face, fingers pinching the bridge of his nose as he slowly shook his head. 'It's like some sort of nightmare.'

'What happened then?' McKenzie asked gently.

He dropped his hands and met her gaze.

'It just went quiet. I drove here as fast as I could. I was sure she'd be here. I don't know where else...' He broke off and cast a look down the long driveway.

McKenzie turned and looked over at the wall of photographs. Most showed their host standing next to an incredibly attractive woman with long, dark, almost black hair. Aged around thirty, she must have been at least ten years younger than her husband.

'What was Fern supposed to be doing today?'

'Catching up on the housework. The same as every Monday.'

McKenzie shelved her surprise. Having taken in the affluent surroundings, she'd assumed the couple would have had a cleaner.

'She doesn't work?' she asked.

'No. She volunteers at a local animal rescue place a couple of days a week but that's all.'

'Could she be visiting friends or family?'

'She has no family. Her parents died in a car crash when she was twenty. Besides, she would have told me if she'd planned on going out.'

'Could she have decided to switch her routines around and gone shopping?'

7

'Like I said, if she was planning on going out, she'd have said something.'

'People do do things on the spur of the moment.'

'Not Fern.'

'When did you last see her?'

'This morning when I left for work about quarter to eight.'

'And how were things between you?'

Marshall looked surprised at the question.

'Fine… Better than fine.'

'No recent arguments?'

'We're not the type to argue. Look, I appreciate these are questions you have to ask, but can't you save them for later and start looking for her while it's still daylight?'

'Where do we look?' McKenzie replied. 'She could be anywhere.'

'Can't you find out from the GPS on her phone?'

'Yeah, we can do that,' Crawley said, nodding. He reached into his pocket for his phone and the missing woman's number.

'Hang on,' McKenzie said, raising a hand. 'I take it you've tried ringing all of your wife's friends and anyone else she sees regularly?'

'I've already told you; she wouldn't have gone anywhere without letting me know.'

'What if one of her friends called with a problem and asked for her help?'

'But what about the phone call… the screaming?' Marshall replied.

'It's not uncommon for people to accidentally call from their mobiles. Are you sure she was screaming and not laughing? Sometimes hysterical laughter can sound similar.'

Marshall shot her a piercing look.

'She was screaming. She sounded terrified.'

'Do you know your wife's security password for her phone?'

'What? No,' Marshall said, seeming confused by the question.

'Then you don't know how secure it is? Most aren't… secure, I mean. 1234 and 0000 are two of the most common passwords. I wonder whether someone has got hold of your wife's phone and played a particularly cruel trick on you.'

'I don't know anyone who would do something that childish. Besides, I know Fern and I know her voice. I'm telling you it was my wife.'

McKenzie gave him a sympathetic smile. Of course he thought it was his wife. He'd had a call from her number and heard a female scream. In the height of what would have been a truly stressful situation he was bound to believe what he perceived to be true.

'Okay, well, I think that's all the questions for now. If you don't mind, I'd like to take a look around.'

'Those other two already did that. She's not here.'

'I'd still like to take a look for myself. It's not a problem, is it?'

'No. I just don't want to waste any more time.'

'We'll be as quick as we can. In the meantime, you can help by calling her friends.'

3.

'What are we looking for?' Crawley asked as they entered the lounge.

McKenzie pulled a pair of latex gloves out of her pocket and snapped them on.

'Anything that jars.'

But the stylish, modern space was immaculate and recently vacuumed, judging by the tram lines visible on the thick-pile carpet. Not so much as a plumped-up cushion or cashmere throw draped over the back of the Italian leather sofa was out of place. The formal dining room, sporting a vast glass table, looked equally pristine. McKenzie trailed a finger over its surface and inspected it for dust. Spotless. A search of the downstairs study, cloakroom and TV room all came up similarly fruitless.

'What's the deal about tracing her phone? Crawley asked, as they made their way upstairs. 'I thought it sounded like a good idea.'

'What if she doesn't want to be found? For all we know, she might be hiding out in a domestic abuse shelter.'

'But what about the phone call?'

'Her way of getting back at him, maybe? It could have been her venting at him or maybe she wanted to embarrass him.' She noticed Crawley screw his nose up. 'All I'm saying is don't take everything at face value. We need to check things out before we declare her disappearance as suspicious and call in the cavalry.' On reaching the landing, she turned and pointed to the room opposite. 'I'll start in there. You take the next one along.'

Stepping into the large double-aspect room it was obvious it was the master suite. An oversized sleigh bed almost filled the far wall. The bed was made and dressed with a collection of scatter cushions and bookended by a pair of bedside tables, either side of which was a closed door. McKenzie walked over and knelt down to look under the bed. Nothing. She dusted the cream carpet fibres off the knees of her black trousers and made for the door in the left-hand corner of the room. She found herself in a large dressing room. Two rows of rails running down one side of the room were filled with clothes, all on identical hangers, all facing the same direction. It looked like something from a photoshoot for a lifestyle magazine. She picked through some of the women's clothing — skirts, dresses, blouses and trousers — all tailored for a tall and slender size eight. On the opposite side, a long run of built-in drawers catered for underwear and sportswear, all of which was neatly folded in short stacks. One drawer contained a handful of tee-shirts and a couple of pairs of jeans, all size eight. The drawer was half-empty. Perhaps the missing woman wasn't a jeans and tee-shirt sort of person. Or perhaps she was and there was a hastily packed case somewhere filled with the rest of her clothes.

She exited the dressing room and walked around the bed and through the other door into a lavishly appointed bathroom. Backlit glass shelves illuminated his and hers electric toothbrushes and an extensive range of men's and women's cosmetics. The surfaces were gleaming; no tell-tale rings of dust here to indicate the odd missing item.

Crawley poked his head around the door.

'You done yet?'

'Nearly. How'd you get on? Any joy?'

'No. The place looks like a show home.'

'There is only the two of them, I suppose.'

Then she thought of her own place. There was only her... and Harvey. Yet you wouldn't find anyone comparing her house to a show home any time soon.

Back in the bedroom, Crawley gestured to a framed photograph on the dressing table that sat under one of two large sash windows.

'Nice car.'

McKenzie walked over and took a closer look. In the shot, Fern Marshall, dressed in a black silk trouser suit, was leaning against the bonnet of a flash sports car looking like a film star.

'Not short of a bob or two, are they?' he said.

Next to the photo, a jewellery box with an intricate design made of mother-of-pearl sat amongst an array of perfumes. She flipped open the lid to reveal an enviable collection of gems. Not short of a bob or two, indeed.

She snapped the lid shut.

'Come on. We're wasting time,' she said, starting for the door.

Marshall was on the phone when they passed on their way to the utility room.

'The washing machine's been run but not emptied,' McKenzie commented as they made their way outside. Standing on the expansive patio, she looked around, then turned to Crawley. 'You take the garage. I'll go check those out,' she said, gesturing to a couple of structures at the bottom of the garden that had caught her eye.

The first was a wooden potting shed. An oiled, rust-free padlock hung open from the lock. She stepped inside and let slip a 'wow' from under her breath. A wall of windows on her right

12

overlooked a well-tended vegetable patch. Underneath was a wide shelf, which ran the full length of the shed. A handmade wooden trug housed a pair of red-handled secateurs and some leather gardening gloves. The opposite wall was home to shelves filled with stacks of plant pots, jars of seeds and nets of bulbs, all neatly labelled. A peg-board held a collection of trowels, forks and other hand tools. Everything was clean and well cared for. As she turned to leave, she noticed a cork noticeboard on the back of the door. On it was a photograph, half-hidden behind a gardening article. McKenzie unpinned it and stared down at Fern Marshall in scruffy jeans and an old jumper, bottle feeding a tiny lamb. Unlike in the posed-for shots in the house, her face radiated happiness; her eyes bright, her smile brighter still. On the reverse, in an untidy scrawl were the words:

Thank you for saving me

McKenzie slipped the photo into her pocket before leaving the shed and moving on to the next structure, a rough weatherboarded shack with a corrugated metal roof. Inside, a large ride-on mower sat surrounded by a jumble of garden furniture. She took a quick look around and after satisfying herself there were no bodies hidden in the corners, she started back up the path towards the house. The light was failing now, the sun having dipped below the tree-line. Ahead, light emanated from the open door on the side of the garage. It was an oak-framed affair with a tall, pitched roof accommodating a second storey. Inside, racks of shelving filled the back wall, containing enough car accessories, household items and sports equipment to open a store with. In the middle of the floor a silver soft-top Jaguar sports car posed like a supermodel. It was the same car as in the photo in the bedroom. McKenzie walked over and opened the driver's door, only moderately surprised to find it unlocked. She leaned in and popped the boot before walking to the back of the car and taking a look inside the small cavity. Not enough room for a set of golf clubs, let alone a dead body. A sound from above caused her to look over to the wooden stairs that ran down the wall by the door. Crawley was making his way down.

'Anything?' she called, slamming the boot shut.

'Nope.' He came over to join her and ran a hand over the gleaming paintwork. 'Now what?'

McKenzie thought through the options. The phone call could have been his wife playing silly buggers, though nothing she'd seen so far suggested she was the type. And while it was possible someone had got hold of her phone and thought it would be a fun prank to play, it didn't explain why Fern Marshall wasn't at home, washing dried, looking forward to dinner with her husband.

'Now we go and see how Mr Marshall's got on with that list.'

Karl Marshall was where they left him. Only he'd dispensed with the mug; instead, he was nursing a glass tumbler. An open bottle of whisky sat at his elbow. He observed them morosely.

'I take it the Jaguar in the garage is your wife's car,' McKenzie said.

'Yes. I bought it for her last birthday.'

'So, if she left here under her own steam, she must have walked. Is there anywhere in walking distance she regularly visits?'

'Not as far as I know. Anyway, she prefers to cycle rather than walk.'

'I didn't see a bike,' McKenzie said. She looked at Crawley, who shook his head. 'Where's the bike normally kept?'

'Just inside the side door to the garage.'

'Well it's not there now.'

Had Fern Marshall been out riding and had some sort of accident and tried to call her husband for help? An image of the missing woman lying injured at the side of the road suddenly accosted her.

Marshall's imagination must have conjured up a more sinister impression, as he said, 'She must have been out on her bike when someone attacked her.'

'Let's not think the worst just yet.' McKenzie gestured to the pad and pen on the counter, next to Marshall's mobile. 'How did you get on with her friends?'

He shunted the pad across the quartz surface. McKenzie picked it up.

'That's it? Three names.'

'They're the only ones I can think of. Fern doesn't go out much.'

McKenzie's gaze returned to the photographs adorning the walls.

'You surprise me. You look like a couple who are used to socialising.'

Marshall pointed to a photo of Fern posing at a busy racecourse. In it she was wearing a teal and purple cocktail dress and an intricate fascinator of peacock feathers that picked up the green of her eyes.

'Ascot, two years ago, in the royal enclosure. My firm had just put a new security system in. The tickets were by way of a thank-you.' He motioned to another picture. This one had both of them in it. He was wearing a black tuxedo and red bow tie. Fern was next to him, a hand draped on his arm, looking stunning in an emerald green silk evening dress and pearl choker. 'That was a VIP party the evening after the men's finals at Wimbledon ...' He took a step over to another picture. 'This one—'

'It's okay. I get the idea,' McKenzie interrupted. 'So, this list…' She flapped the pad in her hand. 'Are any of these close friends of your wife's?'

Marshall lips twisted into a grimace.

'Not particularly.' He pointed to the name at the top of the list. 'Karen's the logistics manager for my company. She and Fern used to hang out when Fern worked there. The next one's her hairdresser and the last one's a neighbour. Fern sometimes walks her dog for her. I've called all three and none of them have any idea where she might be.'

McKenzie felt a pang of pity for the missing woman, until it occurred to her that were she to compile a list of her own friends, it wouldn't be too dissimilar and she was happy enough… wasn't she?

'You mentioned that your wife volunteers somewhere.'

Marshall nodded.

'Freedom Farm. It's an animal rescue place not far from here.'

'Hasn't she any friends there?'

'If she has, she hasn't said anything to me. She mainly goes for the animals.'

Reminded of the photograph she'd found, McKenzie pulled it from her pocket and passed it over.

'Do you know anything about this? Who took it or when?'

'Where did you get this?' He turned it over. Scowling on seeing the message written on the back.

'It was in the potting shed.'

'It'll just be someone at the animal place.' He went to slip the photo in his pocket only McKenzie beckoned to him to hand it back.

'I'd like to keep hold of that if you don't mind. We need a recent photograph.'

'I can get you a better one.' He glanced down and screwed his nose up. 'Fern doesn't usually look this dishevelled.'

'That one's fine.' The missing woman seemed so much more alive in the candid snapshot than in the photos adorning the walls. 'Do you have an address for the animal rescue place?' she asked, dropping the photo into her bag.

'I can't remember the name of the lane but if you turn right at the end of the drive, then take the next right, it's about a mile on. You can't miss it.'

'I take it you've rung to check she's not there?'

Marshall shook his head.

'No.' McKenzie darted him a look and he quickly added, 'There's no point. She only goes on Tuesdays and Thursdays.'

'Couldn't they have called and asked her to swap days?'

'If they had, I would have expected her home by now. And if you haven't noticed, she's not here.' He threw his arms wide and looked from side to side to make the point.

'Mr Marshall, I understand you're upset but there's no need to be antagonistic.'

He set both hands flat on the worktop, displaying a set of perfectly manicured nails, and closed his eyes. A moment later, he looked from detective to detective. 'Look. I can see you're both trying to do your job, and God forbid anyone should say you're anything but thorough, but when the hell are you going to start looking for my wife?'

Crawley tugged up his shirt cuff and glanced down at the oversized diver's watch that dwarfed his wrist. He caught McKenzie's eye and nodded in the direction of the door. She dismissed him with a small shake of the head.

'How long have you been married?' McKenzie asked.

'Three years,' Marshall replied.

'How did you meet?'

17

'Fern came to work for the company. She was temping. Maternity cover for one of our project managers.'

'Were you both single?'

'What?'

'People have affairs.'

He set a hand to his brow and began to rub.

'Yes. We were both single.'

'I have to ask, and I'm sorry if it causes any upset, but has there been anyone else since you've been married... on either side?'

'Absolutely not,' he said, with an accompanying glare. 'Fern is a devoted, loving and loyal wife. And the idea that I would cheat on her is simply preposterous.' For a moment his eyes lost focus, then he gave a short shake of the head, fixed them with a sincere look and said, 'I just couldn't.'

'Okay,' McKenzie said, nodding. 'I know you've given me your wife's mobile number, but we also need details of her service provider, plus the numbers for the landline here and your mobile. I'd like her bank and credit card details as well. We'll check to see if there have been any withdrawals or purchases made since you got that call and get markers put on the accounts to alert us if there's any activity moving forward.'

Marshall opened the pad on the worktop to a clean sheet and started to scribble down numbers.

'She doesn't have any bank cards,' he said without looking up, thereby missing the shocked expression that crossed McKenzie's face. 'And the credit cards are in both our names, so I get notified when there's any spend on them. There's been no action on them today.'

'She doesn't have her own bank or building society accounts?' McKenzie asked.

'She doesn't need to. I let her have whatever she wants, whenever she wants it.'

'Okay,' she said, trying not to judge.

He handed her the sheet with the requested details. She passed it to Crawley while she dug around in her bag for a business card.

'Well, I think we've got enough to be going on with.' She set the card down onto the worktop. 'My details. If you hear from your wife or get an idea of where she might be, please call. We can see ourselves out.'

Crawley felt about in his jacket pockets. Pulling out a card, he pressed it into Marshall's hand. 'Don't worry sir, we'll find your wife.'

'That's it?' Marshall said as the two detectives made for the door.

McKenzie turned and found him looking at them, incredulous.

'We need to go and make some enquiries. If she hasn't turned up by tomorrow, we'll review it then. Oh, I nearly forgot... your security system. I'd like to see the film from today. If you could email it over, I'd appreciate it. We'll be in touch if we get any news.'

4.

Back in the car, McKenzie twisted to reach for her seat belt. Out of the corner of her eye, she glimpsed Karl Marshall watching them from the kitchen window. Shadows played across his face, transforming it into a hollow mask. She turned back to the wheel and started the engine.

As they pulled off the drive, Crawley pointed over his shoulder.

'You're going the wrong way. We came from that direction.'

'We're not going back yet. Freedom Farm's only up the road. Marshall might not think there's any point checking whether she's there or not, but I disagree. She could have been asked to switch her days and just lost track of time.'

'Why don't we phone them?'

'It's literally two minutes up the road.'

Crawley shook his head.

'What's the point? If she was there, how'd you explain the phone call?'

'It's a farm. Maybe it was a pig squealing.' She didn't need Crawley's snort of a laugh to know how ridiculous she sounded.

'You could be right though,' he said, seconds later. 'About her having made the call without realising it. She could have accidentally rolled onto her phone while having a quickie with some other bloke. You get women like that. You know, scream like a banshee.' McKenzie shot him a look, but said nothing. 'I bet she shows up ten minutes before hubbie normally gets home.'

McKenzie glanced at the clock. Not yet six. It was possible. She should have asked Marshall what time he usually got in.

'We'll find out soon enough if you're right.'

A few minutes later they were at Freedom Farm. McKenzie said a silent prayer for her suspension as they bounced along a dirt drive punctuated with potholes the size of elephants' feet. She brought the car to a stop in front of a metal gate that barred entry to the yard beyond and climbed out. They started towards the large farm building ahead, McKenzie marching across the cobbles, while Crawley picked a path through dobs of mud and muck, a dull glow of yellow at its windows guiding them in. McKenzie banged a closed fist on the solid wooden door as Crawley busied himself wiping the soles of his polished leather shoes on the side of the step.

Shortly the door swung open and a woman with grey-streaked blonde hair gathered into a pony tail peered out at them.

'Yes?'

'Police.' McKenzie raised her warrant card.

A flicker of shock crossed the woman's face.

'Has something happened?'

'It's nothing to worry about. Could we come in?'

'Of course.' She stepped back to admit them. 'I'm Celia Heart. I run this place... for my sins.'

She led them along a corridor, its dirt-ingrained walls fashioned from cheap ply tacked to a softwood frame. Bare bulbs, hanging from cracked plastic sockets, cast long shadows, giving the place an eerie glow. The air was ripe with animal musk and ammonia. In contrast, the room she took them to was filled with the pungent scent of curry. She made for a scarred, wooden desk on which sat a Tupperware container, steam rising from its surface.

'Lunch, believe it or not. It's been one of those days.' She snapped the lid closed. 'You're the first folk today not to turn up with some poor animal in tow.' She cleared a couple of chairs, setting the contents on the floor between stacks of animal transit crates and feed sacks. 'Please, take a seat.'

McKenzie eased herself down onto a rickety wooden stool, while Crawley looked disdainfully at the tattered chair nearest to him, its fabric seat pad mottled with a myriad of stains.

He tugged at his jacket and said, 'I'm alright, thanks.'

Heart rolled out an office chair from under the desk, spun it around and sank down. She gave a warm smile.

'So, how can I help?'

'Fern Marshall. I understand she volunteers here,' McKenzie said.

'That's right. Tuesdays and Thursdays.'

'You haven't seen her today then?'

'No but as I said, I wouldn't expect to.' A concerned look flitted across her face. 'Is there a problem?'

'She's not at home and her husband is worried.'

'I'm sorry. I'd like to be able to help but I don't know the first thing about what she does when she's not here.'

'Have you been here all day?'

'Pretty much. Apart from a couple of hours around lunchtime. Though I'm sure if she'd shown up someone would have mentioned it.' She gave a tired laugh. 'In fact, they probably would have strong-armed her into staying and lending a hand.'

'Would it be possible to check?'

'Of course. Kath Winters, the deputy manager, has been here all day. We can go and ask her.'

She led them outside, back across the cobbles to a long stable block. She stopped at the first of six doors.

'She should be in here feeding the lambs with a couple of volunteers.'

'I do love a nice leg of lamb,' Crawley said, with no indication he was being ironic.

Heart shot him a look that could cleave granite.

'We're a no-kill sanctuary,' she said, in a voice that suggested she would happily make an exception for him, causing florid pink spots to bloom on his cheeks. She turned and addressed McKenzie, 'I'll get Kath for you.'

'It's okay. We'll go in. Save disturbing her,' McKenzie said.

'I'll wait here,' Crawley said, scraping his heel on the side of a stone. McKenzie glared at him, causing him to add, 'What? It doesn't take both of us.'

Inside the stall, three people, a woman and two men, were kneeling on a thick carpet of straw. Tiny lambs were clambering over their legs, bleating loudly as they competed to be fed.

'Has anyone seen Fern Marshall today?' Celia Heart asked.

'Fern doesn't do Mondays,' the woman on the floor replied.

One of the others, a young man with a severe expression that matched his square-cut fringe and thick-framed glasses said, 'Miss Winters that's not correct. Mrs Marshall doesn't *usually* do Mondays.' He pushed his spectacles up his thin nose. 'But sometimes she does. At Christmas she came in on Monday because Christmas day was on a Tuesday and Boxing Day was on a Wednesday and—'

'Yes, thank you Oliver,' Heart said, before turning to McKenzie. 'Oliver likes to get the detail right.'

The kneeling woman gently lifted the two lambs she was nursing off her lap and passed her bottles to the other teenager. McKenzie could just make out a rash of acne behind the curtain of thick, black hair that hung down to his shoulders. The two abandoned lambs ran to him, bleating.

'I'm getting too old for this. These hard floors play havoc with my knees,' Kath Winters said, groaning as she clambered to her feet. She came to join the other two women. 'Has something happened?'

'This lady is with the police. Mrs Marshall's husband has reported her as missing,' Heart said.

'Oh dear. I'm sorry, but I don't have the first idea where she might be.'

'Do you know if she's made any particular friends here?'

Winters shook her head and said, 'Fern's pleasant enough but she's not really the making friends sort.'

The long-haired teen mumbled something.

'I'm sorry, did you say something?' McKenzie asked, turning to look at him.

Only the boy didn't answer. He remained looking down at the lambs vying for attention on his lap.

'Danny…' Heart said, taking a step towards him. 'If you've got any idea where Mrs Marshall might be, you need to say.'

Without looking up, Danny shook his head.

Back outside, Heart closed the door. She turned to McKenzie.

'How long has Fern been missing?'

'Her husband last saw her before he left for work this morning.'

A look of surprise flashed across the other woman's face.

'This morning? I just assumed… Couldn't she have gone to visit a friend or something?'

'She hasn't got any,' Crawley said.

'Darren, why don't you go and wait in the car?' McKenzie passed him her keys. As he walked away, she said to Heart, 'What he meant is her husband doesn't have the contact details of many

24

of her friends. When we heard she spent a lot of her spare time here, we thought we'd better drop by.'

'I'm sorry we haven't been able to help.'

'That's okay.' McKenzie took a last look around at the muck-laden ground and the animal enclosures, all grey and drab in the day's fading light. She thought back to all the glamour shots hanging around the Marshalls' home.

'What exactly does Mrs Marshall do when she's here?'

'Whatever's needed. Feeding, mucking out, changing bedding, treating sick animals… any one of a long list of jobs.'

'Doesn't mind getting her hands dirty then?'

'God no. Wouldn't be much use to us around here if that was the case.'

5.

'Someone's in a hurry to get home, 'McKenzie said, noticing Crawley pull his car keys from his pocket as soon as she pulled into the station car park.

'Got a hot date. You can drop me here, thanks,' he said, escaping out of the door before she'd even engaged the handbrake.

A minute later, McKenzie was climbing out of her car, as he raced past in his black BMW sports coupe.

Inside the station, the serious crimes team office was quiet. DI York's glass-walled box was also empty, though the corporate screensaver bouncing around on his screen suggested he was around somewhere. At her own desk, McKenzie dropped off her bag before grabbing a coffee. Settled in her seat, she reached for the phone and started to ring around the county's accident and emergency departments. The good news was that no one matching Fern Marshall's description had been admitted, nor had there been any accidents involving a push bike that day. The bad news was it meant they were still no closer to knowing where the missing woman might be. She turned her computer on and started to trawl social media, hoping for some insight.

Fern Marshall's digital footprint was surprisingly scant. Apart from an old Facebook account that hadn't been updated for a long time, Twitter, Instagram, LinkedIn and every other media platform McKenzie could think of drew a blank. The only recent images she could find of the missing woman had been posted by Karl Marshall, who appeared to use the social media networks extensively. Photos of him accepting trophies and medals from one sport or another sat alongside images of him and Fern living the dream: sunning themselves on the prow of a super yacht; diving in the Maldives; dressed to impress at centre court of Wimbledon at the men's finals.

McKenzie thought about the snapshot in her bag... Fern Marshall in her comfy clothes, cuddling a lamb and radiating happiness.

Who was the real Fern Marshall? The glamorous lady of leisure or the grafter with dirt under her nails? And which one had left the house earlier that day? She couldn't help but think that the answer to that was the key to finding the missing woman. Perhaps the footage from the home security system could help? She logged into her emails. Nothing from Karl Marshall. She looked in her bag for the sheet of paper with his contact details only to remember that Crawley had taken it. He'd also got Mrs Marshall's mobile number, so she couldn't even contact the telecoms company to find out where the phone was at the time Fern had called her husband. She drummed her fingers on the desk. Thwarted at every turn.

'Sorry Darren, date or no date, I need that information,' she muttered, reaching for the phone.

It rang straight through to voicemail. She was in the process of leaving a message, when she heard footsteps ringing out from the direction of the corridor. She twisted in her seat just as York walked in, a takeaway pizza box in one hand, can of Coke in the other. He saw her, gave a wave and ambled over.

'Didn't realise you were coming back in,' he said, setting the pizza box and Coke down and perching on the edge of her desk. 'Help yourself. It's pepperoni but you could always pick the meat off.'

'I'm good thanks.'

'So, what you up to?' he asked, picking up a slice and taking a bite.

'Doing some digging into the missing woman who called her husband screaming.'

'Still no sign of her?'

'Nope.'

'You think something's happened to her?'

'I don't know. They're loaded, but not like millionaires — at least I don't think they are — so kidnapping feels a bit of a stretch. And anyway, if she's been kidnapped, I'd have expected someone to have made contact by now. I suppose it's possible someone snatched her off the street. It does happen, thankfully not often, but if that is the case, it's odd she was able to make that call.'

'She could have hit redial without her attackers realising?'

'True.'

'Maybe she had an accident and managed to phone before passing out.'

'I called all the hospitals. Nobody remotely matching her description has been admitted, though there's always the chance she's lying in a ditch somewhere.'

'But you don't think so?'

'I can't put my finger on why, but no, I don't. She was supposed to be at home all day. The fact she wasn't makes me think there's more to it.'

'Have you tried the women's refuges?'

'I was going to do that in the morning but again, the phone call to her husband makes me think it's unlikely we'll find her in one.'

'I take it you've asked for a trace of where she was when she made the call?'

'I would have done but Darren took her mobile details. He shot off the second we got back. I've tried calling him but he's not answering.'

'Could she just be out with friends, somewhere like Thorpe Park? That might explain the screams.'

'She'd be home by now.'

'Not if she went for a meal afterwards.' He picked up another slice of pizza and paused before taking a bite to ask, 'How's Darren getting on?'

'Okay,' she replied hesitantly. 'Let's just say he won't be winning any prizes for tact anytime soon. Forgets to engage his brain before opening his mouth.'

'He's young. We were all there once.' He clicked open the Coke and swigged straight from the can.

'You know what his theory is?' McKenzie said. 'He reckons she rolled on her phone while having some you-know-what with a bit on the side.'

York gave a lop-sided grin.

'I doubt it'd be the first time. Did anyone apart from the husband hear the screams?'

'Possibly. He was in a meeting at the time.'

'Check. If someone did overhear, they might have picked up on something he missed. Don't forget, his adrenalin would have been on overdrive. The brain can play all sorts of tricks at times like that.'

'Will do.'

York eased himself off the side of her desk and picked up his pizza box and can.

'It sounds like you've done as much as you can for tonight. Why don't you go home and see how the land lies in the morning? You never know — she might have turned up by then.'

Reluctantly she agreed and with the smell of pizza still lingering in the air she packed her bag and headed home. Later, with her own dinner seen to and the dog fed and walked, she moved to the lounge and had just settled in front of the TV when her landline started to ring. Easing Harvey's substantial weight off her lap — her plan to put the British Bulldog on a diet still an idle threat — she grabbed the handset from its base and glanced at the caller ID. It was Phil. She and Phil had been seeing each other, or at least trying to, for almost a year now. The fifty miles between them and the fact they were both detectives married to their jobs made it a hit and miss affair.

'Hi, stranger,' she said, flopping back in the sofa and making herself comfortable.

'Sorry. I know I said I'd call last weekend, but work sort of got in the way.'

'It's alright, I know what it's like. I've only just sat down myself. Thought I'd watch TV for half an hour before bed. So how's it going?'

'Slow. I've been holed up in a disused warehouse in the middle of nowhere on a surveillance job all week.'

'A new case?'

'Sort of. We got word one of the OCGs is expanding. Setting up a new warehouse. Just hope our intel can be trusted. I've been here two nights and so far, nothing. How about you... busy?'

'Quite busy, yeah. Just got a new case, could prove interesting. Though it couldn't be any further removed from staking out an organised crime group. I'm looking for a woman who's gone missing. She'll either turn up wondering what all the fuss has been about and it'll have been a total waste of time, or something terrible has happened to her.'

'I take it something happened to get serious crime involved.'

'Her husband got a call from her mobile this afternoon, she was screaming like her life depended on it. When he got home there was no sign of her or any disturbance.'

'She's probably gone out with some friends and sat on her phone by accident. Noises out of context are easy to mix up.'

'That's what everyone keeps saying. I imagine it'll turn out to be a complete non-event. Anyway, how's Bethany?' Phil's five-year-old daughter was the love of his life.

'She's good. Her first few weeks at school went better than expected. She can't stop talking about all the new friends she's made. I'm going to really miss hearing all about it.'

'What? Why? Don't tell me her mum's being awkward about custody again?'

'No. In fact, Penny's been really good this time. It's this job I'm on, plus the fact the team's a bit light at the moment, which means I'm going to have to do a fair bit of overtime, at least until this undercover op ends. I thought it best if I don't arrange to have Bethany stay over until I know I'm not going to have to let her down.'

'How long's that likely to be for?'

'As long as it takes. Two… three weeks. Four at the outside. That was one of the reasons for phoning. It might be kind of difficult for us to hook up for a while.'

She let her head fall back against the cushion and stifled a sigh. She should have known.

'You want me to cancel the table at Vita's?'

Vita's was her favourite restaurant; an Italian with an impressively large vegetarian menu. The booking, which was in two weeks' time, was made months ago. They'd both promised to make every effort to make it happen after a run of cancellations.

'I was thinking more postpone. Until this job's finished.'

'Fine. I'll call them in the morning. I won't book a new date until I hear from you as to when.' The long pause that followed made her wonder if there was more to it. With most of their relationship having taken place over the phone she'd become adept at knowing when he was not being straight with her. Now was one of those times. 'Unless...?'

There was a pause, then, 'It's not like that. Look, don't cancel just yet. I'll see what I can do.'

They said their goodbyes. She flung the phone down onto the coffee table, climbed out of her seat and trudged into the kitchen, returning a couple of minutes later with a glass of white wine. She turned the sound up on the TV but she was too deep in her own thoughts to concentrate and it simply washed over her. It wasn't the first time she was left wondering what either of them was getting out of the relationship. Not that long ago she'd been set to call time on it. Until someone reminded her if she did, she'd have no one in her life. And what with the hours she gave to the job, it would stay that way for some time to come. And that was back when they actually managed to see each other, albeit infrequently. Nowadays it was all bounced dates, short calls and half-hearted apologies. What was the point? Why didn't she just call him back and end it on her terms?

But she didn't. Because she could remember how good it had been and knew how good it could be again, provided they both wanted it and were prepared to work for it.

She knew she was prepared to try; the question was, was he?

6.

McKenzie sat with the phone to her ear, fingers drumming the desk as the ringtone droned on. At her elbow the directory was open at the page listing women's refuges in Kent. It was 7:50 a.m. Tuesday morning and she had just dialled the first number. She heard the door open and twisted in her seat just as DC Wynchcombe entered. He strode across the room towards his desk, giving a cheery 'Morning.'

She covered the mouthpiece of her phone.

'Hey Spence, don't suppose you saw Darren in the car park?' So far, she'd left Crawley three voicemail messages, two texts and an email.

'No. He's probably still at home nursing a hangover, seeing as they won.'

'Who won?'

'Arsenal. He was at the match last night.'

'I'll kill him,' she said, under her breath. Some hot date.

She shook her head. The ringtone continued to trill in her ear. She ended the call and was about to punch in the next number on the list, when her mobile started to ring.

'DC McKenzie. How can I help?'

'Detective. It's Karl Marshall. I wondered if you had any news?'

33

'No. I'm sorry. Nothing yet. I take it you've still no idea where she might be?'

'No and I've called everyone I can think of. Nobody knows anything. You've got to do something. Please.'

'We're working on it, Mr Marshall. The good news is, as of last night, your wife was not in any of the county's hospitals.'

'What about the phone records? You must know where she was when she called by now?'

McKenzie winced.

'We're still waiting on that information. As soon as I have anything you'll be the first to hear.'

She ended the call and returned to the list of women's refuges. It didn't take long to work her way through them all and after hanging up on the last one, she closed the directory and leaned back in her seat, staring at the ceiling. Nothing. Not a single one of the safe havens had had any contact from anyone matching Fern Marshall's description.

She picked up her mobile and tried Crawley's number… again. Behind her came a familiar ringtone. She looked over her shoulder to see Crawley walk in. He made straight for his desk, openly ignoring the ringing coming from his pocket. He flopped down into his chair and finally reached for his phone, swiping a thumb over the screen, terminating the call, without so much as a glance to see who was calling.

McKenzie marched over.

'That was me you just hung up on. I've been trying to get hold of you all morning. Where the hell have you been?'

He rolled his head and stared up at her with tired eyes.

'I think you'll find I am entitled to a life out of the office.' He yawned and turned to face his computer, hitting the on button.

'Do you want to call Mr Marshall and tell him that?'

'She hasn't turned up then?'

'No. And apart from checking the hospitals and the women's refuges — which drew a blank, by the way — I haven't been able to do anything because you've got all the information. It wouldn't have taken you two minutes to send it over. I left enough messages.'

Crawley reached into his jacket pocket and pulled out the sheets of paper Marshall had given him. He pasted on a tight smile and held them out to her.

'All yours.'

She snatched them from his grasp.

'And the footage from the Marshalls' CCTV. I assume he sent it to you because I haven't got it.'

Crawley turned to his keyboard and jabbed at a few keys, opening up his email account.

'Yep. I'll start on that now.'

And spend the morning staring at the screen and call it work? I don't think so.

'Email it over. You can call the telecoms company. Find out where she was when she made that call.'

'I would but…' He looked at the sheets of paper in her hand.

She threw them down on his desk and started to walk away. Without bothering to turn around, she said over her shoulder, 'And when you've done that, you can get back on to the hospitals and check she didn't turn up overnight.'

With a steaming mug of coffee at her elbow, McKenzie opened the email containing the footage from the Marshalls' security cameras from the previous day. She fast forwarded to just before Marshall said he'd left for work and waited. With the on-screen clock showing a little after 8:15 a.m., the front door opened and Marshall left the house. He walked over to a dark blue Range Rover Evoque with blacked out windows and a private plate — the same car that had been at the house the day before — put a black briefcase and a large sports holdall onto the back seat then drove off. Setting the film to quadruple speed, she settled back in her seat and watched. At just before noon, the front door opened and the figure of a woman flitted across the screen. McKenzie pressed pause and rewound it a couple of minutes before setting it to play at normal speed. Shortly, Fern Marshall came out of the house, walked across the drive and entered the garage by the side door. A minute later, she emerged pushing a sturdy looking bike with purple paintwork and a basket on the front. She was wearing a grey hoodie, black capri pants and dark-coloured Converse on her feet. A small backpack completed the ensemble. She pushed the bike through the gate, then, mounting it in one easy movement, pedalled off up the lane and out of view.

McKenzie set the recording to play again. Fern Marshall certainly didn't look like a woman with any worries. In fact, if she wasn't mistaken, McKenzie thought she could see a small smile playing at her lips. After watching it a second time, she settled back and watched the rest of the afternoon's footage zip past in quadruple time. During the four and a half hours that followed not so much as a neighbour's cat strayed beyond the gate.

She looked over to Crawley, who was busy on the phone. She waited until he hung up, then walked over.

'How are you getting on?'

'Not having much luck.' He looked down at his notes. 'The telecoms company confirmed a call lasting seventeen seconds was made from Mrs Marshall's mobile at 16:05 to her husband's number. They couldn't nail the location down with any accuracy due to the lack of masts in the area. In addition to which, the location services on her phone are disabled so there's no GPS data to go from. Best they could do was triangulate it to an area just over a mile wide not far from the Marshalls' house.' He reclined in his chair and stared up at her. 'In a nutshell, it's no help at all.'

'At least we know she's not at Thorpe Park.'

'What?'

'Nothing. Have you got details of the triangulated area?'

He turned to his computer and called up a map, a portion of which was highlighted yellow. McKenzie leaned forward and started to scrutinise the screen.

'How did you get on?' Crawley asked.

'Mrs Marshall left the house on her bike just after twelve. After that no one else came or went.' She tapped a property within the highlighted area with her pen. 'That's Freedom Farm. Perhaps we should pay them another visit?'

'What for? We already know she didn't go there.'

'Just because the people we spoke to didn't see her doesn't mean no one did. The manager said they'd been rushed off their feet. Maybe someone saw her on her own, recognised an opportunity and took it.'

'Why would she have gone there? They all said she didn't do Mondays.'

'I don't know.'

The image of Fern Marshall leaving the house popped in her mind — she'd hardly looked dressed for an afternoon on the farm. Her gaze drifted across the room. Spotting York sitting in his glass box office, tapping at his keyboard, reminded her of their conversation the previous evening.

'Okay. Forget that. I've got a better idea. We'll drive over to Marshall's office, have a chat to his PA, see what she remembers about the call. And while we're at it, we can see if Fern's friend who works there is available to talk to us. You never know, she might know something she didn't feel comfortable telling Marshall. If we take your car I can call ahead and make the necessary arrangements on the way.'

They'd been on the road fifteen minutes and McKenzie had just hung up, having set up meetings with the two women, when her mobile rang.

'Caitlyn. It's your mother.'

'Mum. I'm working. Can I call you back later?'

'I only called to find out if you're staying for lunch on the twenty-fifth?'

'The twenty-fifth? What day is that?'

'It's a Sunday. The crematorium... you haven't forgotten?'

Shit. She had too. Every year, on the Sunday nearest to the anniversary of her brother Pete's death, her parents went to the crematorium to put flowers by the bench they sponsored. Personally, she'd have preferred to have planted a rose bush in the garden and left it at that, but that was her.

'Caitlyn, are you still there?'

'Sorry. No. I hadn't forgotten. I was just thinking. I'll definitely be able to make the crematorium but I'm not sure about afterwards. It depends what's happening work-wise.'

'Oh...' She could hear the disappointment in her mother's voice. 'But I've already bought you something from the Waitrose vegetarian range.'

'I thought the whole point of calling was to see if I was staying for lunch?'

'I only said that to be polite. Of course, we're expecting you to stay.'

'And you bought it already? It's a few weeks away yet.'

'I put it in the freezer.'

McKenzie rolled her eyes.

'Then it won't matter if I can make it or not, will it?'

'Of course it matters.'

'I'll do what I can.'

She ended the call.

'Someone close?' Crawley asked.

'What?'

'The funeral.'

'Oh, no. There's no funeral. It's the anniversary of my brother's death.'

'Ah, the great Pete McKenzie.'

She cast him a curious look. Was he being sarcastic?

'I didn't realise you knew him.'

'I didn't. My dad did. They worked together for a while.'

Pete joined the force straight from school, as a result, he'd worked with a lot of people. Still, it always came as a surprise when anyone said they'd known him.

'I didn't know your dad is on the force?'

'He isn't. Not any more. He retired a couple of years ago. Made detective sergeant though. Worked in Vice, mainly.'

'Is that the reason you joined... inspired by your old man?' Crawley said nothing as he navigated the car over a couple of busy roundabouts. She went on, 'That happens a lot. I know I wouldn't be in the job if it wasn't for Pete.'

'I'm surprised you wanted to join after what happened to him.'

'What do you mean?'

'Him getting killed.'

'It was a hit and run. It had nothing to do with the job.'

Crawley glanced at her.

'That's not what I heard.'

'What did you hear?'

'Only that he couldn't keep his nose out of things.'

'What sort of things? Do you know something?'

Crawley shook his head and turned his attention back to the road. They didn't speak again for the remainder of the journey.

A little while later, he pulled off the main road onto a wide tree-lined drive that led to a sprawling single-storey building clad in a blue, mirrored material. SoftCommTech Ltd stood out in shining aluminium lettering emblazoned above the front door. Crawley found a vacant visitor's space close to the entrance and the pair climbed out and made their way to a set of wide glass doors. Inside, cream leather sofas lined the pale green walls of the ultra-modern lobby. A smartly dressed woman looked up at them from behind a curved desk fashioned from black granite.

'Can I help you?'

McKenzie flashed her warrant card. 'We're here to see Karen Brodie and Dawn Butler. They should be expecting us.'

The woman's painted lips parted a fraction as surprise registered on her face.

'If you'd like to take a seat. I'll let them know you're here.'

They chose a pair of sofas separated by a smoked glass table. Crawley threw his arm across the back and crossed an ankle over a knee.

'Why do you insist on seeing people face-to-face? You'd save a lot of time talking to them on the phone.'

She was about to explain the gains to be had by observing body language when Crawley looked away, drawn by the sound of heels on the cold stone floor. A slim woman with a sharp bob and even sharper navy suit was heading towards them.

'Karen Brodie,' she said in a faint Scottish burr, extending a hand.

McKenzie jumped up and introduced herself. Brodie clinched her fingers in a tight grip. After Crawley had followed suit, Brodie took them through to her office. She rounded her desk, coming to sit behind it, while McKenzie and Crawley took the chairs opposite. A pair of intelligent eyes peered at them through black-framed glasses.

'I can't believe she's still missing. I was sure someone would have heard from her by now. Though I suppose the phone call does change things, doesn't it?'

'What were your first thoughts, when you heard what had happened?' McKenzie asked.

'I thought she must have rung Karl's number by mistake and that she'd been laughing, or it was some other noise he'd heard. I've done it myself — sat on my phone and accidentally called someone. But this morning, Dawn, Karl's PA, told me she'd heard it and said it was definitely a woman screaming. Knowing that, what else is there to think, other than someone's abducted her?'

'Mr Marshall told us you and Fern were good friends.' Karen Brodie had been at the top of the list.

'We used to be, back in the day. I haven't seen her for nearly a year and it's been at least six months since we last spoke — I called to see if she was interested in going to a get together for a mutual friend's birthday. Unfortunately, she'd got something else on that weekend. We said we'd reschedule, but we never did.'

'All the same, as an old friend you must have some idea of where she might be?'

'I'm sorry but I really don't. I called some of the girls last night. A group of us, including Fern, used to go out… coffees, lunches, drinks after work, that sort of thing. None of them have got any ideas either. You're better off talking to the people she hangs around with now.'

'We would if we knew who they were.'

'Oh.' Surprise alighted on her face. 'I assumed she had a shiny new set of friends to go with the shiny new lifestyle.' Karen Brodie waved a hand. 'Ignore me. I shouldn't have said that. I'm only jealous.'

'Jealous of what?'

'Being a kept lady. Actually, I'm not really — not my cup of tea.'

'But Fern enjoys being a lady of leisure?"

'I assume so.' She let out a sigh. 'I say that, but I don't really know. She used to be one of the girls: up for a laugh and didn't take herself too seriously. The last time I saw her she was dolled up to the nines, hanging off Karl's arm and sipping champagne. I get that it was a corporate function and you'd hardly expect her to be chugging pints, and... well, she said all the right things, but there was something that felt off about it all.'

'In what way?'

'She seemed aloof and distant.' She gave a shrug. 'I don't know if she was because she was unhappy or whether it was because I wasn't part of her new glitzy lifestyle.'

'It sounds like she's changed a lot.'

Brodie's gaze slid from the ergonomically shaped desk made from a pale, plasticky wood to the bland walls where, in the corner, a limp Swiss-cheese plant was leaning towards the window, as if looking to make its escape. She gave a wistful smile.

'I guess we all have to grow up eventually. Hit your thirties and life suddenly gets all serious.'

'How long ago did she leave here?'

'It must be nearly three years now.'

'So not long after she was married then?'

'No. It was quite soon after.'

'And she gave it up to do nothing?'

'She didn't exactly give it up. The job she was doing was deleted. She'd been on a contract providing maternity cover. When the woman who'd had the baby said she wasn't coming back, it was decided to get rid of the post. It all happened quite quickly. I didn't see Fern very often after that and when I did, she seemed reluctant to talk about work. I imagine she didn't want to rub everyone's nose into the fact she didn't need to work any more.'

McKenzie nodded.

'You said a minute ago, you thought her being a bit offish might have been because she was unhappy. Could she be depressed, do you think?'

She shook her head.

'Fern's not the type. Did someone tell you she was?'

'No. It's just something we have to consider in any missing person case.'

'If she was, she'd do something about it.'

Crawley shifted in his seat

'You mean like kill herself?' He turned and looked at McKenzie. 'Perhaps she changed her mind at the last minute and called her husband only it was too late.' He sounded unduly excited by the idea.

'I didn't mean that at all,' Brodie said sharply. 'I meant she'd change whatever was making her unhappy. She's not one for sitting around feeling sorry for herself. Whatever the problem is, she just gets on with it. You know she walked out on a guy she was living with once. It was just before she came to work here. Now, what was his name…?' Brodie steepled her fingers in front of her mouth and stared at the desk.

Whilst the woman opposite dredged her memory, McKenzie was thinking the chances of finding the missing woman unharmed might not be as low as first feared.

After a second, Brodie looked back across at them. 'Simon Parry. I knew I knew it. I used to go to school with someone with the same name. Anyway, Fern found out he was cheating on her. At the time, they were living together *an* she was working for him. He had a business hiring marquees or something like that. The cheating thing upset her so much she just walked out with no place to live, no job, no car, just a suitcase of clothes. And I never heard her moan about it once. She just got on with rebuilding her life. Got herself the job here, bought a car, found a flat and eventually a new man.'

'As in Karl Marshall?' McKenzie asked.

Karen Brodie gave a nod.

'Funny really. When she first came, she was all, "I'm off men for life", and I think she meant it. Ironically, I think that made Karl all the keener. There she was, a real stunner and playing hard to get — he never could resist a challenge. But I think it came at the right time for both of them.'

'Tell me about this other guy,' McKenzie said. 'When she left him, did she tell him she was leaving or did he get home only to find her gone?'

There was a moment's pause, then Brodie said, 'I think he was away on business at the time. I remember Fern saying something about having left him a note listing all his shortcomings. It was the sort of thing you read about in Cosmopolitan. We had quite a laugh about it.'

McKenzie could imagine the caustic words scribed from the pen of a woman scorned. Perhaps this time she'd taken it one step further?

'It sounds like Fern isn't the type to pull any punches. How far do you think she would go? What about playing tricks or jokes?'

Brodie gave her a questioning look.

'You mean the phone call?' McKenzie nodded but Brodie shook her head. 'I don't think so. It's a bit juvenile, isn't it? Fern's older now and they're married. Besides, I can't imagine Karl cheating on her, he dotes on her. More than he did his first wife.'

'He was married before?'

'Yes. Natalie. She looked a lot like Fern. No one saw it coming. One day they're the perfect couple, then next they've split up. I guess it often happens that way. There's a lot you don't see.'

'When was this?'

'A couple of years before Karl and Fern hooked up.'

'And she just disappeared?'

'What? Oh no. Sorry. I didn't mean like that. No. I saw her shortly afterwards. I was visiting a friend in West Sussex and happened to bump into her in Sainsbury's. I didn't get chance to talk to her. She was in a hurry. But she looked well enough.'

7.

'Obvious innit? She's done a runner,' Crawley said as soon as he and McKenzie were on their own. They'd been shown into a small meeting room to wait for Dawn Butler, Karl Marshall's PA.

Crawley walked over to a long cabinet and picked up the flask of fresh coffee. He poured himself a cup, grabbed a couple of chocolate digestives, then headed over to a huddle of low-slung chairs in the corner of the room. By the time McKenzie had helped herself to a drink and joined him, all that was left of the biscuits was crumbs.

She took the seat opposite and asked, 'If that's the case, why did she leave and why make the phone call?'

'Marshall cheated on her and she wanted to get him back.' After a second, he added, 'Though he must be a frigging idiot. She's a real looker... and that bod. I wouldn't chuck her out of bed, that's for sure.' He took a gulp of coffee. 'You know, yesterday, when I said about her rolling on the phone while shagging. I only said it as a bit of a joke, but a good-looking woman like that, it's not that hard to believe.'

McKenzie regarded him.

'Have you ever heard a woman in the throes of an orgasm?'

'Course.' He leaned back in his seat.

'Well if you think the sound could be confused with the screams of a woman being murdered then I reckon you must be doing something wrong.' A flurry of pink blotches blossomed across his face. Realising she'd embarrassed him, she said, 'Sorry. That wasn't very professional of me. But you're right. Not all screams are a result of someone being murdered. Let's see what Marshall's PA says. She was in the room when the call came through. We talk to her and if it sounds like he could have misinterpreted it, then the risk level drops.'

'And we can hand it over to the misper unit and get ourselves a proper case?'

This *is* a proper case, she wanted to say, but still feeling guilty about her previous jibe she decided to cut him some slack.

'Maybe. But I wouldn't get your hopes up. It sounds like from what Karen Brodie was saying, the PA confirms Marshall's version of events.'

Dawn Butler was a formidable woman in her late fifties with wiry, salt and pepper hair in a no-mess short crop. She was wearing a white button-up blouse that was tucked into the waistband of a pair of fawn trousers that strained at the waist. She took a seat, perched on the edge of a chair opposite the two detectives.

'Sorry about the delay,' she said, after the introductions. 'I've been busy rescheduling Mr Marshall's appointments.' After a short pause, she asked, 'Do you think I ought to go over? It must be awful being in that house, on his own, just waiting.'

'Mr Marshall's not in today?'

'No. He's staying at home. In case she shows up.'

'Do you think she will… show up?'

Dawn Butler shook her head.

'That call… You don't scream like that then walk through the door the next day as though nothing has happened.'

'Did you actually hear the screams?'

'Yes. Mr Marshall was chairing a project development meeting when it happened. We had just started when his phone began to ring. He's usually a stickler for everyone switching their phones to silent before we start. When his mobile started to ring, I was expecting him to turn it off, but he saw it was her number and made some joke about it being a domestic emergency — like what to make him for dinner — before answering it. The screaming started straightaway.'

'And when you heard it, what did you think was happening?'

'I don't know. I suppose at first, I thought she must have hurt herself, but then it soon became obvious she was being attacked. It was awful, like something out of a horror movie. It sent a chill down my spine.' She shook her head, as though trying to shake from it her memory. 'Something terrible must have happened to her. People don't make those sorts of noises unless they are in fear for their lives.'

'What changed… to make you think she was being attacked?'

'Gosh. Good question.' Butler's eyes lost focus for a moment, then she said, 'To start with it was just a scream… well, screams, then in between the screams she said "no". That's what made me think someone was attacking her.'

'Just the one no, or did she say it more than once?' McKenzie asked.

'More than once. I think she might have actually said, "no, please"; or maybe "no, please don't".'

'She said please?' Crawley said, casting McKenzie a knowing look.

'As in please don't,' Butler replied. 'I'm sorry, I can't be any more precise. It all happened so fast.'

'That's okay,' McKenzie reassured. 'You're being a great help. It's good that you managed to hear so much.'

'Well it was so loud everyone in the room could hear it.'

'What happened then?'

'Mr Marshall tried to get her to calm down; kept asking what was happening, and then the phone went dead. He told me to call the police, which I did straight away.'

'He asked you to make the call?'

'Yes.'

'Why didn't he do it? Presumably he was standing there with his phone in his hand.'

'Yes, but he was in a hurry to get home to get to his wife. He grabbed his car keys and rushed out.'

'Was there anything about the call that gave the impression Mrs Marshall was at home?'

The PA looked at her as though she ought to know better and said, 'Mrs Marshall is always at home on a Monday. That's the day she does the housework.' She must have clocked the surprise on McKenzie's face, as she said, 'I know all of their routines.'

McKenzie gave a smile and nodded.

'Do you know Mrs Marshall well?'

'Not particularly. Of course, I knew her when she used to work here but she was quite different back then.'

'Different how?'

'More… frivolous. Not elegant and sophisticated as the wife of a senior executive should be.'

'From the photographs at their home, she certainly looks very refined these days.'

'Oh, I know. Mr Marshall often shows me photographs from the different events they go to. He's very proud of her. Rightly so, she always looks so beautiful.'

'Has he talked much about her voluntary work at a local animal sanctuary?'

Dawn Butler leaned forward and said in a conspiratorially hushed tone. 'Yes and he's not happy about it. He's told me a few times he'd prefer it if she gave it up. Ironically, it was his suggestion she volunteer somewhere, but he was thinking more of a position on a board of trustees, not grubbing around with farm animals.' She eased back in her seat. 'To be honest, I'm surprised she's still there, after the trouble earlier in the year. Mr Marshall said he was going to insist she stop going and find something else to do. Something safer. Obviously, she got her own way on that one.'

'What trouble was that?' McKenzie asked.

Dawn Butler frowned.

'The police *were* involved.'

With an overwhelming feeling she was being judged and found lacking, McKenzie said, 'It must have been my day off. Humour me.'

'All I know is that a rather unpleasant man who owns a local abattoir and some of his farmer friends forced their way into the sanctuary looking for some stolen animals. They caused quite a commotion, which is why the police were called. Since it happened, Mr Marshall has definitely been more anxious about Mrs Marshall. He gets very worried about her.'

'Okay. I think that's all the questions covered, unless...' McKenzie looked at Crawley. 'Darren, is there's anything you'd like to ask?'

He shook his head. McKenzie turned back to the PA.

'There is just one more thing. If it's not too much trouble, I'd like to take a look at the room you were in when the call came through.'

McKenzie spotted Crawley roll his eyes. Thankfully, Dawn Butler appeared not to notice. She rose from her seat and led them down a corridor and into a moderately sized office. An impeccably tidy desk sat in the centre of the room; a row of filing cabinets filled the wall behind it. On the desk, next to the computer, was a photograph showing Dawn Butler standing between two young women who bore a striking similarity to her.

'The meeting was in here.' Butler led them across the room to a door in the corner. 'This is Mr Marshall's office.'

A massive boardroom table dominated the large room, while a substantial glass desk resided at the far end, offering extensive views over a neighbouring golf course. McKenzie had long harboured the opinion that you could learn a lot about a person from the spaces they occupied. In here, the carpet was plush, the desk sleek, and the large solid walnut boardroom table with ten leather-upholstered chairs commanded attention. But it was little details that caught her eye: the desk was empty apart from a monitor, keyboard and phone. On the far wall, a bookcase showcased framed photographs and various sporting trophies.

'Very impressive,' she said, gesturing to all of the awards.

Dawn Butler beamed proudly.

'Mr Marshall is a very accomplished sportsman.'

'What about Mrs Marshall?'

'She's a very good tennis player, I believe.' She walked over to the shelves and gestured to a large silver cup. 'They won this at a doubles tournament at their tennis club last year. Mr Marshall's hoping to make it two years in a row.' Her lips twitched. 'At least, he was.'

McKenzie nodded and turned to face the table.

'Where was Mr Marshall when his phone rang?'

Dawn Butler walked over and laid her hands on the back of the chair at the head of the table.

'He was here. I was here…' She indicated an adjacent chair. 'Taking the minutes.'

'And after it rang, did he stay seated?'

'No. He got up and walked towards his desk.'

The distance between the desk and his chair was at least three metres. Had the people at the table been sufficiently close enough to him to be sure of what they had heard?

As though reading her thoughts, Dawn Butler said, 'The screams were so loud he had to pull the phone away from his ear, which meant we could all hear it.'

McKenzie nodded. Out of questions, she thanked the woman for her time and brought their meeting to an end. Shortly, she and Crawley were standing in the car park next to his car. She was on her phone while Crawley was leaning on the bonnet playing games on his mobile, seeming happy enough.

'Dawn Butler was right,' she said, ending the call and rounding the bonnet to the passenger door. 'There was an incident at Freedom Farm earlier this year. Two patrol cars were despatched after a complaint came in that some lambs had been stolen from a local abattoir. The owner of the abattoir accused the sanctuary of taking them. He turned up at the sanctuary mob-handed. The staff there denied it and it all kicked off.'

'When was that?' Crawley asked.

'March.'

He looked across at her.

'That was ages ago. Fern Marshall might not have even been volunteering there then.'

'She must have been. Dawn Butler said Marshall wanted her to stop volunteering because of the trouble.'

'It's still ancient history. You can't really think her going missing has got anything to do with a six-month-old squabble over a few lambs. She's done a bunk. She did it before and now she's done it again. So can we stop pissing around and leave it to the misper team to find her?'

McKenzie fixed him with a steely glare.

'The last time Fern Marshall walked out it was because her boyfriend had cheated on her. She took her things and left a note. This time, there's no evidence her husband has cheated, she's taken nothing, left no note, and then there's the phone call. Whatever you want to believe, this isn't a typical missing person's case. If you want to go to Alex and ask to be put on a different case, you do that, but I'm not giving up until I know exactly where Fern Marshall is.'

Out of the corner of her eye, she saw Crawley shake his head. He climbed into the car and started the engine. McKenzie was still buckling up, when he jammed the car into gear and stamped his foot to the floor. The car took off, tyres squealing.

McKenzie turned and stared out of the window, a resolute set to her jaw.

8.

Back in the office, McKenzie picked up the phone and punched in the number for Freedom Farm. As she waited, she watched Crawley cross the room and slump into an empty chair next to DS Bob Bells' desk. He started to talk, punctuating his words with a succession of rolled eyes and shakes of the head. At one point, he looked over and caught her staring. He glanced away just as Celia Heart came on the line.

'Hello. Ms Heart, it's DC McKenzie. I'm sorry to trouble you again.'

'It's no problem. I take it you still haven't found Fern?'

'Unfortunately, no.'

'Oh dear. How can I help?'

'I understand that earlier this year you had some trouble... somebody accused you of stealing their lambs.'

'Ah, yes, the delightful Mr Skinner, the owner of a local abattoir. Mr Skinner turned up with a handful of lackeys, shouting the odds, accusing us of stealing lambs he claimed were in a holding pen at his slaughterhouse. When I told him we didn't have his lambs he started throwing his weight around, so I rang for you lot.'

'What made Mr Skinner think you'd taken them?'

'Because of what we do and the fact we're against everything he stands for. We've had several run-ins with him over the years.

Some of them instigated by us. Let's just say you won't hear the words best practice and Don Skinner in the same sentence too often.'

'Did it get resolved in the end?'

'Not in a way any civilised person would consider resolved. On the day, the police officers took a look around and confirmed there were no lambs here. You'd think that would be the end of the matter, but no. Skinner is a nasty bastard. Pardon my French. A week after it happened, I arrived one morning and found six of our sheep dumped at the entrance to the drive with their throats cut. The marks on their coats matched those of a flock of about thirty ewes we had in a field next to the road. Obviously, we had no evidence he had anything to do with it, but half a dozen of our sheep against the same number of his lambs, it was hardly going to be anyone else.'

McKenzie frowned and quickly typed something into her computer.

'I can't see anything about dead sheep on our system.'

'I didn't report it. What was the point? He'd have only done something else. I just wanted an end to it.'

Lamentably it was a common enough reaction.

'Was Fern around when all this happened?'

'Err… Oh, yes! When Skinner and his goons first showed up, I tried reasoning with them to no effect. They were determined to cause trouble. They pushed through the gate and started towards the main building. Fern was bloody marvellous, quite a force to be reckoned with. She stopped Skinner in his tracks and told him he'd be charged with trespass if he and his cronies didn't leave. They didn't, but they did stop to argue the toss long enough for us to have time to call the police.' She paused, then said, 'You don't think that's got anything to do with Fern disappearing, do you… surely not over a few stolen lambs?'

55

McKenzie didn't reply at first. She was thinking about the young lambs in the stable being bottle-fed the previous evening. What if something similar had happened recently, only instead of causing an affray, the slaughterman and his lackeys decided to ramp up the stakes?

'Those lambs I saw, yesterday,' McKenzie said. 'Where did they come from?' An uncomfortable silence filled the air. 'Ms Heart?'

'I don't know, is the truth. Someone left them tethered to the gate at the end of last week. Nobody saw who did it. But that's not that uncommon for a rescue centre. People leave all manner of waifs and strays at our door.'

'Who found them?'

Another pause. Another deep breath. 'Fern. Fern found them when she arrived on Thursday morning.'

***

'It seems a bit extreme,' DI York said five minutes later, after McKenzie filled him in. 'Abducting a woman for the sake of a few lambs.'

Crawley nodded keenly. He'd joined the pair within seconds of McKenzie having walked into York's office.

'They retaliated by killing six sheep before,' she replied. 'What if they were planning on doing something similar only Fern happened to be in the wrong place at the wrong time? She could have been out on her bike on Monday and was passing Freedom Farm and saw something going down and interrupted them. We know she tackled the abattoir owner before.'

'In broad daylight?' Crawley said. He shook his head, 'I don't buy it.'

'I agree it sounds a bit out there, but I've got a bad feeling about this one,' she said. 'I'd like to carry on with the investigation. At least until we run out of leads.'

York rubbed his chin. The seconds ticked by. Eventually, he said, 'I'll give you to the end of the week. If you haven't got anything more substantial by then, you'll have to hand it over to the misper unit. I can't afford to have two detectives working a missing person case that's going nowhere.'

'Sir,' Crawley said. 'Maybe Cat could work it on her own. That way you won't be losing two detectives.'

McKenzie shrugged, more than happy to go it alone.

'I appreciate the offer, Darren,' York said, 'but the two of you should be able to cover a lot more ground in a shorter space of time, so stick with it for now.' Crawley nodded, a miserable expression on his face. York transferred his gaze to McKenzie. 'And Cat... you've only got a few more days. Make them count.'

'Right, first thing we need to do is go knock on a few doors,' McKenzie said to Crawley as they crossed the room to their desks. 'See if we can find anyone who saw Mrs Marshall after she left the house.'

'House to house? Forget it. I didn't become a detective to do a uniform's job,' Crawley said before stalking off.

'Darren!'

He ignored her and kept walking, past his own desk, returning to the empty chair by DS Bells.

Ignoring the impulse to go and tell him exactly what she thought of grown adults acting like sulky children, McKenzie returned to her own workstation and pulled up a map of the area surrounding the Marshalls' home. A scattering of houses peppered the network of lanes; not too many, provided they shared it between them. She printed a couple of copies of the map, highlighted half the houses on one sheet, the second half on the other, then went to get Crawley. Only Crawley was nowhere to be seen. Nor was DS Bells.

'Spence, any idea where Darren is?'

'With Bob in Alex's office,' he said without looking up.

She stood up and approached York's glass-walled box. The door was open but she knocked all the same.

'Cat, come in.' York beckoned her over. She took a couple of steps forward, but remained in the doorway. York turned to Bells, 'You were saying, Bob?'

'Just that me and Sanj are struggling to make any ground on those two rapes. An extra pair of hands would really help.' McKenzie noticed Crawley dart a smug grin in her direction. Bells went on, 'I want to do a canvass of the area, see if anyone has been the victim of an attempted attack and not reported it. If we've got a serial rapist on our patch, we need to nail them as soon as possible. In which case, does it make sense to have two of the team out looking for some posh bird who's left her husband? I just wondered if that was a good use of resources. Sir.'

'We don't know that she's left him,' McKenzie jumped in. 'In fact, it's looking less likely by the hour.' She turned to York. 'You're not going to let him walk away from a case just because it's not exciting enough?'

York turned to look at Crawley, fixing him with an impenetrable stare.

'You keep saying she's run off... what evidence have you got?'

'She did it before. It's history repeating itself.'

'She was a lot younger then and the guy she was living with was cheating on her,' McKenzie hit back.

'You don't know that her husband isn't cheating on her this time,' Crawley parried.

'Exactly,' York said, causing a look of satisfaction to curl on Crawley's lips, though it wasn't there long when York continued,

'We don't know. Which is why, before we go making any decisions on how to proceed, you need to get out there and find some evidence. Discussion over.' He gestured to the door. Bells and Crawley stood up and started towards the door. 'Oh, and Darren...' Crawley paused and turned to look back at York. 'Stop pissing around. Pull your finger out and get some answers. That's how you'll get yourself allocated a new case.'

McKenzie stepped out first, Crawley followed. He glowered at her, lips pursed, eyes narrowed. Bells pulled the door closed and clapped Crawley on the shoulder.

'Never mind, lad. It was worth a try.'

'The car. Five minutes,' McKenzie said over her shoulder as she walked away.

Forty minutes later they pulled up outside the Marshalls' home for a second time. Karl Marshall met them at the door, radiating hope like a child awaiting news on a lost kitten. McKenzie shook her head and a haunted look descended on his face. Indoors, he led them through to the lounge, where he slumped down onto the modish, grey leather L-shaped sofa sited in front of an over-sized TV mounted above a generous open fireplace.

'So...?' He looked from one detective to the other.

'We're following a number of lines of enquiry and hope to get a lead on your wife's situation soon.' McKenzie said.

'Situation? You say it like she's just popped out to the shops. There is no situation. Someone has taken my wife and done God knows what to her. Why are you even here? Why aren't you out there, getting a search party organised? Better still, get some sniffer dogs,' he said, brow knotted angrily.

She kept her face devoid of emotion and her voice calm.

'We're not quite at that stage yet, though we will be looking around the area, as soon as we finish here.' She didn't think it a good idea to let him know it was only going to be her and

59

Crawley. Deftly changing the subject, she said, 'Earlier in the year there was some trouble over at Freedom Farm — they'd been accused of stealing some lambs. Your wife was there when it happened.' Marshall nodded. 'Did she say much about it?'

'Actually, it was one of the few times we argued.'

'Oh?'

'I asked her to stop volunteering there and find something else to do, somewhere run by people who don't try to turn everyone into animal rights activists.'

'Is that what your wife has become… an animal rights activist?'

'No. Fern is far too sensible for that. Doesn't stop them trying though, does it? Look, what has this got to do with her disappearance?'

'Maybe nothing. We're just considering every possibility.'

'Did your wife ever say anything about feeling as though she was being watched?' Crawley asked.

McKenzie shot him a perplexed look. Where the hell had that come from?

'You mean like a stalker?' Marshall replied.

'Not necessarily. It's just that if someone did intend to do her harm, they might have spent some time familiarising themselves with her routine.'

Marshall shook his head.

'She never mentioned anything.'

'There's a good chance she wouldn't have noticed,' Crawley said. He turned to McKenzie. 'I think we need to take a look at the footage from the security system going back a few weeks. If somebody was watching her, it's possible the camera caught them. It could be a critical lead. So critical, I think I really should do it next.'

McKenzie clamped her jaw, biting back her irritation. They'd already got their morning mapped out, but if Darren was so determined to avoid having to knock on doors, she knew he'd only do a crap job of it. For once she wished Bob Bells had got what he'd asked for. The pair of them deserved one another.

She looked at Marshall.

'Is that okay with you?'

He looked at her, then at Crawley, and after a moment's pause, said, 'Whatever you think will help.'

9.

While Karl Marshall was showing Crawley to his study-cum-den and giving him access to the couple's home security system, McKenzie was heading down the lane in the direction Fern Marshall was last seen cycling away in, praying she wasn't wasting her time. Prayers that she quickly felt must have fallen on deaf ears after the first two houses she visited proved fruitless, as although both sets of neighbours had been at home on Monday, neither had seen the missing woman that day. She continued down the lane, and turned left. The next three properties were equally unrewarding. With no one at home, they would all require a return visit. According to the map, another turning, this time right, some half a mile on, led to another lane that looped around and joined back onto the same road a mile later. She took the turning and soon came across the next property.

The ramshackle farmhouse sat behind a broken picket fence, like an unloved child left to wallow in its playpen. Encouraged by the sight of an old, white Escort van on a driveway comprising a patch of gravel containing a collection of weeds, McKenzie walked through the gap in the fence where a gate might once have been and approached the front door. She gave an emphatic knock. Inside a dog began to bark. She waited, listening for the sound of footfall or the click of a lock. After a minute, she was still waiting.

The house was silent; even the barking had tailed off. She knocked again, setting the dog off for a second time, then walked over to the window, cupped her hands around her face and peered in, trying to see beyond a set of grubby lace curtains. Sensing a shadow of movement at the back of the room, she tapped on the glass and called, 'Hello… Police. Anyone home?'

Nothing.

Maybe it had been the dog she'd seen? Though even that had grown quiet.

***

Robbie Skinner shifted uncomfortably. His back ached and his legs felt cramped having sat on the hard wooden floor for so long. Funny how he'd never had that problem before, all the hours he'd spent there, though then he'd had other things on his mind. His stomach rumbled loudly, breakfast a distant memory. He stood up and walked over to the paneless window and looked out, but the leaves of the great oak, though a rich coffee-bean brown, were hanging on doggedly, blocking the view of the road beyond. Back in the house the dog started to bark. Robbie turned his head and listened. The dog quietened. He was about to sit back down when he heard a knocking. He started towards the square hole in the tree-house's floor and dropped through, legs clutching the sides of the ladder as he rode it down to the ground below before sprinting back to the house. The knocking had set the dog off again. Robbie entered through the back door.

'Shane!' he called in a whisper. The dog came running, turning circles, tail wagging enthusiastically. A knock at the window made him jump. He pulled the dog into the kitchen and pulled the door to. 'Good boy. Stay!' Robbie slipped back around the door and, keeping close to the wall, walked slowly over to the window and peered through a tiny gap in the lace. A tall, slim woman, with long dark hair was walking back down the path. She was half-way down when she stopped and turned. For a moment it was as though she was looking straight at him, but Robbie held his nerve and his position, hidden behind the net curtain.

The woman started back towards the road and climbed into a white Skoda. A minute later she was gone.

***

McKenzie started down the path. The dog's silence bothered her. She turned and looked back at the house. Instinct told her someone was there, but there was nothing she could do about it. Not everyone was prepared to answer the door to strangers. After a moment, she gave up and started for the car. Another one to try again later. Maybe she'd get Crawley to do the second visits when he'd finished at the Marshalls' place.

The next property, a little further along the lane and on the opposite side, was a small bungalow, plain but tidily kept. An old man in an olive cable-knit cardigan answered the door. He was bent over a walking frame, his hands resting heavily on its plastic grips; his knuckles, inflamed and misshapen with arthritis, looked like livid bee stings. A pair of rheumy eyes regarded her as she explained the reason for her visit.

He shook his head. 'I'm very sorry. I wish I could help but I don't get out much these days, apart from the odd trip to the hospital.'

'Do you live alone, Mr...?'

'Tomkinson. Yes. Laura, my wife, passed almost five years ago. I have a couple of smashing girls from the care agency come, help me dress and get me my meals.'

'What times do they normally visit?'

'They start ever so early. They're here at six in the morning, then they're back at four to do my tea and then at nine. When they first started coming, I used to think nine o'clock was far too early to go to bed.' He leaned in conspiratorially. 'To be honest, I'd struggle to stay awake much later than that these days.'

McKenzie reciprocated with a kindly smile.

'No one comes to help with lunch?'

'No need. They make me a sandwich in the morning and leave it in the fridge. I can get around on my own. I'm just a bit slow is all.'

'It sounds as though you're coping admirably.'

'I have the girls to thank for that. Their visits cheer me up no end.'

'I bet. Is it possible to get the details of the care agency?'

After thanking the old man for his time, she called the agency and asked for the contact details of the carer assigned Mr Tomkinson's Monday teatime visit, before continuing on to the next house. This one was situated right at the end of the lane, at the junction with the road that looped back around to where McKenzie started. The pretty cottage had white weatherboarding and a red tile roof and was nestled in the bosom of the two lanes. There was a small five-year-old red Nissan on the driveway, which McKenzie hoped meant someone was at home. She pulled up in front of a wooden gate and climbed out. As she reached for the latch, a trio of terriers rushed towards her in a crescendo of yapping. She snatched her hand back as they jumped up to greet her.

'You're alright. They won't bite,' a woman called over from the path at the side of the house. Early sixties, tall and slim, she wore her henna-dyed hair in a neat pixie cut. 'They might lick you to death though,' she said, half laughing.

McKenzie slipped around the side of the gate, making sure the dogs didn't escape. She needn't have worried, as they were far too interested in her trouser legs to make a run for it.

The woman slapped the side of her thigh, calling to the dogs.

'It's okay. They can probably smell my dog,' McKenzie said, bending down and giving them some fuss.

The woman approached, wiping her hands on a towel.

'Do you need help with directions?'

'Detective Constable McKenzie.' She flashed her warrant card. 'I'm making enquiries about a woman who has gone missing. Does anyone else live at this address, Mrs...?'

'Forker. Bridget Forker. No. I lost my husband a couple of years ago and my daughter and son-in-law live over in Australia. They come back when they can, only... well, it's such a long way, isn't it?'

'It must be difficult.'

'I've got the dogs at least.'

McKenzie reached into her bag and pulled out the photograph. She handed it over.

'This is the woman; name of Fern Marshall.'

Mrs Forker looked down at the picture. Straightaway McKenzie noticed a flicker of recognition in her eyes.

'I saw her yesterday when I took the dogs out. She passed me on her bike about half a mile down the lane.' She pointed down the road, in the same direction that McKenzie was travelling in.

'Can you remember what time it was?'

'Let me think...' Mrs Forker stared into the distance. 'It would have been about ten-past twelve. I had a Tesco delivery booked between eleven and twelve and they came right at the end of the slot. I went out as soon as they'd gone. I often see her out. I usually leave just before twelve and am normally at the top of the road when our paths cross, but yesterday she was almost at the gate.'

'The gate?' McKenzie asked.

'It leads to the garden of one of the properties on that lane there.' She gestured to the road McKenzie had just driven down. 'The road loops around. The house has a plot that runs all the way back to join this road here,' she said, indicating the lane they were on now. Mrs Forker looked back down at the photograph; a frown crimped her brow. 'It might be nothing, but sometimes I've noticed her bike parked next to the gate, hidden behind a large holly bush. I say her bike, it might not be. I've never seen her getting on or off it, it's only that it looks similar — same sort of colour and with a carrier-box on the front. I've often wondered where she goes when she leaves it there. It's not like there's anything nearby. There aren't even any footpaths.'

'Is she usually alone?'

'Always. Though I suppose she might leave the bike there and go off with someone. Actually, yesterday there was a van parked on the verge, not far from the gate.'

'Was anyone in it?'

'No. I thought perhaps the driver had pulled over for a call of nature.'

'Can you describe the van?'

'White. Smallish. I haven't got a clue what type. I've never been any good with cars. They all look the same to me. But it was quite old. You don't see many around these days.'

'Was it boxy with a stubby front, or did it look more like a normal car, sort of like an estate but with the back panels blanked out?'

'More like a car. It wasn't like the ones you see delivery drivers belting up and down in.'

McKenzie thought about the van parked on the drive at the farmhouse she'd just been to. If that was the property the gate led to, it could have been the same van.

'Was it like the old Ford Escort vans?'

Mrs Forker shrugged.

'I really don't know. Sorry.'

'And you've never seen it parked there before?'

'Well, I couldn't say with any certainty. I mean I don't recall seeing it recently, but as for never... I wouldn't like to say.'

So, the owner of the farmhouse might have parked around the back of their property. Not exactly a ground-breaking revelation. McKenzie gave a nod.

'Going back to yesterday... did you see anything that seemed out of the ordinary?'

'No.' She passed the snapshot back. McKenzie was returning it to her bag, when Mrs Forker added, 'Not yesterday.' McKenzie looked at her sharply. 'It might be nothing, but this morning, I was out walking the dogs after breakfast, about half past seven. I saw a man not far from where the van had been. He was on the verge, bending over. It looked like he was looking for something.'

'Did you get a look at him?'

'Not at first. He had a baseball cap on and kept his head down, so I couldn't see his face, but after we'd passed him, one of the dogs dropped her ball — she carries it everywhere with her — I stopped to pick it up and glanced back. I don't think he noticed but I did catch a glimpse of his face. He was gone by the time I walked back. I let the dogs have a bit of a sniff, but I couldn't see anything. I took it that he'd found what he was looking for.'

'What did he look like?'

'Not young. But then not that old. He was wearing one of those sweatshirt tops with a hood and tracksuit bottoms. I thought he must have been jogging and dropped something.'

After getting directions to the gate and a rough location of where the man had been scouring the verge, McKenzie thanked Mrs Forker and set off down the lane, keeping her eyes peeled.

Soon she spotted a holly bush next to a wide five-bar gate and pulled over. She walked over to the bush and looked behind it. There was no bike but the grass was heavily trampled.

McKenzie turned and looked around. On the opposite side of the road, behind an overgrown ditch and hawthorn hedge, fields stretched off into the distance. Why would Fern Marshall stow her bike there? Did she come here to meet someone? Someone who took her somewhere else? If so, who and where had they gone?

She returned to her car and reached through the open window for her map. Bridget Forker was right. Behind the gate was the garden of the farmhouse she'd visited earlier, its plot bridging the two lanes. She thought about the patch of flattened grass. What if the owner of the farmhouse had come in the white van to the back of the property and discovered Fern Marshall stowing her bike there? It was hardly trespass, but perhaps the sight of an attractive woman on her own was too much to resist? The garden was tantalisingly close and the gate would be nothing more than a minor inconvenience for someone with as much strength as intent.

She approached the gate and looked over. A weed-riddled gravel path wound its way through a screen of overgrown shrubs, blocking the view beyond. She thought back to the van on the drive and the feeling that someone was inside, watching. She set a foot on the first bar of the gate. An image of Alex bawling her out for going in without a warrant suddenly flashed through her mind. Quickly followed by the thought that she could even lose her job, were she to get caught.

… but not if she thought a woman's life might be at risk.

She cupped a hand to her ear. Was that a faint cry she could hear?

Before she could talk herself out of it, she vaulted the gate and started to advance up the gravel path, hugging the bushes for cover whilst scouring the area for signs of a recent disturbance. Trees loomed tall. At ground level, a wilderness of greenery rendered some parts unpassable. High in the sky above, steely clouds closed in, muffling the light. She gave an involuntary shudder at the sudden drop in temperature and took refuge behind a large laurel bush, letting her gaze drift, taking as much in as she could. As gardens go, it was a shabby, sorry affair dominated by an enormous oak tree. She spotted a ladder at the base of the trunk, running skywards, up to a large treehouse constructed of planks of greying wood. Her eyes tracked right, crossing the path ahead, to where a collection of decrepit wooden hutches and coops lay rotting. All were empty and didn't look to have been suitable for housing anything for some years. The only sign anyone had been there recently was a table-sized rectangle of yellowed grass where a hutch or coop must have rested until recently.

Keeping a keen eye on the house at the end of the path, she stepped out from behind the laurel, set to venture further into the garden, when her phone began to ring. A volley of barks erupted from inside the house. She raced to the gate, launched herself over and sprinted to the safety of her car, ringtone still singing from her pocket. With shaking, fumbling fingers, she fought with the key, trying to get it into the ignition. Finally, it went in. The roar of the engine cut through the relative silence of the country lane, as she accelerated away.

After rounding a corner, safely out of view of the gate, she allowed herself to slow down and let out a long release of breath.

That was close.

She pulled her phone from her pocket and scanned the screen. One missed call from Crawley. She dropped the phone in the centre console and called him back on the car's Bluetooth.

'Has she turned up?' she asked, still breathing heavily.

'What? No. I've finished looking at the security footage, so I'm ready to leave.'

'What do you think I am, a bloody chauffeur? You'll have to wait. I've still got a couple of houses to do. Unless you want to do them?'

'Don't bother. It looks like I was right all along about there being a boyfriend.'

She could hear the glee in his voice. For some inexplicable reason she felt disappointment wash over her.

'Oh. Okay. Well, good result.' It was a good outcome, right? At least the woman wasn't lying dead in a ditch somewhere. 'I'll come straight there. Make sure you get a copy of the recording.'

'Will do. What do I tell Mr Marshall?

'Nothing for the time being. If he asks, just say you need more time to look at it.'

Karl Marshall answered the door and ushered McKenzie through to the kitchen. Crawley was sitting at the island, mug in hand.

He greeted her with a nod then gestured to a large book lying on the counter in front of him.

'Check this out. These are all the cars Karl's had over the years.'

She walked over and glanced down; saw it was actually a photograph album. She pressed it closed.

'Right, Mr Marshall. We'll be off now. I'll be in touch as soon as we get any news.' She started for the door, Crawley following behind.

'Wait! Did you find out anything? Has anyone seen her?' Marshall asked, eyes pleading.

71

McKenzie looked back at him.

'I'm afraid I didn't have a lot of luck. Most people were either out or didn't see your wife yesterday. There was one person who saw Mrs Marshall around midday as she was cycling past, but of course, she could have gone anywhere after that.'

Marshall shook his head, looking bewildered.

'How can she have just disappeared?'

McKenzie looked down at the floor, unable to think of anything to say of any value. After a moment, she looked him in the eye.

'I promise we'll be in touch as soon as we get anything.' Back in the car she turned to Crawley. 'Okay, what's the deal with the boyfriend?'

'I'd say he's about the same age as Karl. Looks like he takes care of himself. Dresses well — he was wearing a Paul Smith shirt — and drives a BMW M5 convertible. Such a cool car.'

'How often has he been here and how long do his visits tend to last?'

'He was here a couple of weeks ago. Got a box out of the boot and took it up to the door. He was in there for over an hour.'

'And?'

'That's it.'

'That's it? From that you surmise she was having an affair?'

'It's obvious.'

'How is it obvious? He could be anyone; a door-to-door salesman, a guy come to service the boiler, their mortgage advisor.'

'How about an old boyfriend?' He sounded all cocky. McKenzie eyed him suspiciously. 'I checked out his number plate,' he said, smirking. 'Name's Simon Parry. Ring any bells?'

Forget bells, a klaxon went off in McKenzie's head.

'The ex-boyfriend.'

'The one and the same. Now can we hand it over to Missing Persons and let them deal with it?'

'Not so fast. So he went round to see her. It hardly proves they're having an affair.'

'He was there over an hour. Marshall didn't know anything about it. Before I looked at the film, I asked him if she had any friends that regularly visited, so I could discount them. He said she didn't.'

'I don't mean to disillusion you, but wives don't tell their husbands everything. It doesn't necessarily follow they're having an affair. Let's get hold of this Simon Parry, see what he has to say before we go jumping to any conclusions.'

Crawley's eyes flicked to the clock on the dashboard. It was close to 5:00 p.m.

'What, now?'

'No.'

'Good.'

'We'll do it when we've finished talking to the neighbours. The ones who weren't in earlier might be home by now.'

10.

There was still no one at home at two of the houses on the same lane as the Marshalls'. Next stop was the old farmhouse, the one with an overgrown wilderness for a garden. Once again, McKenzie's knocks were met by a flurry of barks. This time, they were swiftly silenced and the sound of heavy footsteps could be heard through the scuffed front door. It swung open and a young, broad-set man with a thatch of blond hair stared back at them.

'Yes?'

'I'm DC McKenzie and this is DC Crawley. We're investigating the disappearance of a woman who was last seen in the area yesterday lunchtime.'

'I was at work all day.'

'Perhaps we could come in for a minute, Mr...?' McKenzie said.

'It's Robbie.' He leaned forward and glanced up and down the lane. 'Now's not a good time.'

'It won't take long.'

Reluctantly, he took a step back and admitted them into the narrow hallway.

'Do you live here on your own?' McKenzie asked.

'No. My dad lives here too.'

McKenzie looked at him, reckoning him to be in his early thirties, only a year or two older than her. And while plenty of people their age still lived with their parents, for some reason it always surprised her.

Robbie led them into a lounge-cum-dining room that spanned the length of the house. The place looked old and dishevelled, its décor in serious need of a lick of paint, and the furnishings, of which there were few, looked genuinely vintage. In the rear half of the room, a pair of wooden spindle-back chairs sat either side of a small pine table. A tired kitchen could be seen through an open door leading off to the left.

'Is your father home? It'll save time if we could speak to you both together.'

'He's not back from work yet.'

'Okay. Well, as I said, we're talking to everyone in the neighbourhood. The woman, a Mrs Fern Marshall, was last seen—'

Suddenly a loud bang in the hallway caused them all to look towards the door as a giant of a man staggered into the room. He had a gut like a beer keg and sported a greasy, dirty grey comb-over. Crawley stepped away from the door to avoid being trodden on.

'What the fuck is this, eh lad?' the man snarled.

Lad?

McKenzie looked back at Robbie, whose face had noticeably paled.

'Get out of my house. You're not welcome.' He flung a hand out and pointed to the door.

Crawley hurried out. Not easily frightened, McKenzie stood her ground. She stepped forward and held out her warrant card.

'I'm DC McKenzie and this is—'

'Are you deaf or stupid? I said get out!' He advanced on her.

She put out a hand and said, 'Sir, this is an official police investigation. A woman is missing. We're asking everyone in the neighbourhood whether they've seen her.'

'No.' He took a step forward.

'How do you know? You don't know what she looks like.'

'I don't hold no truck with women. I haven't seen any and don't want to see any. Including you.' He took another step towards her, giving her little option but to back away, but not before he'd got close enough for her to smell the alcohol on him. She stopped retreating and sniffed theatrically.

'Been drinking, sir? I hope we don't find a car with a hot bonnet outside.'

His loud guffaw took her by surprise.

'What you gonna do if there is? Not much I'll wager, seeing as you can't prove it was me who drove it.' He glowered at her for a moment, then added, 'Make sure you shut the door behind you.'

McKenzie decided to try a last-ditch attempt.

'Sir, if you would give just one minute of your time. The woman hasn't been seen since yesterday lunchtime. All I need to know is—'

The man rounded on her and shuffled his considerable weight towards her, forcing her backwards. He didn't stop until she was over the threshold, where he slammed the door in her face.

'Well, that went well,' Crawley said.

McKenzie was fuming. She bent down and shouted through the letterbox, 'A woman's life could be hanging in the balance.'

Peering through the slit, she was surprised to see the big man's florid, pock-marked face staring back at her.

'Fuck off!' he growled.

McKenzie let the metal flap over the letter box snap shut and stood up.

'The guy's had a skinful,' Crawley said. 'There's no point trying to talk to anyone when they're like that.'

She knew he was right, but there was the son and he wasn't drunk. She bent over and pushed the letterbox open a second time.

'Robbie! Would you mind coming outside so we can talk to you?' she called. 'Robbie… Please…?'

The dog started to bark and they could hear a series of crashes coming from inside. McKenzie was contemplating sending for backup when the door opened a crack.

'Please, go away,' Robbie hissed through a three-inch gap. 'You'll only make him worse.'

'We can leave him for now, but I'd still like to talk to you, now that we're here.'

'I'm sorry, I can't help. I don't know anything. Please go.'

McKenzie plucked a card out of her bag and slipped it through the gap.

'Her name is Fern Marshall. She was last heard from around four o'clock yesterday afternoon and was seen on a push bike near here at lunchtime. Call me if you think of anything that might be relevant. Anything at all. Please.'

Robbie nodded, before pressing the door shut on them.

Walking back to the car, McKenzie stared at the black Discovery on the drive, engine still ticking as it cooled. She reached for her phone. A minute later, she hung up.

'Well, that's interesting, The car's registered to a Mr Donald Skinner.'

'The name sounds familiar.'

'That's because he's the abattoir owner who was involved in that trouble at Freedom Farm.' She thought back to the rescued lambs at the sanctuary. 'Is it just coincidence Fern Marshall parked her bike at the back of his property?' Her mind conjured up a picture of the rectangle of yellowed grass. Something had been there and recently moved. 'What if she came to see if they kept any animals out the back and they happened to come home and found her snooping? A woman up the road said she spotted a white van parked around the back at lunchtime, around the same time as she saw Fern cycle past. There was a white van parked on the drive, right there, when I came around earlier.' She gestured to the driveway, where the Discovery now sat. She shook her head, dismissing the thought. 'I'm doing your trick and jumping to conclusions. The woman said she'd seen Mrs Marshall's bike parked by the gate a few times. I can't see her making a habit of stopping to see whether there were any animals here.'

'There are white vans everywhere these days. It's all those delivery drivers.' Crawley reached up a hand and grabbed the handle above his head. 'Come on, time to call it a day.'

McKenzie started the ignition.

A minute later, Crawley twisted in his seat and said, 'What if she was having an affair with the driver of the white van? She could have left her bike and gone off in his van.'

'If that's the case, where's the bike now?' She thought about if for a second, then offered, 'What if she was meeting someone but someone else saw her and grabbed her while she was waiting? Imagine it, she's standing on the roadside waiting, someone spots her and takes a shine. When her date turns up and she's not there, they leave, thinking they've been stood up.'

'How's that any better than my suggestion? You've still got the fact the bike's gone.'

'Whoever took her, could have taken the bike too,' she said. 'So we wouldn't know where she was when they took her.'

'You think someone grabbed her, stuck her in their car, or van, then pissed around trying to get the bike in as well? Have you ever tried to stick a bike in the back of a car? Hardly a quick getaway.'

After a minute, he said, 'My money's still on her having done a bunk.'

'Yes. I think I've got that. Thank you.'

Fifteen minutes later, the police station logo shone like a beacon from the roadside. Crawley pulled his car keys out of his pocket and started to toss them in his hand. 'You can drop me in the overflow car park. I couldn't get a space anywhere else when I got in this morning.'

'You're going home?' she said and, ignoring his request, headed straight for the space nearest the station door.

'People to see, places to go.'

'You're not interested in what this ex-boyfriend might have to say? I thought you were banking on him to lead us to her.'

'If I'm right, she'll still be with him in the morning.'

McKenzie pulled on the handbrake. Crawley reached for the door handle.

'Not so fast.' She held out her hand. 'I need that USB with the CCTV footage.'

Crawley felt about in his pocket. After passing her the device, he climbed out of the car and scurried across the car park.

The office was quiet, with only a handful of people still working. McKenzie made straight for her desk. Wasting no time, she inserted the USB stick into her computer and settled down to watch the footage from the Marshalls' security system. She navigated to the time when Crawley said he'd seen Fern Marshall's ex arrive at the house. A silver BMW soft-top pulled in front of the gate. A tall, slim man with sandy hair got out. He walked around to the boot, where he pulled out a cardboard box about the size of a microwave oven. Hooking it under one arm, he started up the drive. McKenzie pressed pause and took a closer look at him. He had a rugged charm. She pressed play and watched him disappear into the house, then fast-forwarded until he re-emerged without the box, seventy-two minutes later.

A quick internet search furnished her with the fact that Simon Parry ran his own events business. She reached for her pad and scribbled down a contact number, adding it to the address Crawley had got from the number plate search. Social media furnished her with a plethora of photographs of Parry flashing a Buzz Lightyear smile, usually with an attractive woman on his arm. Fern Marshall failed to feature in any of the shots. Not that that proved anything, particularly if the pair were having an affair. She reached for her phone and dialled the number on Parry's website. It rang straight through to voicemail. Without giving away the reason for her having contacted him, she left a message asking him to return her call, turned her computer off and headed for her car. Her gym bag was on the back seat, reminding her of her good intentions, but with Harvey at home wondering where his dinner was, a workout would have to wait.

She had been on the road for ten minutes and was on the outskirts of town when a sign caught her eye. Acting on impulse, she took the turning. Soon the traffic thinned and the route began to meander through a string of bucolic villages. Shortly, she passed a signpost announcing her arrival in the village Simon Parry called home. She slowed her speed and kept a watchful eye on the house signs punctuating the roadside and it wasn't long before she spotted a post from which three house signs hung. She pulled off the road and started up the long drive.

The first property she came to was a handsome Georgian manor house. She continued past that and the next house, a wisteria-clad brick cottage, before finally coming to a stop in front of a large converted barn at the top of the drive. The place was cast in darkness. Her hopes sank. She climbed out and crossed to the front door, a fifteen-foot-tall slab of wood flanked by two

80

tall, narrow windows that wouldn't have looked out of place in a cathedral. She pressed the bell and stepped back, scanning the windows. After a minute, with no dim glow or sound of movement coming from within, she returned to her car and started back down the drive. A short distance on, a pair of headlights bore down on her. She pulled over, lowered the window and stuck a hand out, flagging down the approaching vehicle. The driver of the car, a green Vauxhall Corsa, obligingly stopped and began to wind the window down.

A slight, white-haired, ruddy cheeked man peered out at her.

'Can I help you?'

'I'm looking for a Mr Simon Parry,' McKenzie replied.

'You're at the right place but he's away at the moment.'

'Any idea when he'll be back?'

The man's crow's-feet crimped suspiciously.

'I'm sorry.' She reached for her warrant card and held it up at the open window. 'Detective Constable McKenzie. I was hoping to speak to Mr Parry about an ongoing investigation. A woman's gone missing. An old friend of his.' She fished the photograph of Mrs Marshall out of her pocket and passed it over.

A shocked expression flashed across the old man's face.

'That's Fern. She used to live there, with Simon.' He nodded towards the barn. 'I'm going back a few years now, mind.'

'Have you seen her recently?'

'No. Not since she left.' He handed the picture back. 'She was a lovely girl. I always thought Simon was mad to let her go.'

'Let her go? I thought she left him.'

'Oh no. I'm sure it was the other way around. I got the impression she was looking to get married and… well, I remember Simon saying he was too young to be tied down.'

'Do you know when Mr Parry is due back?'

'At the weekend, I think. He's up north somewhere, working.'

'Okay. Well, thank you for stopping.'

McKenzie pressed a finger to the window control.

'I hope you find her soon,' the old man said through the diminishing gap.

On the drive home, she thought about the different accounts she'd heard. Which was true? Had Fern left Parry or was he the one who ended it? Perhaps Parry had said that to save face. Whichever one it was, the question was, had they rekindled their relationship as Crawley believed, or was she wasting her time on a wild goose chase?

She drove straight home. Harvey met her at the door, bottom wagging. He led her into the kitchen and stood by his empty food bowl, slobber laces trailing from his flabby chops. She emptied a tin of dog food into his bowl. The British bulldog virtually inhaled the contents and looked at her with puppy-dog eyes pleading for seconds. Relenting, she threw down a handful of kibble before scouring the fridge for something for herself, her rumbling stomach reminding her that the last time she'd eaten had been at breakfast, not having had time for lunch. Ten minutes later, she padded through to the lounge with a cheese and pickle toasted sandwich and a bottle of lager. The answer machine blinked at her from across the room. She frowned. No one called her on the landline any more… apart from her mother. Probably checking to see if she was still okay for the crematorium and lunch afterwards. Well, she'd have to wait, the cheese toastie beckoned. She turned the TV on and settled back to enjoy a few moments of vacuous nothingness while she ate her sandwich and drank her beer.

Harvey trotted in just in time to beg for the last mouthful. She dropped the last corner of crust, watching him snatch it out of the air, then rose from her seat and crossed the room for the phone. She set the message to play and sat back. Nothing but dead air. She thumbed the key pad, surprise registering on her face on seeing Phil's name on the caller ID. She slipped her mobile from her pocket — no missed calls. Odd for him to call her at home. Perhaps he didn't want to risk her being somewhere they couldn't talk in private. If that was the case, it didn't bode well. She might end up cancelling that restaurant booking after all.

There was only one way to find out.

Her call bounced straight through to voicemail. She left a brief message and set the phone back down. A weight of loneliness suddenly descended on her. Whatever problems she and Phil had encountered trying to keep the embers of their long-distance relationship alive, it used to feel good knowing she had someone there to talk to, even if it was only at the other end of the phone. Her thoughts drifted to the missing woman. Had Mrs Marshall been lonely too? Lonely enough to seek solace in the arms of another man? If it wasn't for the phone call to her husband, they'd have already put it down as a case of history repeating itself and passed it on to missing persons. But nothing about it felt that straightforward.

11.

Robbie Skinner woke to a pounding pain in his temple. He tried to open his eyes and knew it was bad when all he could see out of his left eye was a thin slit of light. He slipped a hand from under the duvet into the cold air of the unheated room and sensitively probed his face, trying to ascertain the size of the swelling. It felt like someone had glued half a hard-boiled egg into the socket. He threw back the covers and padded over to a chest of drawers under the window, retrieving a tube of arnica from the top drawer.

By the time Don Skinner woke he too had a pounding pain in his temple, only his was entirely self-induced — a result of the previous night's excesses. He went through his daily ritual, washing and dressing in his trademark suit, shirt and tie, before heading downstairs, where he took a seat at the small table on which a rack of toast was growing cold. Robbie slid two perfectly fried eggs onto a plate already laden with bacon, sausages and beans and set it down in front of his father, along with a mug of tea, then returned to the kitchen, where he mixed a bowl of porridge oats with milk and put it in the microwave.

Don loaded his knife with butter and reached for a slice of toast.

'This is cold,' he grumbled.

'Sorry. I kept it warm in the oven for as long as I could but it was starting to dry out.'

'Bloody useless.' He flung the slice across the room. It hit Robbie on the shoulder and dropped to his feet. 'Make me some more.'

Robbie slipped two fresh slices of bread into the toaster while, despite his complaints, his father buttered another of the cold slices and ate it without any obvious difficulty. Fifteen minutes later, with his plate empty and the two extra slices of toast untouched, his father made his way upstairs.

At the same time that Robbie was breakfasting on a bowl of cold porridge, McKenzie arrived at the office. It was still early and apart from DI York there was no one about.

'Morning,' she called as she passed.

'Hey, how did you get on yesterday?'

She stopped and sauntered over. York was sitting at his desk. A McDonald's box and coffee carton lay in front of him. She couldn't help but wonder how things were going at home. Not that long ago they were close enough for her to feel able to ask. But that was the problem it seems. According to Alex, they'd been too close. Now she was lucky if he shared a coffee break with her let alone details of his private life.

He beckoned her in.

'We made good progress,' she said, taking a seat. 'There are a number of lines of enquiry that might prove lucrative. We've managed to track down her previous boyfriend. Darren spotted him visiting the house on the footage from the home security system. Of course, there could be a perfectly reasonable explanation for why he should visit when her husband wasn't there. He's away at the moment, something to do with his work. I called and left a message asking him to call me back. I also managed to find someone, a Mrs Bridget Forker, who saw Mrs

Marshall out on her bike on Monday afternoon. Mrs Forker lives about a mile away from the Marshalls. She said she quite often sees Mrs Marshall out on her bike. Interestingly, she said she sometimes sees the bike parked behind a bush outside one of her neighbour's houses. The neighbour happens to be Mr Don Skinner, a local abattoir owner. The same man responsible for the trouble at Freedom Farm earlier in the year.' York's eyebrows shot up. McKenzie nodded. 'I know. No such thing as coincidence, eh? We tried to talk to him last night but he'd been drinking and kicked us out. As soon as Darren turns up, we'll head over to the abattoir, see if we can get anything out of him once he's sobered up.'

Back at her desk, while waiting for Crawley to grace them with his presence, McKenzie set about trawling the internet's social media sites for any mention of Don Skinner and his son. The only reference she could find was a newspaper report commenting on the trouble at Freedom Farm, where the slaughterman had openly accused the sanctuary of stealing the lambs. Next, she tried the police databases. Robbie Skinner came up clean. His father's record, on the other hand, was as dirty as a schoolboy's neck. She found a history of arrests for offences ranging from affray to attempted ABH. But it was the last database entry that caused her breath to catch in her throat: a report into the death of Ms Margaret Beech.

Ms Beech, once known as Mrs Skinner, had been Robbie's mother and Don Skinner's wife, before she left him, citing physical and emotional cruelty as grounds for the divorce. She had died as a result of a hit and run, some seventeen years ago. McKenzie felt her skin crawl as old memories resurfaced. Her brother Pete had been similarly killed — ploughed down by an unknown vehicle and left for dead at the roadside, run over so many times there was barely a bone in his body that hadn't been broken. She took a deep breath, forcing her emotions down, and started to read.

Margaret Beech had been making her way home after her shift as a cleaner at a bank in town, one of two part-time jobs she held. At 7:30 p.m. on a cold, drizzly December night she had taken the number twelve bus from the stop outside the bank. The bus driver remembered her alighting at her usual stop, recalled seeing her in his rear-view mirror struggling with her umbrella as he drove away. That was the last time anyone saw her alive. A short while later a group of youths on their way to the pub found her body. Meanwhile, thirteen-year-old Robbie had been home alone doing his homework to the backdrop of EastEnders. No witnesses ever came forward.

Not surprisingly, Don Skinner had been interviewed. Despite the divorce having been some two years earlier, it was known to have been acrimonious. When detectives went to see him and broke the news, Skinner did little to disguise his disdain for the woman who had once shared his name and his bed, comfortable in the knowledge he had an alibi, as on the night in question he'd been with a friend. No other suspects were ever investigated and the case was never closed.

12.

'Don't get comfortable. We're going straight out,' McKenzie said, as Crawley slunk past her desk on the way to his own.

'Has something happened?'

'Not as far as I know. We're going over to the abattoir to see Skinner senior. We'll try talking to him again, now that he's sober.'

McKenzie spent the first ten minutes of the twenty-minute journey updating Crawley on what she'd learned about father and son. She was just about to run through her planned approach when her mobile started to ring. She flicked a switch on her steering wheel.

'DC Cat McKenzie,' she said into the microphone in the corner of the windscreen.

'Hi Cat. It's Phil. I just wanted to apologise. I should have—'

'Phil,' she quickly jumped in. 'I'm in the car, on speakerphone. I've got a colleague with me.'

'Oh, right. Sorry I missed your call last night. I was out on surveillance. Call me back when you're free to talk.' The line went dead.

McKenzie could feel a flush of colour creep up her neck.

'Boyfriend troubles, eh?' Crawley said. After a few moments of silence, 'He must be mad if he's cheating on you.'

She glared at him.

'Who says he's cheating?'

'Overnight surveillance? Total giveaway. I've used that line more than once.' She transferred her gaze back to the road, biting back her irritation. Crawley went on, 'You know the best thing to do when that happens? Get your own back. See someone else then let him find out.' After a moment's pause, he added, 'I'd be up for it, if you want?'

She turned to look at him.

'What do you mean, you'd be up for it?'

'Friends with benefits.' He gave her a wink. 'What about it... you and me?'

She gripped the steering wheel tight. Was he joking?

'I thought you had a girlfriend?'

He shrugged.

'I've got plenty of friends who are girls. Some who, well, you know, hang out... in my bed.'

McKenzie looked at him. She took in the needy, sex-obsessed look, usually seen in teenage boys, and realised she needed to deal with him the same way she'd dealt with them in school. She cracked a laugh.

'Very funny. You had me going for a minute.' She returned her gaze to the road, though not before she'd seen Crawley cringe with embarrassment before turning to look out of the window.

For the rest of the journey, she drove hard and fast, taking her frustration out on the road. First Phil, then Crawley. By the time they reached the abattoir, she was ready for whatever games Don Skinner wanted to play.

Skinner's Yard was a sprawling site, in the middle of which sat a large industrial building constructed from corrugated grey concrete walls and a rusting steel roof. The whole place was surrounded by a tall metal fence punctuated by a pair of sturdy metal gates that opened onto a wide concrete apron. McKenzie parked in one of the bays marked for visitors. Climbing out, she wrinkled her nose at the stench of manure congealed with the foul ferrous smell of blood. There was something else too — something she was struggling to place — the reek of fear perhaps.

She had never been to an abattoir before. Having been a committed vegetarian since her early teens, it wasn't anywhere she'd ever envisaged needing to go. Crawley, on the other hand, didn't seem to share her discomfort.

'My uncle's a butcher. My granddad was too,' he said, rounding the car. 'He used to tell us stories about the old days when they used to do the killing out the back of the shop. They used to eat anything back then, you know. Especially in the war. If they could catch it, they'd eat it. Even horses. People used to think they'd go to the knacker's yard for dog meat and glue, but that was only the bits people wouldn't eat, like the heads and hooves.'

McKenzie swallowed, bile already rising. She clenched her jaw. She could do this.

'Actually, I'd prefer it if you could save the stories until… well, like never.'

Crawley smirked.

'I didn't peg you as the squeamish sort.'

She shook her head and cast a look around. The place seemed deserted. She spotted a black Discovery parked towards the rear of the building that looked a match for Don Skinner's. Behind it, a hint of a white bonnet poked out. She took a couple of steps towards it, satisfying herself it was the same white Escort van she'd seen the day before.

'Hello!' A man's voice called. McKenzie turned to see its owner standing in the doorway. She took in the grey overalls and long blue plastic apron that was soiled with a collection of dark, wet patches. 'We're not open to the public.'

'We're here to see Don Skinner.'

'Do you have an appointment?'

'No. We're—'

'Mr Skinner only sees people with an appointment.' The man, twenty-something with a weaselly face and lank, floppy hair, turned to go back inside.

'We're police!' she called back. He paused and looked back over to her. She flashed her warrant card. 'If you could take us to Mr Skinner now, I'd appreciate it.'

The man darted a look through the open door. He wore a troubled expression and seemed to be having difficulty in coming to a decision, eventually he nodded.

'Is Robbie Skinner here too?' McKenzie asked, as she approached.

'He'll be in the office if he is.' He turned and stepped through into the slaughterhouse. 'This way.'

Crawley followed him in, while McKenzie, despite her best intentions, stalled at the threshold. She balled her hands into fists, steeling herself for what she might see and stepped inside.

The vast space was brightly lit and surprisingly noisy. An array of ropes, pulleys and hooks hung from the walls and ceiling. Blood ran in slick rivulets over the concrete floor into a gulley. The smell of death hung heavy in the air. She wished she'd had the foresight to daub a smear of Vicks under her nose before getting out of the car. It went some way to helping whenever she had to go to a post mortem. This felt no different. The weaselly looking man gestured to them to follow. Fighting to stop herself from gagging, she kept her breathing shallow and her eyes trained against the nearside wall, away from the swinging carcasses, and tried desperately to calm her raging nerves.

The weaselly man cast McKenzie a curious look, to which Crawley rolled his eyes and replied, 'Vegetarian.'

With a firm set to her jaw, McKenzie said, 'Could you just go and find Mr Skinner for us please?'

The weasel-man turned and yelled, 'Mr Skinner! Visitors!'

Out of the corner of her eye, McKenzie saw someone turn and look at them. She tore her gaze away from the wall and dared a glance in their direction. Don Skinner, also dressed in a slick wet apron, glowered at her, his puffy features corrugated in a scowl. He walked towards them with a ponderous tread. He must have seen something in McKenzie's expression or perhaps it was her anaemic pallor, which was as bloodless as the carcasses surrounding them, as he said, with no hint of humour in his dark, brooding eyes, 'You've missed the fun. The killing's over for today. Although we could always arrange a private demonstration. What will it be? How about a suckling lamb?'

'She's one of those vegetarians,' weasel-man said, with a tone that suggested she be declared a witch and accordingly burnt at the stake.

'Is she now?' Skinner's grin grew wider, like the wolf fixing Red Riding Hood in his sights. He jerked his head in the direction he'd come from. 'Go and give Jim a hand taking that bin of heads out.' Weasel-man gave a subservient nod and scuttled off.

McKenzie turned to Skinner.

'We only have a few questions sir, then we'll leave you in peace. As you know we're investigating the disappearance of—'

'You must be deaf or stupid, or both. I told you last night, I know nowt about any missing woman.' Weasel-man and another, Jim presumably, struggled past, carting a heavy-duty plastic container the size of a dustbin. Skinner said, 'Hey, hold up.' He turned to the two detectives. 'Either of you got a dog?'

Sensing an ambush, McKenzie said nothing.

Crawley nudged her with his elbow.

'You've got a dog, haven't you?'

Skinner walked over to the bin and eased the lid off. He reached in and appeared to feeling around for something. A minute later he pulled out a blood-soaked hand.

'Here… a present for Fido.' He threw what looked like a small ball in McKenzie's direction. She stepped back and instinctively squealed. A cow's eyeball sat on the floor at her feet, staring up at her. The men started to laugh, including Crawley.

'What's the matter?' Skinner said, feigning upset. 'Eyes are good for dogs. Helps them to see in the dark.' He looked at Crawley and winked.

McKenzie dug her nails into her palms. She spotted a door at the back of the room.

'I understand there's an office in here somewhere. We can go and talk in there.'

Skinner didn't move.

'I already told you, I—'

'Mr Skinner,' she snapped, cutting him off mid-flow. 'We *will* ask our questions. Here or at the station. It's your call. If you don't want your day disrupted any more than necessary then I suggest you find us somewhere quiet where we can ask our questions and you will answer them and then we'll let you go about your business.'

Don Skinner narrowed his eyes. The seconds crawled by, until eventually he stomped towards the rear of the room. McKenzie stepped over the eyeball and followed. The door opened into a short corridor, which led to a dirty-walled office. A battered, old-fashioned wooden desk sat in front of a fire door and side-on to a mesh-covered window. McKenzie took in the phone and mountain of paperwork that covered much of its surface, including an open ledger, a pencil marking the page, next to which was a mug of black coffee, steam rising from the drink's slick surface.

'Get on with it then,' Skinner growled. 'Ask your questions.'

McKenzie reached into her pocket and pulled out the photograph of Fern Marshall nursing the lamb. She held it out for Skinner to see.

'Do you recognise this woman?'

He barely glanced at the picture.

'No.'

'Take a closer look.' She held the photograph in front of his face.

'Do you recognise her?' McKenzie pressed.

He snatched the snapshot out of her hands.

'Is she one of those do-gooders from that rescue place? No better than common thieves, the bloody lot of them.' He thrust the photo back at her. 'Maybe she stole from the wrong person this time.'

'What do you mean by that?'

'Some people don't take kindly to folks thieving off them. If it means no more of my stock goes missing then I reckon I owe them a favour.' He glowered at her, as though daring her to challenge him.

Instead, she decided to change tack.

'How did the lambs get taken? I mean, those are some serious gates you've got out front.'

'Brazen, was what it was. It was early. Everyone was inside having a cuppa. The lambs were in a holding pen out the back. Someone must have driven in, loaded the lambs into their own van and taken off.'

'Why were you so sure it was someone from Freedom Farm?'

'Because that's what they do. Always banging on about rescuing poor defenceless animals. They don't realise, those lambs are worth money. What they're doing is taking away my livelihood.'

'How would anyone from Freedom Farm know you had lambs on site, if they were being held out at the back?'

'Who knows? They could have been planning on taking anything they found.'

'Have you had any other animals taken?'

He went to speak but stopped himself and regarded McKenzie down his ruddy, bulbous nose.

'I've answered your questions. I think we're done.'

'Not quite. Where were you Monday afternoon?'

'What?'

'It's a simple question. Monday afternoon, where were you?'

'Here. Like I am every Monday. You can ask the lads.'

'Don't worry, we will.' Skinner started for the door. Crawley made to follow. McKenzie set a hand out, stopping him. 'Mr Skinner, we're not finished yet.' Skinner turned back to face her. She went on, 'While we're here we'd like to talk to your son. If you'd be kind enough to fetch him.'

'If he's not in here, then he's not around.'

McKenzie gestured to the chipped coffee mug next to the open ledger.

'Isn't that his drink?'

The fat man's top lip curled into a sneer. 'If I say he isn't here, he isn't here.'

'Well, he isn't now,' McKenzie said, wondering whether Skinner junior was lying low somewhere on the premises. 'Where was your son on Monday?'

'Here. All day.' Skinner looked from McKenzie to Crawley. 'If that's everything.' He turned and walked out.

McKenzie hurried after him.

'We still need confirmation of your whereabouts on Monday.'

He pushed through the door and, as soon as McKenzie joined him, clapped his hands, attracting the attention of the five men who were busy hosing down the concrete floors, dancing between the racks of hanging carcasses.

'Lads...!' The men all looked over. 'Mondays — am I here all day, half-eight till six, or what?' Every head nodded in agreement. 'I take it that puts me in the clear?' He looked at McKenzie, his face blank and eyes cold. 'Now that really must be everything.' He started to steamroller the two detectives towards the open door and slammed it shut the second they stepped outside.

'That was a waste of time,' Crawley said, walking to the car.

'Oh, I wouldn't say that,' McKenzie replied, her gaze having come to rest at the empty space beside the black Discovery.

13.

'Looks like Robbie Skinner saw us and did a runner, 'McKenzie said as they climbed into the car.

'How do you know he was here? Could have been anyone's coffee,' Crawley said.

'But not anyone's van.' She ignored the look of confusion that crossed his face. 'I thought at first the van parked at the back of the house Monday lunchtime was unrelated. Now I'm not so sure. What if he grabbed Mrs Marshall and held her somewhere?'

'His old man said he was here all day.'

'Oh yes. And, of course, it would have been impossible for him to have slipped out without anyone noticing.'

'Okay. Say he nipped out at lunchtime and grabbed her, what then — at four he gave her her phone back and let her call her husband? You're so desperate to make this case into something worth investigating.'

'I still think it warrants a little chat.' McKenzie started the engine, gripped the steering wheel and turned to Crawley, 'Oh, and talking about little chats... if you ever embarrass me in front of a potential suspect again, maybe next time Alex asks me how you're getting on I'll just have to tell him exactly what I think.'

'What do you mean embarrass?'

'She's a vegetarian,' she said in a mock falsetto. 'And then there was the: she's got a dog.' Crawley's mouth twitched as a smile threatened to break. He clamped his lips together. McKenzie held her gaze until he started to squirm then twisted back in her seat and slipped the car into gear with a final shot across the bows, 'I mean it Darren.'

The fifteen-minute journey to the Skinners' farmhouse proved futile. There was no sign of the white van and no answer at the door, apart from the dog's barks. If Robbie Skinner was in, he was lying low. McKenzie walked over to the garage and scanned its wooden doors looking for a gap, but despite the peeling paintwork, the wood underneath was sound enough to thwart any chance of peering inside.

She tried knocking again, banging hard with the side of her closed fist, then crouched down and yelled through the letterbox, 'Mr Skinner! Robbie! It's DC McKenzie. I need to talk to you.'

'I think it's safe to say, he's not in,' Crawley called over. He was leaning against the bonnet of her car, arms folded, a bored expression on his face.

Reluctantly she agreed.

Back at the station. DI York waved them over as soon as they walked through the door.

'How did you get on?'

'Skinner senior says he knows nothing and his staff alibi him all day Monday,' McKenzie said. 'We didn't get to talk to Robbie, the son. He wasn't there. Though I'm sure he was when we arrived. It looks like he slipped out through a fire exit. That said, according to his father he was at the abattoir all day too.'

'Is there anything to link the son to the missing woman?' York asked.

'Not specifically. Apart from the trouble at Freedom Farm perhaps. But that neighbour I told you about, the one who'd seen

Mrs Marshall out on her bike Monday lunchtime, she also said she'd seen a white van parked at the back of the Skinners' place around the same time. Robbie Skinner drives a white Escort van.'

'Lot of white vans around these days, Cat. Could have been a delivery van. They're everywhere these days.'

'I said that,' Crawley said.

'Of course, that's a possibility,' McKenzie said, 'but from the neighbour's description it didn't sound like a transit, plus she said it looked quite old, which fits with Robbie Skinner's van. One thing that occurred to me was whether the Skinners keep any animals at their place — maybe Fern was planning on a rescue attempt, and Skinner junior came back and found her on the property.'

'Did you say the neighbour saw the van at lunchtime?' York asked.

'Yes. Around midday.'

'The phone call was later in the afternoon. It can't be relevant,' Crawley said.

'You don't think so?' Alex asked, causing a look of confusion to cross Crawley's face.

'Well... I... err... I suppose she could have been abducted earlier and kept somewhere.'

McKenzie stared at him, open mouthed. The cheeky git. That had been her argument.

York nodded.

'It's possible. Okay, well we're going to need some answers soon; I've had the DCI on to me. She's had the Chief Super on the blower. Seems Mr Marshall knows him from golf. Anyway, the word is, the Chief Super's less than happy with how we're dealing with Mrs Marshall's disappearance and wants the search ramped up.'

'We're doing our best,' McKenzie said, annoyed at having to defend herself when she'd been the only one taking it seriously from the start.

'I know Cat, but we need to try harder. Get hold of this Robbie Skinner, and see if we can corroborate his movements on Monday. And call that ex-boyfriend again. Even if he doesn't know where she is, he might know something useful, seeing as they met recently. We'll meet back here at six and reassess the situation. In the meantime, try and find anything that takes us in the right direction.'

'Can we make it half-six?' McKenzie asked, resulting in a dirty look from Crawley. 'We don't know what time Robbie Skinner is going to show and we'll need time to get back here.'

'Actually, sir,' Crawley said. 'I think it makes more sense if we go to their house first thing in the morning, before Robbie leaves for work, when he's not expecting us. If we go this afternoon, he'll ignore the knocks on the door or if his dad's there we'll just get told to sod off again.'

York gave it a moment's thought then nodded.

'Fair point. You've got until ten tomorrow morning. The Chief Super's pressing for a public appeal. It would be good to have something to report. He actually wanted a fingertip search in the area she was last seen, but given we know Mrs Marshall was alive four hours after she was seen by the dog walker and there's nothing to suggest she remained in the area, I managed to persuade him to leave it for now. I think we'll—'

McKenzie's mobile started to ring.

She pulled it out of her pocket and hit answer.

'DC McKenzie.' A smile slipped across her lips. 'Hello Mr Parry. Thank you for calling me back.'

She pointed towards the door. York gave her a thumbs-up and she stepped out of his office. Crawley followed her out. He skirted around her and headed over to DS Bells' desk and pulled over a chair. Back at her own desk, McKenzie began to quiz Parry about his relationship with the missing woman. A burst of laughter at the far end of the room caused her to glance over. She found DS Bells looking her way, wearing an expression thick with malicious satisfaction. Crawley said something to him and he started to laugh, again. McKenzie swivelled in her seat, turning her back on them, and focussed on the conversation with Simon Parry.

After the call ended, she returned to York's office, intending on updating him, only his chair was empty. She grabbed her mug and headed for the kettle instead. It had just boiled when she saw him walk through the door from the corridor. He looked over and started towards her.

She gestured to a clean mug on the side.

'Want one?'

'Go on then,' he said, passing her the coffee jar. 'What did the ex-boyfriend have to say?'

'He was open about his recent visit. Said they'd bumped into each other a few months back and he'd mentioned he still had some of her things from when she left. They arranged for him to drop them around. Says he's got no idea where she is now. He's been in Hull since last Friday, working at some music festival.' She poured the hot water onto the granules and started to stir.

'Milk and two sugars for me, cheers,' Crawley said, coming from behind her and putting his mug down next to York's. 'So, was I right? Is she with him?'

McKenzie spooned some sugar into his mug and said, 'No. He hasn't seen her since the day he visited the house.'

'So he says,' Crawley scoffed. 'He's hardly going to admit it, is he? Not if she doesn't want her husband to find out where she is.'

York turned to McKenzie.

'Do you think he's telling the truth?'

'I told him we were on the verge of launching a major investigation. I made it clear he'd be in serious trouble if he was lying.'

'That's not much of a threat to some folk,' York said. 'Remember Shannon Matthews?'

'Who's Shannon Matthews?' Crawley asked.

'A kid who went missing on her way back from school. Must have been 2007 or 2008. Only nine years old. Her mother was regularly seen raw-eyed on the news appealing for information. Yorkshire Police spent millions on a hunt that lasted nearly a month, only to find the mother had lied through her teeth and had known exactly where Shannon was the whole time. In fact, she'd helped organise the so-called abduction. It was all part of some cock-eyed plan to get hold of reward money.'

'What if Parry's killed her?' Crawley said.

'He's been in Hull since the weekend,' McKenzie said.

Crawley turned on her.

'He could have slipped back.'

York looked at her.

'He's got a point, Cat.'

'Fine. I'll go and check his alibi out.' She passed them both their drinks.

Crawley peered into his mug. A confused look appearing on his face at the insipid mixture.

'What's this?'

'Milk with two sugars, like you asked for.' She turned to York. 'I can drive up to Hull tonight. Darren will have to go and see Robbie Skinner on his own.'

'It'll take too long,' York said. 'It's a five-hundred-mile round trip. I was thinking more of checking the ANPR system, see if there are any hits for his number plate in Kent on Monday afternoon. In fact, Darren could do that while you take a closer look at the Skinners.'

'Yeah Cat, you could give old man Skinner a bit of an eyeballing, eh?' Crawley said, mimicking DS Bells' malicious grin from earlier.

Arriving home that evening, McKenzie stepped through the door to find Harvey greeting her as he always did, with a view of his derriere retreating down the hallway towards his food bowl in the kitchen. She dropped her bags and followed, glancing into the lounge as she passed. The steady glow from the light on her answer machine reminded her of her promise to call Phil. A heavy lump of dread settled in her stomach.

Later, with the dog fed and dinner dispensed with, she settled down in the lounge, her laptop resting on her knees and Harvey asleep at her feet. She started by documenting everything she knew about Robbie Skinner. Every so often her gaze slid over to the coffee table, where her mobile rested, and she'd think about calling Phil, then just as quickly she'd dismiss the idea — bad news could always wait.

Back to Robbie Skinner.

If he was involved in Fern Marshall's disappearance, had their paths crossed beforehand or had it been a chance encounter? She called up the press articles that had resulted from the fracas at Freedom Farm. There was no mention of him in any of the reports nor was he in any of the photographs published by the papers.

She thought back to the photograph of Mrs Marshall holding the lamb and the note on the back: *Thank you for saving me.* Who had written it? The person responsible for rescuing the animals or someone Fern had helped? Who could she have saved? And from what?

She shook her head and snapped the laptop shut. Working through the evening might make her feel like she was doing something, but in reality, it was getting her nowhere.

Ten minutes later, with a mug of tea on the table in front of her and Harvey snoring like a pneumatic drill, she gave in to the inevitable and reached for her mobile.

'Hello…?' came a female voice.

She felt her stomach flip.

'I'm sorry, who is this?'

'Are you after Phil? He's just—' She became aware of a male voice in the background and steeled herself as she listened to a hushed conversation before Phil came on the line. 'Cat. Hi. Sorry about that. I was—'

'Sorry if I called at a bad time,' she interrupted.

'No, no. Now's fine. I've finished for the day.'

'Honestly, it sounds like you've got company. I can call back another time.'

'Cat, it's fine.'

'But if you're still at your stakeout…'

'I'm not. I'm at home. Got in about five minutes ago.'

'Shouldn't you be tending to your guest, rather than chatting to me?'

'That's okay. Lolly, err… Charlotte is working with me on the surveillance op. You know how it is. We haven't eaten for hours. Thought we'd send out for pizza. She's just calling our order through so I can spare a couple of minutes.'

How kind.

In the background, she heard Lolly ask where the corkscrew was.

'Sounds like you're needed. I better let you and *Lolly* get back to it then. Maybe you can call me when you're not otherwise engaged?' She terminated the call before he could reply and flung her phone down on the sofa. Straightaway it started to ring. She snatched it up. 'Look Phil. We're both adults. I know when—'

'Hello. Is that DC McKenzie?' It was a man's voice and it wasn't Phil.

14.

The road was empty save for a marked patrol car and a white transit van with a Forensic Services decal emblazoned down its flanks. McKenzie pulled in behind them and climbed out. The air was cold and damp and smelled of autumn. She zipped up her fleece and started to walk. Ahead, a portable halogen rig cast a harsh light, scorching a hole in the dark night and sketching long shadows onto the hedgerow. Standing underneath were two uniformed officers — a slender, young Asian woman and an older rotund man. They looked over as she approached.

'DC McKenzie. Where's the bike?'

The woman pointed towards the verge. McKenzie stepped forward and looked down into an overgrown ditch. Nestled in the long grass lay a bicycle. Its purple paintwork glinted between the long swathes of green and McKenzie felt a sudden wretched sensation that whatever they did now, it was already too late for Mrs Marshall.

A man in an all-in-one scene suit rustled past. Moving cautiously, he side-stepped down into the ditch, where he started to secure plastic bags over the handlebars.

McKenzie moved forward, careful not to block his light and called, 'Hi, DC McKenzie. Is there any damage to the bike?'

The CSI officer looked up, squinting.

'There might be a few scratches but nothing obvious.'

McKenzie nodded, before turning back to the two uniforms.

'Do we know who reported it?'

'All we know is a member of the public called after seeing one of the posters,' the female PC replied.

'Posters?'

'On the telegraph poles.'

'There's one down the road,' her partner added, hooking a thumb in the opposite direction to the one McKenzie had come from.

McKenzie started walking. A short distance down the lane, an A4 sheet glowed in the moonlight. She pulled her torch out of her pocket and trained it on the page. Fern Marshall's eyes peered out from below the brim of some milliner's lavish creation. The text urged anyone who had seen the missing woman since she'd left the house on Monday or who had any information about her current whereabouts to contact the local police station. A description of her bicycle completed the plea. Obviously, the handiwork of Karl Marshall. He'd even helpfully included the station's phone number.

She stuffed her torch into her pocket and reached for her phone.

'Thought you'd want to know,' she said after updating DI York on the find, while walking back to her car. 'I take it this changes things?'

'Just a bit.'

She went on, 'What I don't get is why no one spotted the bike before. Loads of locals must use this road. I mentioned the bike to everyone I spoke to. Even I've driven up here a few times in the last couple of days and haven't seen it.'

'Maybe it hasn't been there the whole time,' York suggested.

'Yeah. Maybe. Do you want me to call Mr Marshall and let him know?'

'No. I think we leave it until the morning. He's coming in to the station first thing to film the public appeal. I'll tell him then.'

***

The following morning, it was still dark when McKenzie left home. It was a little after seven by the time she arrived at the Skinners' house and the sky was a fuzzy glow of peaches and pinks. She continued on past their drive, where Don Skinner's Discovery was parked in front of the garage, and came to a stop a short distance away so that her car couldn't be seen from any of the windows. With one eye on the rear-view mirror, she reached for her mobile and called Crawley. No answer. She left a message asking him, when he finally surfaced, to call everyone living near to where the bike had been found — excluding the Skinners — and find out whether anyone had seen it. She then pocketed the phone and settled back in her seat, watching in the wing mirror for someone to make an appearance.

At 7.34 a.m. the front door swung open and Don Skinner emerged wearing a brown overcoat and flat cap. He walked straight to his car, climbed in and drove away in the opposite direction to McKenzie, as she'd hoped he would. As soon as he was out of view, she slipped her Skoda into reverse and backed up the road and onto the drive. If Robbie Skinner's van was in the garage, it was going nowhere.

She climbed out and approached the front door. If she knocked, she knew there was a good chance Robbie would take a look through the yellowed lace curtains and decide to lie low. She needed to play it smarter than that. Instead, she pulled her notepad out of her pocket and started to punch a number into her phone. She waited, listening to the sound of a familiar tring-tring coming from inside the house. Shortly, the ringing stopped.

'Hello?' came a man's voice.

'Robbie, it's DC McKenzie. We spoke yesterday.' The phone went dead. McKenzie crossed to the window and rapped on the glass with her fist. 'Mr Skinner,' she yelled. 'I know you're in there… Mr Skinner, if you don't open up, I'll have no choice but to force entry. Mr Skinner…'

There was a click behind her. She turned as the front door eased open an inch.

'What do you want?' Robbie Skinner asked through the gap.

'Mr Skinner. I need to talk to you. Please let me in.' She took a step forward.

Robbie shrank back into the shadows.

'Please go away. I can't help you. I don't know anything.'

She pressed a hand to the door and pushed. Finding no resistance, she opened it fully and stepped inside. Robbie was standing with his back to her. She moved forwards and stepped around to face him, taking in the patchwork of bruises that sullied his face and the swollen eye peeping through a slit in an eyelid that looked like chopped liver.

'What happened?' she asked.

'I tripped,' he mumbled through split lips as he headed into the living room.

She rolled her eyes and followed him through.

'More original than walking into a door… though only just. Is that why you did a disappearing act yesterday?'

'I don't know what you mean.'

'You left the abattoir while we were there. Don't say you didn't because I noticed your van was there when we arrived.'

He turned away from her gaze.

'I had errands to run.'

She slipped the photograph of Mrs Marshall from her pocket and held it out. Robbie looked away. A very definite reaction. McKenzie felt her pulse quicken.

'I already told you I don't know where she is.' She kept the picture held out. Eventually he couldn't help but look.

'Do you know her?' Taking in his unfaltering gaze, she said, 'It's clear that you do.'

'We were at school together.' He slipped his hands into his trouser pockets, perhaps to stop his worrying fingers give anything away.

'When did you last see her?'

He shook his head and shrugged.

'Have you seen her recently?' He looked down at the floor and gave another shrug. 'I've been told she regularly rides her bike in this area. Maybe you've seen her around?' He shook his head. 'What about her bike then? Purple, with a basket on the front.' Again, he shook his head. 'Only it was found not far from here.'

A frown pinched his brow as suddenly as if someone had cinched it together with the pull of a cord. She noticed him swallow.

'Robbie, when did you last see Fern Marshall?'

'Not Monday,' he said firmly. 'I was at work all day.'

'Until what time?'

'About four.'

'What about lunchtime? Did you nip home for any reason?'

'No. Not this week. Dad wanted to go out, so I had to stay. He insists one of us is always there.'

'Your father went out Monday lunchtime?'

Robbie nodded.

'He told us he'd been at the yard all day.'

Momentarily a look of surprise flitted across Robbie's face.

'He must have forgotten.'

'I take it he doesn't normally go out on a Monday lunchtime?'

'No.'

McKenzie groaned quietly. When Skinner asked his staff to confirm his alibi, he'd asked about Mondays... not *this* Monday. Don Skinner had deliberately misled them. Why? Had it anything to do with the missing woman?

'What do you know about the trouble at Freedom Farm that your dad was involved in?'

Robbie cast her a strange look, perhaps surprised at the change in direction.

'Nothing much. Only that it was to do with some lambs Dad reckoned they'd stolen.'

'Were you involved in the confrontation?'

'No.'

'What about what followed?'

'What do you mean, what followed?'

'The six sheep whose throats were cut.'

'No.' He exploded in a burst of anger. 'You think because I live here and work for him that I'm like him? Well I'm not!' His face bloomed a furious red.

'So why do you? ...live with him and work for him?'

'Because I don't have any choice.' He flashed her a look that screamed shame.

McKenzie considered him for a moment, then reminded herself not to let pity impede the investigation.

'You drive a white Ford Escort van, is that right?'

'Yes.'

'Where is it now?'

'In the garage.'

'Can I take a look?'

'If you want.'

She followed him out of the house, to the garage, where he produced a key from his pocket, slipped it into the lock and threw open the double doors.

She stepped inside. It was a deceptively large space. Although only one car's width, it was long enough to house at least two end-to-end.

McKenzie started a slow stroll around the vehicle. It was clean and in good nick, given its age.

'Who else uses the van?'

'No one.'

'It's never used by your dad or anyone at work?'

'No.'

She opened the door and looked inside. The driver's seat was frayed and sagged in the middle, but other than that it was relatively unscathed.

'When did you last clean it?'

'Saturday.' McKenzie looked at him sharply causing him to add quickly, 'I do it every weekend,'

'Did you clean the back out too?' she asked, walking around to the rear.

'Not this week, no.'

McKenzie gestured to the handle. 'Could you open it up please?'

Robbie stepped forward and did as asked. The inside was empty except for a small toolbox and a few scraps of paper littering the floor. But it was the rings welded onto the side wall and the remnants of nylon rope hanging off in tatters that drew McKenzie's attention.

'What are those for?'

'Securing sheep. Sometimes I have to pick them up from the farms.'

'Do you ever bring any animals back here?'

'No.'

'Ever keep any animals here?'

Robbie gave her a confused look.

'There's the dog…?'

'Apart from the dog.'

'We used to have chickens and I had a rabbit when I was a kid, but nothing for a long time. Why do you want to know?'

McKenzie stared at him, taking in the swollen eye and kaleidoscope of blues and browns covering the side of his cheek. What if Fern Marshall hadn't gone down without a struggle? Just because she went missing on Monday doesn't mean she wasn't being held somewhere. She could still be there now.

'I'm going to need to take those ropes,' she said, slipping on a pair of latex gloves.

'Why?'

She didn't answer. Instead, she climbed into the back of the van and started to tease the knots undone.

'I don't understand. Why are you here? What do you think has happened to her?' Robbie asked, with a slight tremor in his voice.

'That's what we're trying to find out. We're not ruling anything out at this stage.'

McKenzie slipped the segments of rope into an evidence bag and clambered out. She scanned the rest of the garage. Above her head, an old door spanned the rafters, home to a collection of misshapen paint tins edged with thick drips of paint. She let her gaze drop to the floor. Nearby, a stack of storage crates caught her eye.

'Could you open those for me, please?'

Robbie wrenched the lids off each to reveal contents that ranged from car washing paraphernalia to a miscellany of household items, including more ropes.

'Want to take these too?' he asked.

'No. That's fine. Thank you.'

As Robbie started to return the lids back onto the crates, McKenzie walked towards the end of the garage, past the van, over to the far wall where a large chest freezer sat. She swallowed, steeling herself for what she might find, and flung open the lid. Quietly, she let out the breath that had caught in her chest. Inside was an assortment of bagged meat: large leg joints, huge hefts of steak, big sacks of mince and rust-red objects labelled up as hearts, livers and kidneys. Somehow, cut up and frozen like that, it was hard to imagine them as ever having anything to do with a living, breathing animal. She started to move some of the bags, pushing them aside to make sure there was nothing more sinister lurking underneath. Satisfied that wherever Fern Marshall was, she wasn't buried under fifty kilos of offal, she lowered the lid down.

'You still haven't told me when you last saw Mrs Marshall,' she said as they left the garage and returned to the drive.

'Does it matter? I told you it wasn't this week.' After a short pause he said, 'Do you think something bad has happened to her?'

'You seem upset at the prospect.'

Robbie's gaze dropped to the floor. He gave a nod.

'I remember her, from school,' he said, his voice almost a whisper. 'She was nice to me when others weren't.'

15.

After leaving Robbie, McKenzie made her way to the station. She sent the rope to the lab for testing, then went in search of Crawley, who it turned out was nowhere to be seen. The door to York's office was closed and, unusually, the blinds were down. She walked over and stood outside, listening to the murmured voices that could be heard through the glass walls. Men's voices. She leaned in closer, trying to make out their owners, when the door swung open. She jumped back as Karl Marshall stepped out. He gave her a curious look. Next through the door, came one of the force's media team; a slick-haired, smart-suited, thirty-something man whose name McKenzie didn't know. Finally, York emerged.

'Were you looking for me?' he asked.

'I was but it's not urgent.'

'Are you sure?' When she stalled, York turned to the media man. 'Paul, could you take Mr Marshall to the media suite, please? I'll join you in a minute.'

McKenzie watched Karl Marshall leave. If she hadn't known who it was, she would have struggled to recognise him as the same man she'd met only three days ago. Gone was the well-groomed, slick executive. Now, his jaw was covered with stubble, and dark circles, like smudged boot polish, underlined a pair of worried eyes that peered out from a pale and pasty face.

'What is it?'

She turned back to York and said, 'I just wanted to update you on my meeting with Robbie Skinner this morning. He's still saying he doesn't know anything but he did say his dad went out for a couple of hours around lunchtime on Monday, which means Don Skinner lied to us. Seeing that Robbie's van would have been at the abattoir, what if his father took it?'

'Go and talk to Skinner senior again. If he doesn't change his tune, try and get the lads who work there on their own, see if they remember things differently without him around.'

'Will do.' She looked over to Crawley's empty chair. 'Don't suppose you know where Darren is?'

'He was in earlier. If you can't find him, see if Spence can go with you.'

Unable to find Crawley — not that she tried too hard — McKenzie went over to DC Wynchcombe.

'It shouldn't take long,' she said after asking if he was free to accompany her to Skinner's Yard.

'It can take all day as far as I'm concerned,' he said, cracking his knuckles and stretching his back. He grabbed his jacket off the back of his chair. 'It'll be good to get out. Two days I've been sat at my desk, finalising these case files for the CPS. I've almost forgotten what it's like to do some proper work.'

Five minutes into their journey, he said, 'You think this abattoir guy has got something to do with the missing woman then?'

'If he hasn't, why lie?'

'Because he's an arse? Daz was telling us about the eyeball thing. The guy obviously enjoys winding you up.'

'When did Darren tell you that?'

'Last night, in Mickey's.'

'You went to Mickey's with Darren? I didn't realise you two were mates.'

'We're not — I mean he's alright — but the whole team was out.'

McKenzie looked at him, a frown darkening her brow.

'How come I didn't get an invite?'

'Would you have gone if you had?'

'Probably not, but...'

'There you go then.'

He was right. There you go indeed. She couldn't blame anyone other than herself. It was no wonder that lately she'd felt she was becoming increasingly detached from the team when she made so little effort. Though that hadn't always been the case. There had been plenty of fun nights out with too much to drink and not enough sleep, back in the day when it was usually her and Alex being the last men standing. Things had changed a lot over the last twelve months, after Alex's marriage hit rocky ground and he'd decided the answer was to build a few barriers between them. All the same, perhaps it was time to try to be more sociable? Especially as it looked like she might soon be single again.

'Cat...!' Wynchcombe said sharply.

She snapped out of her reverie. The sign for Skinner's Yard fast approaching. She hit the brake and slapped the indicator wand up as she pulled onto the concrete apron.

The first thing she noticed was Robbie's van, parked in the same spot as before. Her gaze moved to the mesh-covered window of the office. Was he in there, watching?

She climbed out and started towards the main building. At the door, the loud baying, bellowing cry of cattle stopped her in her tracks. A background of shouts and bangs and whining machinery completed the cacophony. Her heart started to thump its own tympanic accompaniment in response. She felt the blood drain from her head. This was not her world. Dead people she could deal with; slain animals she could not.

'You alright?' Wynchcombe asked, concern etched on his face. 'You've gone as white as a sheet.'

'I'm not sure I can...' Her eyes darted back to the door. 'I think they're actually killing things.'

'Do you want me to...?'

She shook her head.

'No. I need to just... Oh, I don't know.' She took a deep breath. 'Let's just do this.' She pressed the handle down and pushed the door open.

The air was ripe with the smell of fear and death; a cloying, suffocating smell that threatened to send her rushing back to the comfort of her car. She felt the bile rise and swallowed hard. She clenched her fists by her side, then yelled, 'Mr Skinner!' Slowly the noise level reduced. 'We're here to speak to Don Skinner.'

Skinner senior appeared from in between two hanging carcasses.

'Would you mind stepping outside for a moment, sir?'

'What now?' he growled as he strode towards them, wiping his bloody hands on his blue coveralls, adding a smear of bright red to the morbid collage of rusts and browns.

McKenzie turned and rushed out, exhaling the stale air from her nose and taking in a deep breath, though now even the outside air seemed equally tainted.

'Well...?' Skinner asked.

McKenzie turned to him.

'Monday, where were you?'

'I told you. Here.'

'All day? You didn't happen to go out for a couple of hours at lunchtime?'

Skinner fixed her with a piercing stare. Suddenly a sly smile cracked across his lips.

'You're right, I did go out. It must have slipped my mind. I'm usually here all day on Mondays. What of it?'

She gave a small shake of her head and pulled a notepad and pen from her pocket.

'Exactly where did you go and between what times?'

'Hmm… Let me think.' He rubbed his chin. The glint in his eye told her his thoughtful air was all a sham. Eventually he replied, 'I went to the pub to meet a mate. I left here about twelve, got back about two.'

'Which car did you take?'

'Mine.' He jerked his head towards the black Discovery.

'Not your son's van?'

'Why would I want to drive that piece of shit?'

She ignored the question and said, 'This friend… I need a name, address and phone number, plus the name and address of the pub.'

For a moment it looked like the older man was going to refuse. His jowls wobbled as his mouth opened and then closed. Eventually he relented. After he'd furnished her with the requested details, McKenzie was about to leave when, out of the corner of her eye, she spotted movement at the office window that immediately conjured up an image of Robbie Skinner shrinking back from view.

'What happened to your son, Mr Skinner? How'd his face get all bashed up?'

Skinner looked over at the empty window with a hateful scowl on his face.

'He walked into a door. He's always been a clumsy little shit.'

'Where was he on Monday?'

'Here in the day. Home at night. Like every day.'

'Times?'

'Got here just after me, around eight and left before me. I remember, 'cos he was whinging he hadn't had a break all day.'

'What sort of time?'

'I don't know.'

'Roughly?'

'Around four.'

'Could it have been before or after four?'

'Quarter to, quarter past, it's all the same to me. I don't spend all day clock watching like you lot, wasting bloody taxpayers' money.'

16.

Lunchtime was nearly over by the time they got back to the station. McKenzie dropped her bag off at her desk, then headed for the canteen. On the way, she heard Crawley's voice coming from the opposite direction. A moment later, he rounded the corner, talking at a million miles an hour to Karl Marshall, who was walking alongside him. Neither man acknowledged her.

She stopped and, with a puzzled frown, watched their retreating backs, until they disappeared through the door at the end of the corridor.

McKenzie entered the canteen only to find they had already stopped serving hot food and the refrigerated shelves were almost empty. After spending a minute staring vacuously at the scant offerings, she grabbed a blueberry muffin and mug of tea and was about to make her way to the office when Crawley came through the door. He didn't notice her over by the till, and she stood watching as he made his way over to a table in the far corner, where he joined York and Bells.

She walked over.

'Okay if I join you?'

'Sure.' York gestured to the empty chair next to him.

'How did the filming go?' she asked as she sat down.

'It went well. Marshall made an impassioned plea for anyone who might know something to come forward. I tried to get him to say something directly to his wife, appeal to her to come home in the event she's left voluntarily, but he was having none of it. We just have to hope if she has run out on him, she'll see the film and let us know.'

'How did he seem during the filming?'

'Upset. Clearly worried about his wife. There were no signs he was holding anything back.'

'He's proper devastated,' Crawley said. 'There's no way you can fake that.'

York hooked an eyebrow, an indication that he didn't necessarily agree, but said nothing.

'You were there?' McKenzie asked Crawley.

'Yeah. I was surprised you weren't. It's our case, after all.' Smug didn't begin to describe the look on his face.

'I didn't realise...'

'You should have said if you wanted to be there,' York said. 'Like Darren says, it's your case. I wouldn't have stopped you.'

'You need to show more initiative,' Bells said. 'You're not going to get very far sitting around, waiting for people to spoon-feed you opportunities.'

'I haven't been sitting around waiting for anything! I've been out there working the case. If you're going to accuse anyone of sitting around then I don't think—'

'So how did you and Spence get on?' York interrupted. He gave Bells a warning look.

McKenzie recounted her conversation with Don Skinner, then said, 'We still need to check his alibi, confirm he was at the pub when he said he was. If Robbie spent the day tucked away in the office at the yard, he might not have noticed if his dad took the van.'

'From what Darren's told me, it doesn't matter where he or the van was at lunchtime,' Bells said. 'Fern Marshall was fine until four. That's where the focus of your attention should be.'

McKenzie rounded on him.

'We don't know that. The last time she was seen was midday. She could have been abducted earlier and held somewhere.'

'And she just happened to forget she had her phone on her until four o'clock?' Bells challenged with a smirk.

'Maybe she'd been tied up and then later, when they untied her, she managed to get hold of her phone.'

'That's not a bad hypothesis,' York said. 'The call was short and frantic.'

McKenzie nodded, adding, 'Also Robbie Skinner left the yard earlier than usual. He could be in it with his dad. I found some ropes in his van. I sent them for testing. You never know, we might get lucky and find they come up positive for Fern Marshall's DNA.'

'Were they blood stained or something?' Crawley asked.

'No. It's just that they were fixed on the inside of the van. They could easily be used to restrain someone.'

'Odd that someone used to dealing with livestock might have some method of restraint in their van,' Bells said.

Crawley gave a snigger.

McKenzie looked at him with a blank expression.

'So Darren, how did you get on with the neighbours?'

He gave a puzzled look.

'What about the neighbours?'

'I left a message on your phone first thing, asking you to phone around and see if anyone noticed Mrs Marshall's bike on the side of the road.'

'Yeah, well, I've been tied up in the appeal all morning. I'll do it tomorrow. I was going to do the ANPR search of Parry's

123

number plate next.' Crawley slipped lower in his seat and lifted his mug to his lips.

McKenzie checked her watch.

'There's still plenty of time. If you go now, you should be able to get both done.'

'Actually, we should all go now. Time to get back to work,' York said, pushing his chair back and standing up. 'And Darren... Cat's right. If you get off your arse, there's no reason you can't get everything done today.'

With York heading for the door, Crawley slammed his mug down and scowled at McKenzie. She replied with a shrug, then rose from her seat and started to walk away. Let him scowl. She was past caring. It was about time he started to pull his weight.

Back at her desk, she spent the next hour watching the recording of Karl Marshall's appeal, scrutinising his every movement; every facial expression. She saw what she thought was a tremor of anger ripple beneath his carefully composed words when he talked about Fern and their perfect marriage. Little wonder. Three days and still no sign. She felt her own anger rise at the thought of having been excluded, pushed aside like a bit-player in the investigation. There had been a time, not that long ago, when Alex would have sought out her presence and encouraged her to get involved. She shook her head. She needed to forget about them and keep her focus on the case. The public appeal was done now. All they could hope was that it would move the investigation forward. Maybe Alex was right and the missing woman would see it and realise what a circus her disappearance had caused, though she doubted it. Almost seventy-two hours had passed since that fateful phone call and the chances of Fern Marshall turning up alive and well were looking slimmer than the clothes that filled her dressing room.

With the appeal not due to air until the early evening, feeling tired and jaded McKenzie decided she needed a break and took the opportunity to get some value from her gym membership. The main studio was packed with the after-work crowd. Bodies of all shapes and sizes pounded out a comfortable tattoo on the treadmills. After warming up with a few stretches, she headed over to the weights area, nodding to the occasional familiar face as she made her way to her first station. After slipping a couple of disc weights on to the end of an Olympic barbell, she began her first set of squats. Soon, the stresses of the day were overtaken by the stresses on her muscles and the turbulent thoughts that had been careering around her busy brain began to quiet as her focus turned to maintaining good form. As the worries that had beset her day faded away, her optimism started to rise. An hour later, happily exhausted, she stepped into the cool evening air. Compared to the washed-out blue when she'd arrived, the sky was now a dark petrol colour, courtesy of the slate grey clouds crowding the horizon. She gave a shiver and hurried over to her car.

Leaving the car park, she used her Bluetooth to pick up her voicemail: two new messages. The first was from DI York. The TV appeal had aired and calls were starting to trickle in. He made some parting shot, grumbling about being the only one still at the office — so few words, so much guilt. She felt her resentment bubble up. She'd had every intention of going back in, after a flying visit home to see to the dog. Now if she went back, it would look like she'd buggered off without a care and only returned because of his griping.

She forwarded to the second message. A woman's voice, hesitant and apologetic, filtered through the speakers.

'... Oh, I'm not very good with answer machines. I erm... Hello, this is a message for DC McKenzie. It's Mrs Forker. I spoke to you yesterday, about that missing woman. I'm sorry about the late hour but I just saw the news, with that poor woman's husband. I know they gave a specific number but you did ask me to call you directly. It's about Tuesday; about the man I saw scouring the verge.' The sound of a dog barking could be heard in the background. 'Not now Benji, I'm busy. Oh, hang on...' After a short pause, she was back. 'Sorry, about that. The dog couldn't find his chew toy. Anyway, where was I? Oh, yes. I'm sure it was him, even with the baseball cap on. Oh, and the van, the white one I saw on Monday, I remember now, it was there on Tuesday morning too, only parked further down the lane. Erm, that's everything. I'm at home all evening if you need to call me back. Thank you. Goodbye.'

Who had she recognised?

McKenzie scoured the road ahead for somewhere to stop. Shortly, she pulled over into a layby, where she listened to the message for a second time, a crowd of frowns on her forehead. She hit return call and after a handful of rings, the answer machine kicked in. She left a brief message asking Mrs Forker to call her back and hung up.

Excited now, sure the news appeal was the catalyst they so badly needed, she hurried home, saw to the dog, grabbed a packet of crisps and a granola bar, then headed back to the office. The place was in darkness except for an eerie glow emanating from York's glass-sided box. She looked in and saw him, chin resting on cupped hands, staring at the computer screen. She continued past to her own desk and switched on her lamp. She was reading details of the calls that had come in following the appeal when she heard footsteps approach.

'How long have you been here?' York asked, looking bleary eyed.

'About twenty minutes. You looked busy so I didn't disturb you.' She watched him rub his face with his hands and asked, 'Have you just woken up?'

'I might have nodded off for a few minutes.'

She shook her head, her mouth set in a half-smile. Now she didn't feel so bad about having taken a breather earlier. Which reminded her...

'When you called... I'd only nipped to the gym. I had every intention of coming back in.'

'I figured you would. I just thought you'd want to know how it was going.' He gestured to the report on her desk. 'How many have we had now?'

'Eighteen. Though none seem to be particularly helpful. Looks like there might be a couple of cranks and the rest are from people who saw her out and about, but all before Monday.'

'Where the hell was she between Monday lunchtime and the phone call?'

'How about trapped in a van?'

'You seriously think the white van the dog walker saw has something to do with it?'

'I didn't but I do now. Just after you called me, the woman with the dogs called and left a message.' McKenzie looked at him. 'I did tell you about her seeing a jogger looking in the ditch, didn't I?' York nodded. 'I thought so. Anyway, in her message she says she knows who it is. Annoyingly, she didn't give me a name so I'm waiting for her to call me back.'

'Sounds promising.' He got to his feet.

'How come you're still here anyway?'

'Catching up on paperwork.'

Ever since York's son, Cody, had nearly died of meningitis, he'd been leaving the office no later than seven so he could see his kids before their bedtime. What had changed?

'Couldn't you do that at home?' He didn't answer and evaded her gaze. 'Has something happened?'

'I've moved out… temporarily. Mel and me agreed it would be best while we work through some stuff.' A sad smile tugged at his lips. 'I've got to admit, it's tough not seeing the kids every day.'

She only just managed to keep her jaw from dropping open. She always thought Alex and Mel's marriage was as solid as they come. Then again, she would have said the same was true for her friendship with him. In the past, she would have had no qualms at trying to cheer him up with some beer and sympathy. But that was in the past. Now she couldn't help but think any such offer on her part would only make matters worse.

'Oh Alex, I'm sorry to hear that.'

'Like I said, it's only temporary. I'd appreciate it if you'd keep it to yourself.'

'Of course.'

'Anyway, I'd better let you get on.' He started to walk away. 'Don't stay too late,' he said, over his shoulder.

'I won't. Oh, and I'll get Control to give me a call if anything else comes in so they don't bother you.'

'Don't worry about it, I'll be here for a while yet.'

Later, at home, McKenzie mulled over the conversation. It had left her in a reflective mood. She was pushing a squash curry and pilau rice around her plate, wondering where York was staying, surprised she hadn't thought to ask, when her phone started to ring. She snatched it up and pressed it to her ear.

'Hello?'

'Hi. It's me.'

It was Phil. Shit. She'd managed to put him out of her mind.

128

'Oh… Phil. Hi,' She pushed her plate away and rose from the breakfast bar and started towards the lounge.

'Have I called at a bad time?'

That was her line yesterday.

'No. Why?'

'You don't exactly sound happy to hear from me. Are you still mad… about last night?'

Yes.

'No. We aired a public appeal on that missing person case I'm working. I thought it might have been Control calling with a lead.'

'Still no sign?'

'Nope.'

'Not looking promising then?'

'No.' She sank onto the sofa, slumping back in the seat. and running her fingers thought her hair. 'The only lead is to a father and son. The father, who owns an abattoir, had a run in with her last year, well, not with her directly, only he's got an alibi and while the son hasn't, he's got no obvious motive.'

'An abattoir would be useful for getting rid of a body.'

'Don't I know it. I've been there twice now. Both times reminded me why I'm glad to be veggie. So, how's your stakeout going?' She pursed her lips tightly before she said something about Lolly the interloper she might regret.

'Good. Yeah. We actually made a number of arrests yesterday. There's still some chasing down to do — a couple of gang members who've run to ground — but we're on the right track.'

'Does that mean you'll be free next weekend?'

'I'm not sure.'

'Not sure if you're on duty or not sure…?'

'I don't know Cat. What do you think?'

'Is this about that woman… Lolita?'

She heard him laugh.

'It's Charlotte and no, this isn't about her. She's just a colleague.'

'Really?'

He let out a sigh.

'This isn't going how I expected. I just thought…' But whatever it was he thought died in his throat.

She started to chew on a snag on a thumb nail. This was the point she should placate him, tell him it was okay, that she'd over-reacted. So why didn't she?

Instead, Phil spoke next, 'I'd better go. I've got an early start in the morning. Maybe we should get together next weekend? See if we can… well you know…?'

The call ended politely enough, though a little on the cool side. She set the phone down and returned to the kitchen, sticking the cold, half-eaten bowl of curry in the fridge. She poured herself a generous glass of wine and padded back into the lounge, where she proceeded to watch TV with unseeing eyes.

Why were relationships always so difficult? Everyone she knew seemed to be having problems. Apart from her parents, happy in their own little bubble. Was it too much to want some freedom and a loving relationship; children and a career; the ability to enjoy yourself while making a difference? Her thoughts slipped to Fern Marshall. What had she wanted… and how close had she been to getting it?

17.

6:00 a.m. Friday morning. McKenzie roused slowly as the alarm issued its sleep-ending trill. She rubbed her eyes and hauled herself onto an elbow before reaching for her phone. No new messages. A short shower sloughed away her tiredness, though it did little to lift her growing concern for the missing Mrs Marshall. With every day that had passed, she had grown more weighed down by the feeling that even if they found her... no... *when* they found her, it wouldn't be good news. After putting Harvey's bowl down, she breakfasted on tea and toast while staring morosely out of the window. A musical refrain began to play somewhere nearby. Jolting out of her trance, she raced out of the room, belted up the stairs into her bedroom and snatched up her phone.

'Hello,' she said, chest heaving. 'DC McKenzie.'

'Detective McKenzie. It's Celia Heart. From Freedom Farm.'

'Ms Heart, how can I help?' She glanced at the clock. It wasn't even 7.00 a.m.

'I saw the news last night... the appeal. They said Fern's bike has been found.'

McKenzie's heart rate began to pick up.

'Yes. Do you know something about it?'

'Just that the road they said it was found on, I think that's where Don Skinner lives. You know, the abattoir owner that we had a run-in with. I thought I'd better let you know.'

'I was aware of that, but thank you anyway.'

'Oh, good. Well, that was all. Oh, apart from the locker. I forgot to mention it before. Fern has got a locker at the sanctuary. The staff and volunteers use them to keep their things safe while they're working; some people keep spare clothes in them. Mucking out can be a... well, mucky job. I don't know if there's anything in Fern's. I could take a look and call you if there is?'

'I'd prefer to take a look myself.'

Half an hour later, McKenzie was picking her way across the patchwork of cobbles to the entrance of Freedom Farm.

'Detective!' a female voice called from behind. McKenzie turned to see Celia Heart waving at her while steering a colossal pig across the yard. 'I'll be with you in a minute, just got to get Cyril into his new pen.' Heart slapped the pig's backside with an open palm with no hint of trepidation and guided it through a gate and into a muddy enclosure.

While she waited, McKenzie took a look around at her surroundings. In a nearby paddock two women were grooming a pair of towering piebald horses. Behind them another couple, a man and a woman, were mucking out their stable, shifting forkfuls of soiled straw into an already overflowing wheelbarrow. Her attention drifted back to Cyril, who had made straight for a long concrete trough filled with vegetable scraps and was gorging himself contentedly. Not for the first time, she found herself struggling to imagine the missing woman, with her immaculate attire and polished nails, having any sort of hands-on role at a place where the mainstay of the work involves such vast quantities of muck and mud.

'I can't believe she still hasn't shown up,' Heart said, as she led McKenzie through to the staff room. 'Her husband must be frantic. The poor man. He looked so drawn on the TV last night.' They skirted short stacks of boxes overflowing with a miscellany of bedding, food and animal supplies, and headed towards the back of the room where two rows of battered, rust-edged metal lockers stood, six in each row. 'Like I said on the phone, they're only really for keeping bags and coats in while people are working. We make it clear to everyone not to bring anything of any value in with them. We're not insured if anything gets damaged or stolen.'

McKenzie looked down at the lockers. Most weren't closed, let alone locked, though one did have a shiny padlock hanging from the hasp.

'There's always one,' Heart said. 'We specifically ask them not to put locks on in case someone needs to share. There aren't enough lockers to go around for everyone to have one each.'

'Which one's Fern's?' McKenzie asked.

'I don't know.' Heart started to open them one at a time. 'I'm pretty sure she keeps a pair of wellies in it, so she can cycle here in something more suitable.'

Of the twelve lockers, six were empty, one contained a Tupperware filled with something of an indeterminable origin, and four contained a handful of mud-coated clothing. No wellington boots. Soon only the locker with the padlock remained.

'Let me go and find something to open this with,' Heart said, before leaving the room. A couple of minutes later she was back. 'Someone's fetching the bolt cutters from the workshop. Can I get you a drink while we wait... we have herbal as well as regular tea, or you can have coffee or squash?'

'Coffee for me, thanks. Black, no sugar.'

'You can have milk if you like. We have soya, oat or almond.'

'It's alright, I normally take it without, thanks.'

Heart made her way over to an archaic fridge; a cheap plastic kettle rested on top of it, next to an aged microwave. A couple of minutes later, she was pouring freshly boiled water into two chipped mugs when there was a knock at the door.

'That'll be Oliver... Come in!' she called loudly, adding, 'He won't come in unless asked.'

McKenzie recognised the bespectacled teenager as one of the three people who had been tending the lambs the first time she'd visited. He was clutching a pair of long-handled bolt cutters.

'You can just leave them there, thank you, Oliver.'

But instead of going, Oliver stood staring at McKenzie.

'You're very pretty,' he said.

McKenzie smiled.

'Thank you.'

'Mrs Marshall was pretty too. Danny said she's probably dead. That means she won't be pretty anymore, doesn't it?'

Heart looked at him, aghast.

'Oliver, don't say things like that. Of course, she's not dead. She's just gone away for a while.' She turned to McKenzie. 'I'm sure Danny only said it to wind him up.'

'I don't mind,' Oliver said, sounding unfazed by the idea of Mrs Marshall's demise. 'When my hamster died, he just looked like he was sleeping. I put him in a shoe box and my dad helped bury him in the garden. He said I was brave because I didn't cry. When my Granddad died, I wasn't allowed to see him so I don't know what he looked like but Dad said they dug a *really* big hole for him.'

'Why does Danny think Mrs Marshall is dead?' McKenzie asked.

'He didn't say. Only that she probably deserved it.'

Heart turned to McKenzie.

'I'm sure he didn't say that.' She turned on the earnest young man. 'Oliver, remember what I said before, about not talking about people, whether they can hear you or not.'

Oliver's smooth brow crumpled into a frown. He stood for a moment, blinking, then said, 'The lady asked and Mum says I mustn't lie. Danny did say that. He said it very quietly but I heard him.'

'Is Danny here today?' McKenzie asked. After Heart nodded, McKenzie turned to Oliver. 'Oliver, would you be able to get Danny and tell him Ms Heart would like to see him in the staff room?'

'Yes.'

When he didn't move, Heart said, 'Oliver, would you please go and get Danny now.'

Oliver hustled out of the door.

'You have to make it a direct instruction,' Heart explained. 'If you phrase it as a question, you'll get a yes or no but no action. It takes a bit of getting used to. I'm sure Danny has got nothing to do with Fern's disappearance. He's just a young lad, who says stupid things at times, but he's absolutely harmless.'

They used to say that about Dennis Nilsen.

Heart went on, 'You know what teenagers are like. I imagine he's worried about her but feels the need to make out that he isn't.'

'Worried about her, more than most people?'

'Maybe.' Heart leaned back in her seat. 'When Fern started here, Danny was… what can I say, he was a little besotted; used to follow her around like a lost lamb. Not surprising really, seeing as she could wear a potato sack and still look amazing. She humoured him at first but after a couple of months, when his crush didn't appear to be waning, I suggested she gently give him the brush-off. It seemed to do the trick as he kept his distance after that.'

'All the same, it won't hurt to see what he has to say for himself,' McKenzie said, picking up the bolt cutters. She returned to the locker and presented the blades to the padlock. 'Shall we?'

Wearing latex gloves, McKenzie started to remove the locker's contents. First out, a pair of women's gardening gloves, thin fabric things, more for keeping the hands clean than offering any degree of protection. She placed them into a clear plastic evidence bag she'd brought with her. Next came a pair of mud-spattered cargo pants, the type with a million pockets — all of which would need going through — followed by a blue fleece; a match to the one Mrs Marshall had been wearing in the photograph with the lamb. Lastly, a pair of green wellington boots. Only they weren't the last thing... After taking the boots out, McKenzie spotted a slim, brown A4 envelope leaning up against one of the side walls. She pulled it out and turned it over in her hands. The envelope was unremarkable... no writing, stamp or postmark to sully its surface. It was also unsealed. She was about to take a look inside when the door to the staff room opened.

'Hello...?' came a young man's voice.

'We're over here,' Heart called.

McKenzie slipped the envelope into the evidence bag just as Danny appeared. The scrawny slip of a lad darted a nervous glance at her from under a curtain of lanky, black hair.

He turned to Heart.

'Oliver said you wanted me.'

'Detective, this is Danny Mole. Danny, Detective McKenzie would like to ask you a few questions.'

He cast McKenzie a worried look, letting his gaze slip to the floor, before nodding.

'Why don't we go and sit down...?' she said, gesturing to the eclectic collection of chairs at the other end of the room.

Danny pulled out an office chair from under the desk and slumped down, sending it rolling back on its castors. McKenzie eased herself down on a wooden dining chair that felt a lot ricketier than it looked, which was saying something.

Heart was hovering by the door.

'I'll make myself scarce. Let you two talk in private.'

'No, please join us,' McKenzie said, thinking the other woman's presence might make Danny more at ease.

Heart dragged a chair over and set it next to Danny's. She gave him a motherly smile, cheery and round-cheeked. McKenzie thought all that was needed now was for her to say, 'Isn't this nice?' Only she didn't.

'Danny,' McKenzie started gently. 'Why did you tell Oliver that Mrs Marshall was dead?'

After a few minutes, when he still hadn't said anything, Heart gave his knee a tap.

'Danny, answer the lady.'

He scuffed the floor with the toe of his mud-caked boot.

'I suppose I thought she must be. The news last night said she was still missing.'

'Danny, I understand you're quite fond of Fern.' McKenzie wasn't sure, but she thought she could see a flush of pink creep above the neck of his black cable-knit jumper. 'And you're right, she is still missing and could be in real trouble. Which is why we need everybody to tell us whatever they can to help us find her. Do you know something that might help?' He squirmed under her scrutiny, his face now a mottled collection of reds and pinks.

'Come on Danny,' Heart coaxed. 'You're a friend of Fern's. You used to talk to her all the time when she first started here. Surely you want to help?'

He crossed his arms and sank even further down in his chair, chin buried in his chest.

'She's not my friend,' he said sulkily. 'Not any more.'

'Why not?' McKenzie asked. 'What happened?' He gave an abrupt shake of the head before looking down, appearing to be preoccupied with a torn thumb nail, which he started to pick at. 'What if she's dead? How would that make you feel? Would you be glad?'

She felt Heart's accusatory gaze, but ignored it, too interested in the look of horror that flashed across Danny's face.

'Has she upset you, Danny?' He resumed picking his nail. Silence hung in the air between them. McKenzie bit back her impatience and gently asked, 'What did she do?'

Still nothing. Christ, were all teenagers this annoying?

She tried again, 'She must have done something Danny. You're clearly annoyed with her.'

He darted a glance at her. 'Because she's a liar!' McKenzie let the silence mount and after what felt like an indeterminably long wait, he eventually said, 'I sort of asked her if she wanted to go out some time... just friends, like. She said she couldn't because she was married.' He narrowed his eyes. 'Didn't stop her seeing *him* though, did it?'

McKenzie felt a spike of adrenalin but forced herself to remain calm, at least on the outside.

'*Him?*'

'Her boyfriend. I heard her talking to him on the phone.'

'How do you know it wasn't her husband?'

Danny glared at her.

'Because I'm not stupid. This one time, I heard her telling him her husband would be home late.'

'Maybe it was a friend?'

He huffed out a sigh, crossed his arms and looked down at the ground. 'What's the point?'

'I'm sorry. I'm just trying to understand how you knew it was a boyfriend and not a friend.'

Suddenly, his face crumpled.

'She told him she loved him.' He wrapped his arms around his chest and glared defiantly at the two women, as though they were the ones who had betrayed him.

McKenzie waited a minute, giving him time to pull himself together, before asking the million-dollar question, 'Danny, do you know who Fern's boyfriend is?' He shook his head, while wearing a miserable expression. 'No idea at all?'

'No.'

'Did she say anything that might help identify him? I assume you'd like us to find him? He might have something to do with her disappearance. He could be in a lot of trouble if that's the case,' she said, hoping to persuade him of the merits of helping.

It paid off.

'I think he must be ugly.'

'Why do you say that?'

'I heard her say how her husband would never believe she'd choose someone like him.' He looked at McKenzie hopefully, 'That means there's got to be something wrong with him, right?'

'Let me get this right... she said "My husband would never believe I've chosen someone like you."' McKenzie looked at him, watching for a response.

He nodded.

Maybe he was a she?

'I honestly had no idea about any of that,' Heart said once she and McKenzie were alone. 'Though I don't know why I'm surprised. I'm always the last to know anything. Kath's the one who knows all the gossip.'

'Is she? Maybe I should have a quick chat with her'

'I take it there's no news,' Kath Winters said, taking Danny's vacated seat.

'Unfortunately, no,' McKenzie said.

'I saw the appeal last night. I only wish I could help.'

'There might be something. It's a delicate matter. There's a rumour that Fern may have been having an affair.'

Winters' eyes grew wide.

'Surely not anybody here? I'd know if it was.' She looked affronted that there might be a secret she wasn't party to.

'We don't know,' Heart said. 'Danny overheard her talking to someone on the phone.'

'Ah. I wouldn't pay too much attention to anything Danny tells you about Fern. The lad's smitten. That's what he's probably told himself to explain why she isn't interested in him.'

'Wouldn't the fact she's married be enough to do that?' McKenzie said.

'Who knows how a teenage boy's mind works?'

'Fern never said anything that makes you think there could be some truth to what he's saying?'

'Not at all. But then Fern isn't really the chatty type.'

'Why do you think she volunteers here?' McKenzie asked, looking at the two women opposite.

Heart shrugged.

'People volunteer for all sorts of reasons. Some do it to avoid having to stare at the same four walls every day, others want to make friends with like-minded people, and then there are those where it's all about helping the animals.'

'Fern's definitely in the last category,' Winters said. 'I'm not saying she's antisocial or anything, but now I think about it, she has been a bit remote of late.' After a moment, she added, 'Poor woman. When I saw the news last night and they said her bike had been found by the side of the road, it made my stomach turn.

I thought then, it doesn't look good, does it? She used to go everywhere on that thing.'

With nothing more for her there, McKenzie made to leave. Heart accompanied her back to the car, providing a potted history of the sanctuary and how she came to take up her role. McKenzie thumbed the car's remote as soon as they were close enough. A loud blip rang out, causing some sheep in a nearby field to run away skittishly. McKenzie watched them resume grazing a safe distance away.

'The lambs...' she said. 'The ones Don Skinner said had been taken from his yard. Did you have them?'

For a moment, Heart didn't say anything. Instead, she turned and looked across into the field where sheep, horses and donkeys coexisted amicably.

'You see those three...' She pointed to a group of horses: two chestnut mares with coats as shiny as a nut and a dappled grey pony that looked like every little girl's dream. 'When we first got them, they were flea-bitten, mange-ridden and so malnourished you could play their ribs like a glockenspiel. Look at them now.' McKenzie looked. They all appeared healthy and content. 'They and all the other animals — like the lambs — are what make me so proud of what we achieve here.'

Just then, the two mares set off at a canter, bounding around the field, clearly enjoying themselves.

'You're right to feel proud, but you still haven't answered my question.' When there was no reply, she turned, only to find Celia Heart already making her way back to the farmhouse.

18.

McKenzie was pondering whether or not to go after Heart and demand an answer, when her phone started ringing. She dug it out of her pocket and scanned the display.

'Hi Alex.'

'Cat, where are you?'

'At Freedom Farm. The manager called. Said she had some of Fern's things here. I came by to take a look. Why? What's up?'

'Nothing. I just wondered when you were coming in. We've had more calls in response to the appeal. They could do with being followed up as soon as possible.'

'Can't Darren do it?' she said, climbing into her car and throwing the evidence bag onto the passenger seat. 'I was just about to go and see Mrs Forker. She still hasn't called me back and she only lives around the corner.'

'I thought Darren was with you.'

'I haven't seen him since the canteen yesterday afternoon.'

'Bloody hell. I'll—'

'Don't worry,' she jumped in. 'I'll give him a ring, find out what he's up to. We'll sort something out between us.'

After ending the call, she started the car and set off down the lane. She called Crawley's number.

After a couple of rings his voice came through the speakers, 'Hey Cat. What's up?'

'Where are you?'

'In the car.'

'Where exactly?'

'In the driver's seat.' He gave a laugh that threatened to turn into a choking cough.

'Are you on something?'

'No. I'm just having a bit of fun.'

'Maybe you can save the jokes until after we've found Mrs Marshall.'

'Sorry.' It was a petulant attempt, but better than nothing.

'So where are you?'

'I've been talking to neighbours, asking if they'd seen the bike, like you wanted me to.'

'I thought you were going to do that yesterday.'

'Yeah, I tried, only most people were still out.'

'So how are you getting on?'

'It's been a total waste of time. No one saw anything, even those who go that way regularly. I've got one more address, then I'm done.'

'Okay, well I've just had Alex on the phone. He wants us to go through the calls that have come in following the appeal. When you've finished, if you can get back to the station and make a start, I'll join you as soon as I can.'

She thumbed the button on the steering wheel, ending the call just as she turned the corner onto Mrs Forker's lane. A short distance away, just in front of Bridget Forker's weatherboarded cottage, was a black BMW that looked suspiciously like Crawley's. She pulled up in front of it, catching the surprised expression on Crawley's face through his windscreen. They both climbed out of their vehicles.

'I take it this is your last house,' McKenzie said, slamming the door shut.

Crawley cast her a puzzled look.

'How did you know? I might have just been about to leave and still have one left to do.'

'Because you said no one so far had anything interesting to say. If you'd spoken with Mrs Forker, you wouldn't be saying that. She called me last night and left a message after watching the appeal. Seems it jogged her memory. She now claims she knows who the jogger was.'

'Really? Who?'

'She didn't get that far, which is why I'm here.'

'Good. Well, you can ask her whether she saw the bike while you're at it. No point in us both going in. If I put my foot down, I might just make it back in time for tea break.' He gave her a wink and turned, about to get back in his car.

'Hold your horses, Speedy Gonzales. You can ask her your question and I'll ask mine. At least that way, you'll be able to finish the job you started and write a comprehensive report for a change.' So far, Crawley had yet to do a single piece of paperwork associated with the case and that was going to change, whether he liked it or not.

Crawley rolled his eyes, but started up the path all the same, following McKenzie past the small red car on the drive. As they drew close to the house, a shrill yapping started from behind the wooden front door. It rose to a frenetic climax after Crawley rang the bell.

A minute later, McKenzie nodded towards the door. 'Try again.'

They could hear the chime from outside, so the bell was obviously working. When there was still no reply, McKenzie stepped back and looked the house over. The front room curtains were closed, as were those on the second floor. It was nearly 10.00 a.m. Surely the woman didn't sleep in that late, not with three energetic, hungry pooches to feed. Maybe she was unwell? McKenzie bent down and peered through the letterbox. The dogs came skittering down the hallway, issuing high-pitched whines interspersed with snappy yelps.

'Mrs Forker! It's DC McKenzie. Are you there?' She pressed her ear to the opening and listened. She could hear nothing over the dogs' raucous barks. She let the flap snap shut.

'You stay here in case she answers and I'll take a look around the back.'

McKenzie followed the path around to the rear of the house. An intricate lace curtain blocked the view through the half-glazed door into the kitchen. She knocked then tested the handle. It was locked. In the background she could hear the muffled barks of the dogs start up again. Perhaps Mrs Forker had gone out?

Then she thought of the car on the drive.

She dragged a garden chair off the lawn and set it down by the window, climbed up and peered through. Bridget Forker lay sprawled across the floor in the middle of the room.

'Shit! Crawley!' McKenzie yelled, scouring the area for something to break the back door open with. Spotting a small rock in a nearby border, she prised it free, shrugged out of her jacket and wrapped it around her hand with the rock in it. She thrust the rock hard into the glass just above the door handle. It broke easily and glass fell freely onto the floor inside. Once the hole was big enough, she slipped her hand through and turned the key.

'What's going on?' Crawley asked, rounding the corner.

'Mrs Forker's on the floor inside.' She flung the door open and rushed in. 'Mrs Forker...' Her steps slowed on taking in the grey, flaccid face and unseeing eyes. A mottled patch of purple peeked above the open collar of the dead woman's cream shirt, while a puddle of congealed treacle-like blood spilled out onto the black and white linoleum. She reached out and felt for a pulse she knew wasn't there before pressing the back of her hand to the woman's forehead.

'Stone cold.'

'She's dead?' Crawley asked from over by the door.

'Has been for some time,' McKenzie replied, as she studied the prone figure at her feet.

'Do you reckon it was like a heart attack or something?'

'Or something.' McKenzie stepped back and pointed at the blood on the floor. 'There are marks on her neck as well, like someone tried to strangle her.' A torrent of barks and scratching noises erupted at the door to the hallway. She looked across at Crawley. 'You go and call it in... and tell them there are dogs that'll need taking care of. Oh, and don't forget to let Alex know.'

'What are you going to do?'

'I'm going to get the dogs out. Who knows when they last had anything to eat or drink?'

The pair returned to their cars. McKenzie quickly pulled out a protective suit and overshoes, then grabbed a long length of rope from her boot. Leaving Crawley leaning against the bonnet of his car talking on his phone, she returned to the back door, donned the protective clothing, then crossed the kitchen and the small lounge before slipping around the door into the hallway. The dogs ran to her in a frenzy of barking, baring their teeth while simultaneously wagging their tails. After a few minutes of quiet fuss, they grew compliant enough to let her loop the rope through their collars. Exiting through the front door, she ushered them into the garden and tied them to the picket fence.

Crawley came over just as she was filling a bowl she'd found in the garden with water from an outside tap.

'What are they eating?' he asked. The dogs were ravenously chewing on something.

'Bonios. I always keep some in the car. They're the only currency Harvey understands.' She watched them devour the bone-shaped biscuits. 'Judging by how they're wolfing them down, I'd say Mrs Forker has been dead a while.' Her gaze drifted back to the house, a troubled expression on her face. 'I think I'll go take a look around the rest of the house, make sure there are no more nasty surprises. Could you wait and flag down whoever shows up?'

'Sure.'

After slipping on a fresh pair of plastic overshoes, McKenzie entered the house for a second time. The compact kitchen was tidy. A single plate, knife, fork and glass lay on the stainless-steel drainer, clean and dry. In the corner, three dog bowls sat empty next to a full bowl of water. There was no sign of any weapon or evidence of a struggle. Whoever had killed Mrs Forker had acted swiftly and strongly. So why the two sets of injuries?

Steering clear of the body and the bloody, brown smears on the floor, she moved through to the small but beautifully set out lounge. A comfortable two-seater sofa and single armchair, nestled in front of a log burner, gave it a cosy feel. A book lay open, face down, on the seat of the chair, while a cup of what looked like cold tea sat untouched on an adjacent side table. Moving through to the hallway, McKenzie's nose wrinkled, the smell of dog excrement strong in the small space. She sidestepped a yellow puddle and crossed cautiously to the bottom stair. Smears of what looked like dried blood marred the light oak floor. She looked back into the lounge — there was no sign of any blood on the beige carpet. Had one of the dogs been injured? She hadn't noticed anything. Something to check when she got outside. With one foot poised on the bottom stair, she strained her ears, listening for the slightest sound, but the house was silent, save for the loud ticking of an intricately carved pendulum clock on the wall. She climbed the stairs and, alighting at the top step, scanned the area. All of the doors were open. She walked from room to room. Everything was neat and tidy. Apart from in the bathroom, where the toilet seat and floor around the bowl were splashed with water. She realised the dogs might have gone hungry but at least they'd found something to drink.

Back outside, she passed Crawley by the front door, head buried in his phone. She went over to the dogs and gave them each a quick check over. Satisfied they were all unharmed, she returned to her car just as York pulled up. Behind him came the Forensic Service van. A volley of slamming car doors followed.

York made his way over to her as a pair of crime scene investigators moved to the rear of their vehicle and began unloading their equipment.

'Where is she?' York asked, a grim set to his jaw.

'In the kitchen, around the back. This way...' McKenzie started down the path, with York following close behind.

He nodded to Crawley as he passed, who fell into step with him. York held up a hand.

'Darren, could you stay here please. Point everyone in the right direction when they arrive.'

At the back door, York slipped on some latex gloves.

'The door was locked so I broke the glass to gain entry,' McKenzie explained.

York pushed the door open with a finger and took a look at the frame.

'No evidence of a forced entry.' He pushed the door open wider and peered into the kitchen, taking in the prostrate form of Mrs Forker on the floor.

'I already took a quick look around inside,' McKenzie said. 'There's nothing obvious missing. When we arrived, the dogs were shut in the hallway.' York nodded but said nothing. McKenzie continued, 'There are some marks on her neck but there's also blood on the floor under the body. I also noticed smears of what looks like blood in the hallway. Which is interesting, as I couldn't see any on the carpet between the kitchen and the hallway door.'

'Make sure you let the CSIs know about those.' He turned around at the sound of approaching footsteps. Dr Stuart Fitzwilliam, a red-headed mammoth of a man came striding towards them. Crawley trailed behind him like a shadow.

'Morning, Fitz,' York said.

'Still morning, is it?' Fitzwilliam said in a deep baritone that had earned him the nickname the Jolly Red Giant. 'Feels like I've already put a full day in. Where is the unfortunate lady then?'

York pointed through the open door and stepped back to admit the pathologist. The two CSIs rounded the corner. McKenzie stopped them as they passed and let them know about the stains in the hallway.

As the three detectives waited outside, York paced backwards and forwards. Crawley sat at a small outdoor table bathed in sunlight, while McKenzie stood at the threshold watching the medical man conduct his preliminary inspection of the body.

A few minutes later, Fitzwilliam stepped outside, pulling the door closed behind him. York stopped pacing.

'That's one I haven't come across before. Very macabre,' Fitzwilliam said. 'I can't be certain until I open her up, but it looks like strangulation followed by a bit of post-mortem butchery.'

'Butchery?' York said.

'I think that's an appropriate term, seeing that from what I can tell, whoever killed her also relieved the poor woman of a kidney.'

'They actually took her kidney out in there?'

'Yes. Post-mortem, judging by the relatively small amount of blood.'

'Is the kidney around somewhere?'

'Not that I saw. Though I did overhear one of the technicians say something about traces of blood and tissue in the hallway. Perhaps the killer left it for those yappy little critters tied out front to enjoy. Tests will confirm in due course.'

'What about time of death?' York asked.

'I would estimate that she died anywhere between twelve and fourteen hours ago.'

McKenzie put a hand to her open mouth.

'Mrs Forker phoned me at seven last night.'

'In which case, make that between twelve and thirteen and a half hours ago,' Fitzwilliam said, giving them a nod, before returning to his car.

Crawley nudged McKenzie.

'Just think, if you'd come here last night, instead of this morning, you might have caught her killer red-handed.'

York shot Crawley a disapproving look, then said, 'Cat, you weren't to know she was in any danger. And in any case, I'm sure it would have still been too late.'

'I should have realised something was up when she didn't return my message,' McKenzie said, fighting a feeling of mounting guilt.

'You couldn't have known. Who's to say she wasn't out walking her dogs and missed the fact you'd called?' York said.

But McKenzie wasn't listening. She was too busy thinking through what had happened.

Frowning, she said, 'How did the killer know that she'd recognised him? In her call, it sounded as though it was the appeal that triggered her memory.'

150

'Maybe the appeal reminded her to call you. She could have seen the killer out earlier in the day, recognised him then and given the game away by her reaction,' York suggested.

Crawley thrust his hands in his pockets and propped himself against a sturdy wrought iron table.

'I don't get it. Marshall's missus went missing on Monday and her bike wasn't found till Wednesday. What does it matter who the woman saw Tuesday morning? It's totally unrelated. In fact, didn't she say it was just a guy out jogging?'

'No,' McKenzie replied. 'She said it was a man dressed like a jogger, who appeared to be scouring the verge for something.' Seized with an idea, she added, 'What if he was actually there to ditch the bike but after Mrs Forker passed him with the dogs, he figured she'd come back that way, so changed his mind and did it later?'

'It's possible, I suppose,' York said.

'What do you think the thing is with taking her kidney out?' Crawley asked. Suddenly he looked at them, wide-eyed, like a young lad who's opened a present on Christmas morning to find exactly what he'd asked for. 'What if it's a serial killer? One who collects kidneys as trophies. Mrs Marshall could be lying dead someplace with hers missing.'

'Let's not get carried away,' York said. He glanced over to the closed back door. 'I have to say though, I'm not fancying Mrs Marshall's chances much in the light of this. Come on, let's go in and take a look around, see what we can find.'

Two hours later all they had learned was that Mrs Forker kept a tidy house and enjoyed turning her hand to a bit of cross-stitch. There was no clue, as far as they could tell, as to who had brought her life to a premature end.

'Maybe it's no coincidence Fitzwilliam used the word butchery,' McKenzie said, as they gathered on the path outside of the house.

'You think the Skinners might have had something to do with it?' York said.

'She said the man she saw Tuesday morning was wearing a baseball cap. Hats can make people look quite different. What if she saw Robbie or Don Skinner yesterday, without a cap on, and something else about them made her realise it was them she'd seen? Maybe that's why she mentioned seeing the white van again?'

York was nodding. Crawley also started to nod.

'Killing her to stop her identifying them is one thing, but as Darren said, why take her kidney?' York asked.

Just then, the dogs started to bark excitedly. McKenzie watched as the council's dog warden loaded them into the back of his van. She started to shake her head.

'I don't know. All I know is, whether he fed the organ to the dogs or took it as a souvenir, either way, it's the work of one sick individual.

19.

'I'd better get going,' Alex said after checking his watch. 'I need to let the DCI know where we're at, get a team together and the incident room up and running. You two track down the Skinners. Find out what they were up to last night. Briefing will be at five. '

Crawley left his car outside the dead woman's house and climbed into McKenzie's Skoda.

'A lot of serial killers start with animals,' he said as they started down the road. 'A lot also have some sort of trauma in their childhood.' He twisted in his seat to face her. 'Robbie Skinner's mother died when he was young and he had to go back and live with his dad. That'd be enough to send anyone off their rocker.'

'You think Robbie Skinner's a serial killer and we're going to find jars filled with human organs hidden away in a basement somewhere?'

'Why not?'

She gave him a cynical smile and turned her attention back to the road just in time to avoid an oncoming car.

'Idiot! Did you see that? He was right in the middle of the bloody road.' She released a long breath then went on, 'How does your theory fit with the fact it looks like the kidney was fed to the dogs?'

'We don't know that it was. They might have given the dogs some meat to keep them quiet. Maybe they fed them eyeballs,' he said, laughing loudly.

McKenzie shook her head but said nothing. Her thoughts drifted to Fern Marshall. It seemed increasingly likely that she was lying dead somewhere, killed by the same hand that wielded the knife with Mrs Forker. But if so, where the hell was she and why was she killed? Was she the intended target or was it just the case of wrong time, wrong place? And could it really be the handiwork of a serial killer? Despite her cynicism, she couldn't help but pray Crawley was wrong.

Twenty minutes later they pulled up on the concrete apron at Skinner's Yard. Don Skinner and his cronies were standing outside, nursing mugs from which steam curled into the air.

'Not again,' Don Skinner said as McKenzie climbed out of the car. 'You keep turning up like a bad smell. Don't you lot have anything better to do?'

'Having a break from killing things are you, Mr Skinner?' she said, eyes flashing.

Skinner pushed away from the wall and jerked his head towards the door. 'Break's over lads.'

The men started to retreat indoors.

'Mr Skinner,' McKenzie called. 'We have more questions for you.'

He turned and folded his arms.

'You can ask as many questions as you like, but I already told you everything I know.'

'Where were you between seven and nine last night?'

He regarded her suspiciously.

'Why?'

'Could you just answer the question please.'

'In the pub, with a mate.'

'The whole evening?' He looked at her, hooded eyes narrowing and shrugged. 'We need to know what time you left,' she pressed.

'I left when I was good and ready.' There was a long pause. McKenzie stood there, looking at him, waiting it out. Eventually he folded. 'About seven. Maybe a bit later.'

The time could fit.

'Did you leave on your own?' she asked.

'Course I did. Who am I going to leave with?'

She ignored his question.

'Do you know a Mrs Forker... Bridget Forker?'

She watched a frown cloud his brow. Shortly he shook his head, sending his jowls wobbling.

'Can't say as I do. Who is she? Not another one of those do-gooders gone missing?'

'She was a neighbour of yours.'

'Most of those around our way are too far up their own backsides to be of any interest to me.'

'Mrs Forker was found murdered this morning.'

Skinner's gaze flitted between McKenzie and Crawley. After a short pause he said, 'Like I said, I didn't know the woman.'

'The pub you were in, was it the same one that you went to on Monday?'

'Might have been.'

'This isn't a game Mr Skinner. A woman is dead. If you can't answer a simple question I'm going to start to wonder why.'

'Same pub. Same friend. I gave you the details the last time you were here. I can give you them again, if you've lost them.'

'No, that's fine. We've still got them, thank you.'

Skinner gave a sly smile.

'I expected you to have been in touch with him before now. Thought you were keen on finding out if I was where I said I was.'

McKenzie looked at him flatly.

'Oh, we are. We'll be speaking to him soon, don't worry. Back to last night then, what time did you get home?'

'I can't remember the exact time. Eight, quarter past. Something like that.'

McKenzie frowned. That time of night it couldn't take more than twenty minutes to get from the pub he was claiming to be at to his house.

'Did you go straight home?'

'Apart from pulling over for a piss, yes.' He stared defiantly at her. She knew the type — thought throwing in the odd vulgarity made him more of a man.

'You're saying it took you over an hour to get home?'

'I went the long way on the back roads. It pays to be careful... there are a lot of idiots on the road at that time of night.'

A lot of drunken idiots, McKenzie thought, then asked, 'Had you been drinking?'

He snorted out a laugh.

'Call yourself a detective? What do you think? I'd been to the bloody pub, hadn't I?'

McKenzie looked at him blankly. Skinner returned his own fish-eyed stare, seeming happy to let the silence stretch. Not wanting to turn it into a game, she broke the silence.

'Was your son in when you got home?'

'Course he was. The pathetic little sod doesn't have a life.'

'We'd like to talk to him too then. Is he inside?' She deliberately let her gaze slide to the white van parked a little distance away.

Don Skinner walked towards the building, to the window at the back and rapped on the glass.

'Robbie. Get out here now.'

Shortly, the fire exit swung open. Robbie Skinner peered out.

156

'The filth wants a word.' Don Skinner hooked a thumb in the direction of the detectives before pushing past Robbie and entering the building through the back door.

Robbie started towards them, eyes nervously darting from one to the other. McKenzie studied his bruises; though less livid than they had been, the sallow yellows and greys gave him an unwashed, scruffy appearance.

'Robbie, can you tell us where you were last night, between seven and nine?'

'Why?' His voice cracked. He cleared his throat and went on, 'Has something happened? Have you found her?' With his pinched brows and urgent expression, McKenzie was finding it difficult to tell whether it was fear or concern she was looking at.

'Just answer the question,' Crawley said, sounding more menacing than the situation warranted.

'I was at home. I got in from work about quarter to six and was there all night.'

'Any way of proving that?' Crawley asked.

Robbie shot him a worried look. 'No.'

'What time did your dad get in?' McKenzie asked.

'About quarter to eight. Why? What's happened?'

'Do you know a Mrs Bridget Forker?'

His eyes roamed around, as though the answer might suddenly appear from the air.

Eventually, he shook his head and McKenzie explained, 'She was a neighbour of yours. Used to regularly walk her three dogs past your house.'

His expression lifted.

'I've seen her around but I don't know her.' He frowned. 'You said *was... was* a neighbour. Has something happened to her?'

'Mrs Forker was murdered in her home last night,' McKenzie said. 'We're looking for anyone who might be able to help our enquiries.'

'What do you know about it?' Crawley said, affecting a gruff voice.

'Me?' Robbie's eyes shot wide. He shook his head vehemently. 'I don't know anything. Why would I?'

'Because you saw her earlier and realised she—'

McKenzie set out a hand stopping Crawley mid-flow and said, 'We're trying to talk to anyone who might have seen her yesterday. Did you?'

Robbie looked down at the floor, shook his head and said, 'No.' After a moment he looked back up at McKenzie. 'Can I go now?'

Reluctantly, she agreed and watched him walk away, shoulders slumped, with a growing suspicion that he knew a lot more than he was letting on.

20.

By the time they had finished at the abattoir, it was coming up for 4:30 p.m. McKenzie dropped Crawley back at his car and the pair made their way to the station independently.

McKenzie headed straight to the newly established incident room, where a collection of white boards lined one wall, looking depressingly empty. York and DC Wynchcombe were at the back of the room, bent over a laptop. Wynchcombe tapped at the keyboard and the words 'Operation Elm Tree' slowly appeared on a large white screen hanging on the wall behind them. York looked up as McKenzie approached and nodded towards the evidence bag in her hand.

'Anything interesting?'

'It's the stuff I got from Mrs Marshall's locker at Freedom Farm. I haven't had time to go through it all yet. It's mostly clothes.'

'So, how did you get on with the Skinners?'

'Skinner senior says he was at the pub with a friend until about seven. Same pub and same friend as Monday lunchtime. We didn't have time to check it out and get back here for the briefing, but I made it clear we would be following it up. That didn't seem to faze him. Robbie, on the other hand, has no alibi; says he was at home on his own until his dad got in.'

'But wasn't Robbie at the yard all day Monday, so he can't have anything to do with Mrs Marshall. Is that right?' York said.

'Yes, but we don't know what time he left exactly. All we know was it was some time around four. There's nothing to say it wasn't a little before four, which means there's scope for him to have been with Mrs Marshall around the time she called her husband screaming.'

York shook his head.

'Hardly the makings of a strong case, is it?'

Feeling equally despondent at their lack of progress, McKenzie left him and Wynchcombe working on the presentation and headed for her desk. As she set the evidence bag down, the brown A4 envelope inside caught her eye. With everything that had happened, she'd all but forgotten about it. She reached in her drawer for some gloves, about to take a look, when she became aware of a steady flow of people passing. She glanced at her phone. 16:58. Out of time, she dropped the gloves and grabbed her notepad and pen and hurriedly followed the crowd.

The incident room was nearly full. McKenzie managed to grab one of the last seats in the back row, near to the door. York stood at the front, watching everyone arrive. Behind him, Wynchcombe sat at a desk, computer at the ready. York waited until there were no more stragglers then nodded to a PC at the entrance to the room, who pushed the door closed.

York stepped forward and the chatter slowly died.

'Right, it looks like we're all here, so I'll get started. Welcome to Operation Elm Tree. Elm Tree's remit covers the murder of Mrs Bridget Forker, who was attacked and mutilated in her own home yesterday evening and the disappearance of Mrs Fern Marshall, who was last seen around midday Monday, by Mrs Forker no less.'

McKenzie listened as he outlined the facts and said her piece when asked to outline the different lines of enquiry that had already been followed. The discussion revealed nothing new and after individual tasks had been assigned and the meeting disbanded, she hurried back to her desk, keen to see what the evidence bag had in store for her.

She pulled on a pair of latex gloves and reached into the bag for the envelope. Hoping its plain exterior didn't mean she was in for a disappointment, she prised open the unsealed flap and peered inside. Frowning, she tipped the envelope up and slid its sole contents — a grainy black and white photograph — onto her desk and spun it around to read the small square of text printed on the top corner. She swallowed. Whatever she was expecting, it wasn't that. She reached for her phone and started to take photos.

'Cat…'

She gave a start. She hadn't heard York approach.

'Alex. You need to see this. I found it at the back of Fern Marshall's locker at the rescue place.'

York stepped forward and looked down at the image on her desk.

Crawley suddenly appeared.

'Sorry to interrupt,' he said. 'Boss, I know back there you said you were going to split the work into two strands. I was wondering, wouldn't it be better to have three sub-teams? Two looking into the cases of the two women, like you suggested, but with another one looking into the possibility of a serial killer. I'd be happy to do some data analysis, see if there have been any other murders with the same profile as our killer. What do you think?'

'I think you might be a little premature, seeing as so far we've only got one murder.'

'At the moment sure, but we all know Fern Marshall's feeding the worms somewhere.'

McKenzie screwed her nose up at the unpleasant term.

'If that turns out to be true, I might consider extending the investigation, but at the moment there are other priorities.'

'Okay. Just so you know, I'd be keen on covering the serial killer angle if you do change your mind. A serial killer case'd be cool, huh?'

'Depends on your perspective,' York said. 'Not so cool for anyone in their target demographic, eh?' He turned to McKenzie and gestured to the photograph. 'You think this might be hers then?'

'I don't know. There's no name, only a patient reference number, and while we can't be absolutely certain it's hers, given it was in her locker with her things, I'd say that's a reasonable assumption.'

York leaned in, squinting.

'Is that a date?'

'Yes. It was taken last Wednesday.'

Crawley rounded her desk and stood looking down at the photo.

'What is it?'

'What does it look like?' McKenzie said.

'I don't know. Some grey blobs.'

'It's an image of an ultrasound scan,' York said.

'Of what?'

'What are they usually of?' McKenzie said, returning the photograph to the envelope and slipping it back into the evidence bag. 'It's an image of a foetal scan... looks like Mrs Marshall is expecting a baby.'

'*If* it's her scan,' York cautioned.

'Why don't we just call Mr Marshall and ask him?' Crawley said.

McKenzie shook her head in disbelief.

'You can't do that. It might not be his.'

'Doesn't matter,' Crawley replied. 'He either knows she's pregnant or he doesn't. Either way, he's hardly likely to know if the baby isn't his.'

'He would if they hadn't had sex for a while,' McKenzie said.

'Yeah, right. They've got like this perfect marriage.'

'According to Marshall,' McKenzie said. 'He might be saying that because he wants to save face. Look, why don't I contact the clinic that did the scan and see if they can confirm it is Fern Marshall's? I also think it might be worth me going to see Simon Parry, the ex-boyfriend, in the morning. Even if he doesn't know where she is, we know they had lunch together recently. Fern might have confided in him. When I spoke to him before, she hadn't been missing long. He might have felt it inappropriate to share the content of their conversation with me at that stage. If he does know something, given what's happened to Mrs Forker and the fact we still haven't found Fern, I'm sure he'll talk.'

'Good idea.'

McKenzie turned to Crawley.

'Darren, how did you get on with the ANPR check for Parry's car? We could do with knowing whether he was out of the area when he said he was.'

'I was going to do that next.'

'You said that yesterday.'

'You were the one who wanted that other stuff doing,' he snapped back.

York looked at him.

'Darren, just do it.' He started back towards his office.

McKenzie turned back to her computer. Crawley showed no sign of moving. He indicated the envelope with a flick of a finger.

'How come you didn't mention that in the briefing?'

'I only opened it afterwards.'

'You didn't look at it when you picked it up this morning?'

'No. I got distracted by something else. And then with the discovery of Mrs Forker I forgot all about it.'

'Sure you didn't keep it back so you could do the big reveal to Alex on your own?'

'What? No. Why would I do that?'

But she was talking to empty air. Crawley was already walking away.

21.

That night McKenzie slept fitfully. The fact the missing woman was possibly pregnant played heavily on her mind. She woke early to the sound of rain lashing down on the roof tiles above her head. Thankfully, by the time she finished her tea and toast the downpour was beginning to ease. She donned her raincoat and wellies and grabbed Harvey's lead from the understairs cupboard and headed for the door.

'Come on Harv. Walkies.' Harvey looked up from his bed, his droopy eyes communicating his lack of interest. 'Come on Harvey.' She rattled his lead. Ordinarily that would rouse him. Not this time. 'Harvey. Come on!'

The dog lifted his head, sluggishly moved into a sitting position and eyed the lead. She rubbed a hand around his ears and flabby jowls. 'You alright? Still a bit dozy, hey?' Finally, he clambered to his feet.

Stepping out of the door and into the cold drizzle, McKenzie hiked up her collar and started to walk. The outing was really only for the dog to relieve himself but it also gave her time to think, and this morning her mind was working overtime and the slow pace dictated by Harvey's barrel-shaped body and short legs proved ideal. At the end of the lane, she turned right onto a long, sloping street called Orchard Rise — a row of blocky modern terrace houses fronted by a postage stamp of garden behind a short wall. If it had ever been an orchard, there was little evidence of it now. Cars and vans were parked cheek by jowl against the kerbside, turning the pavement into an enclosed path that corralled pedestrians along it like herded cattle, whether they wanted to go that way or not. As she ambled along, her thoughts turned to Fern Marshall. Did she feel penned in by her perfect life? For many who envied her life of luxury, the question would be risible, but given what she'd learned about Fern Marshall so far, McKenzie wasn't so sure. And if she did feel trapped, was it too big a leap to imagine her having deserted her husband? Perhaps not, especially if you considered it wouldn't be the first time.

And it would all fit too, if it wasn't for that phone call. If Fern Marshall had simply escaped her domestic drudgery, why would she have phoned her husband in such a bizarre way? And if she hadn't made the call, who had, and why?

With her thoughts travelling so fast, it was a while before she realised that her feet weren't travelling at all. She had come to a complete standstill, anchored to the spot by Harvey, who was sitting on the pavement, the full reach of his lead pulled taut behind her. The drizzle was rapidly turning into a downpour. Harvey hated the rain. Given that he'd stopped to personalise every lamppost they'd passed, she was content to head back home and turned to walk back the way they came. Unfortunately, it was raining in that direction too, so Harvey remained stubbornly resolute in his pavement protest.

'This is how it's going to be, is it?' she said, bending over. Her breath exploded from her as she hoisted him up onto her hip and slipped an arm around him.

Cursing herself for never having done anything about the diet she'd repeatedly threatened him with, she staggered up the street.

Ahead, two people emerged from a house. A flash of orange came from a car nearby, which they dashed towards. Moments later as they sped off, McKenzie paused to catch her breath. The patch of dry tarmac left by the departed vehicle caught her eye, causing the first stirring of some memory to surface. It reminded her of something. But what? Not another car. Something more obscure. The rain continued to fall, blurring the car's footprint, and would eventually wipe out any trace of it ever having been there. A trickle ran down the back of her neck, its cold, clammy fingers shaking her out of her daze. She hefted Harvey higher and continued the slow journey home. Back at the house and running late, she quickly changed into her work gear — black trousers and blue polo neck — grabbed her bag, keys and phone and rushed out of the door.

The incident room was buzzing and the air was filled with the smell of fresh coffee and buttered toast.

She nodded to York as she passed his office. 'Morning.'

'Hey!' He called. 'I thought you were going to talk to the ex-boyfriend again this morning.'

'That's the plan. I couldn't remember whether he's back today or tomorrow so I was going to call him first and find out. I thought I'd be civilised about it and leave it until after eight.' She checked her watch. Quarter to. She scanned the room. 'Darren not in yet?'

'Doesn't look like it. How's it going with you two? I sense friction.'

Truth was Crawley irritated the hell out of her, what with his crappy work ethic and total lack of enthusiasm for anything to do with the case they were working. Not to mention his malicious little jibes. But she knew if she told Alex everything it would stir up a whole world of pain... for both of them.

She shrugged.

'I think he gets bored easily. Given where we are with the investigation into Fern Marshall there's not that much for him to do. To be honest, he might be better working on the Bridget Forker case. I know he'd prefer that. He's made no secret of the fact he's not happy stuck working a missing persons case when there's a juicy murder to get stuck into.'

'Ah, but Cat, we can't always get what we want, can we?' He gave an impish smile. So, he'd seen through her attempt at ditching Crawley. 'Just give him a chance. I'm sure he'll soon—'

'Boss!' Wynchcombe appeared behind Cat's shoulder. 'Karl Marshall's downstairs in reception asking for you.'

'Tell him we'll be straight down,' York said, rising from his seat. He started for the door and held a hand out towards McKenzie. 'Ladies first.'

'Bet he's heard about Mrs Forker,' she said, as they skipped down the stairs.

Karl Marshall was waiting by the reception desk.

'Detective Inspector…' he said, hurrying over to them as they came through the door. 'Is it true a woman's been murdered near to where Fern was last seen?'

'Why don't we go somewhere more private?' York held out a hand, gesturing in the direction of the interview rooms.

'You've got to take her disappearance more seriously now?' Marshall said, allowing himself to be ushered into one of the rooms reserved for witnesses.

The space might have been small but the chairs were well padded and, apart from the odd scrape, the walls reasonably clean. Once they were seated, DI York confirmed what Marshall had heard was true and went on to assure him that, irrespective of what had happened to Mrs Forker, they were already working flat out to find his wife.

'What about a fingertip search of the area?' Marshall asked.

'The roads and verges have already been checked since your wife's bike was found,' York replied. 'Unfortunately, there is insufficient evidence that your wife is still in the area to warrant us accessing the private property in the area.'

'What do you mean, no evidence? What about the dead woman?' Marshall flung himself back in his seat. 'This is insane. Surely the woman was murdered because she knew something about Fern.' He turned to McKenzie, an angry scowl on his face. 'Maybe if you'd pulled your finger out and taken my concerns seriously from the off, then maybe this other woman would still be alive today and maybe—'

'Mr Marshall,' York said firmly. 'We are doing everything we can to find your wife. I agree that Mrs Forker's death might be related, which is why both cases are now being looked into by the same team as part of the same investigation.'

Marshall blew out a long stream of breath.

'I'm wasting my time here, aren't I? Perhaps I should see what the police commissioner has to say about it.' He stood up, shunting his chair back roughly.

'There's no need for that,' York said, but the other man was already making for the door.

'Mr Marshall… Would you say your wife is happy?' McKenzie said as he reached for the handle.

He froze, then turned to look at her, his face contorted angrily.

'What are you insinuating?'

'Your wife is an attractive, intelligent woman. How happy is she doing virtually nothing with her life?'

'What? How dare you? Of course she's happy. She wants for nothing. What woman wouldn't be happy?' McKenzie leaned back in her seat and crossed her arms, making it clear that this woman wouldn't be. Marshall went on, 'I've always encouraged her to try different things — yoga classes, coffee mornings, joining the local WI. If she doesn't do them, that's her prerogative.'

'What about a job or a family?'

Marshall turned to York and demanded, 'Why am I the one being interrogated? How are these questions even relevant?'

'They're relevant because they might give us some insight into your wife's recent state of mind,' York replied.

Marshall regarded York with the same spiteful glower he'd so far reserved for McKenzie.

'Fern is an elegant and sophisticated woman. She is not the mumsy type. And as for a job, I make more than enough money to provide for everything she needs.'

'What about her sense of independence or self-esteem?' McKenzie challenged.

After a short pause, Marshall replied, 'If she wants to work, I'm hardly going to stop her.' He turned to York. 'Look, we're wasting precious time. I didn't come here to argue. I know that the murdered woman lived up the road from the people who run the slaughterhouse — the ones who caused the trouble at the animal sanctuary. Did you know that?' York nodded. Marshall continued, 'What if... what if they've taken Fern? What if they've done to her what they did to that other woman?' He buried his face in his hands. 'I couldn't bear it.' He looked at them with a look of anguish. 'I'm sorry. It's just...'

'Mr Marshall, I understand how terrible this is for you,' York said. 'But you need to trust us to do everything in our power to find your wife. As I said, we are looking into every possible angle. I promise, we won't leave any avenue unexplored or any stone unturned.'

It would need to be a bloody big stone to hide anyone for the best part of a week, McKenzie thought, conjuring up an image of a lichen-covered tomb, cold and grey.

A feeling of dread settled uncomfortably in her gut.

22.

'I'd say it's fairly obvious he knows nothing about any baby,' McKenzie said, as they started back up the stairs after seeing Karl Marshall out. 'If the scan is hers but the baby's not his, doesn't it make it more likely she's done a runner? '

'How does that fit with Mrs Forker's murder?' York replied, taking the steps two at a time.

'I don't know. What if she was planning on leaving Marshall but the lover had second thoughts and killed her? We know Mrs Marshall left her bike on the lane. She could have gone off with her lover. Maybe he came back for the bike and Mrs Forker saw him.'

'Did she say anything like that?'

'No, but maybe she had a better recollection after seeing the appeal?'

'I thought she called about the jogger?'

McKenzie let out a sigh.

'You're right. I'm going round in circles. Maybe we should do what Marshall wants and organise a search of the Skinners' place, seeing as that's only a stone's throw from where Mrs Marshall was last seen.'

'We could, but you just said yourself, if she met her lover there, he could have taken her anywhere.' After a moment's pause, he asked, 'You really think she was seeing someone else?'

McKenzie shrugged.

'My gut says yes. That's why I want to go and talk to Simon Parry. He's the only person we know who Mrs Marshall has seen recently... apart from the people at Freedom Farm, none of whom she was particularly friendly with.'

They had reached the office door. York opened it and stepped aside to let McKenzie enter.

'What are you waiting for? Go talk to him. You never know, you might be right, she might have told him something that will give us some clue as to her whereabouts. And while you're at it, find out what he was doing Monday through to Wednesday. And see if he can prove it.'

Fifty minutes later, McKenzie was standing outside the oast house, having learned that Parry was going to be at home all morning. When she left the office Crawley had still to put in an appearance, so she was on her own.

Simon Parry answered the door wearing a faded rugby shirt and jogging bottoms. His tanned feet were bare and his blond hair ruffled but stiff, suggesting it had been moulded in place to look as casual as it did. He was attractive in a rugged, boyish way.

'Come in, please...' He ushered her through a vast double-height atrium dominated by a colossal glass and chrome chandelier, into an expansive kitchen in the heart of the oast. 'Coffee?' Without waiting for a reply, he flicked the switch on a coffee machine that wouldn't have looked out of place in Starbucks and grabbed two mugs from a cupboard. 'Still no sign of her then?'

'I'm afraid not. Which is why I'm talking to everyone again. I wondered if she said anything when you visited recently that might give us a clue as to where she might be.'

Parry looked at her, his blue eyes wide, and shook his head.

'No.'

'Perhaps we could start with how she was?' McKenzie asked, pen poised over her open pad.

'She seemed fine and she looked amazing. Better than ever. In fact, I said as much.'

'I understand the two of you didn't part on the best of terms.'

'Who told you that?'

'A friend of Fern's. She said Fern walked out on you without so much as a goodbye.'

'Water under the bridge.' McKenzie looked up and Parry flashed her a smooth smile. 'Look, I wouldn't have been there, having lunch at her house, if there was any bad feeling, would I?'

The coffee machine gave a subtle ping and Parry turned his attention back to their drinks. After placing McKenzie's unsweetened black coffee in front of her, he set his own drink down on the work surface.

'Did she talk much about her personal life?' McKenzie asked, reaching for her cup.

'She mentioned something about an animal rescue thing she was involved in.'

'You mean the sanctuary she volunteered at — Freedom Farm?'

'Err, yeah, that sounds sort of familiar.'

'She didn't talk about any plans for the future, like getting a job or having children?'

'No.'

'What about her marriage or her husband... or perhaps that would have been too uncomfortable?'

'Funnily enough, she did say something. Had a little gloat. I can't remember how we got on to it, but she said at last she'd found her soul mate. She said, suffice to say he was nothing like me.'

'That must have hurt.'

'Not really.' He broke into a grin. 'I deserved worse.'

McKenzie thought carefully about how to phrase her next question. Slowly her expression grew more serious and she said, 'Mr Parry, obviously in cases like this, we have to cover all the bases. When Fern made that comment about her soul mate, was it obvious she was talking about her husband?'

'Who else would it…' Parry's eyes grew wide. 'She was having an affair?'

'I didn't say that. Only, it's a possibility we can't rule out at this stage.'

'My first reaction is that Fern isn't the type to have an affair. She's quite a moral sort of person, if you know what I mean. But I suppose if she wasn't happy, then, I don't know, maybe if she found herself attracted to someone else…' He shrugged. 'The only thing I'd say is that if that did happen, I shouldn't think it would be long before she left her husband. But as for anything she said to me, I can't think of anything that made me think that was the case.'

'And there's nothing else you can think of that might give us an idea of where she is now?'

'I wish I could help but I wasn't there long and…'

Just then Parry cocked his head. A second later came the sound of a key in a lock.

'That'll be Melissa, my girlfriend. Look, if she asks, can you just say you're talking to everyone who used to know Fern. If she knows I went to see her recently she'll go ballistic. Please?' he hissed, just as a tall, leggy brunette came through the kitchen door, boutique store bags dangling from her hand.

She took one look at McKenzie then threw a scowl in Parry's direction, attacking him with eyes framed with fake lashes and thick, drawn-on brows.

'Hi, darling,' Parry said. He walked over and moved in for a kiss, but she gave him the cold shoulder and dumped her bags down an upholstered chair in the corner of the room.

'Who's she?' she said, flashing an irate look in McKenzie's direction.

'*She* is Detective Constable McKenzie,' McKenzie replied, applying a polite-but-don't-fuck-with-me expression before explaining the reason for her visit and granting Parry his wish, omitting to mention his recent reunion with Mrs Marshall.

Melissa went to stand next to Parry and slipped an arm around his waist.

'Simon's not the type to go sniffing around his exes like an old dog. He prefers fresh challenges. Don't you darling?' she said, giving him a catty look.

'Don't start with that again,' Parry said, extracting himself from her grip. He turned to McKenzie. 'Was there anything else?'

'Just your whereabouts between Monday and Wednesday. We're asking everyone that knows Mrs Marshall.'

'I was in Hull, working at a music festival.'

'Can anyone corroborate that?'

'What do you mean corroborate?' the girlfriend jumped in. 'Is he like, a suspect or something?'

'Not at all,' McKenzie replied.

'It's alright,' Parry said. 'I don't have a problem with that. Lissy, why don't you go and put your new things away?' He glanced at the small mountain of bags and frowned. 'I thought you only went to get your nails done.'

176

'Don't change the subject. I'll stay, thank you. Unless there's something you don't want me to hear.'

'Darling, I've already told you what I was doing. We've been over it like a million times. So please, give it a rest.' He turned to McKenzie. 'From Monday, yes?' McKenzie nodded. 'That was the day after the festival ended. Let me think... I was on site first thing. We were busy dismantling the rigs most of the morning. Then I had some lunch, after that I didn't do anything until that night when Melissa arrived and we went out for dinner.'

'You did nothing at all in the intervening hours?'

'Not really. After lunch I went back to my hotel room and got my head down for a few hours. The festival had been pretty intense. I was knackered, and what with Melissa due that evening — we'd booked to stay the rest of the week — I knew she'd want to paint the town red. I thought I'd make the most of the chance to have a bit of downtime.'

McKenzie turned to Melissa.

'What time did you arrive?'

'Eight. And imagine my surprise when Simon wasn't there to greet me.' She fixed Parry with a fiery glare.

'I've already told you, I nipped out for a coffee.'

'Course they don't do coffee in the hotel, do they?' Melissa snapped.

'Honey, are you going to bang on about this forever? All week we've done exactly what you wanted. What more do you want?' He softened his tone and said, 'Please, just go. I'll finished in a minute then you can show me what you've bought.'

Melissa ran her manicured fingers through her mane of auburn hair, before snatching up her shopping bags and flouncing out of the room.

As soon as they were on their own, Parry said, 'I'm sorry about that. She gets so insanely jealous.' McKenzie closed her notepad and returned it to her bag. 'How about you? Your boyfriend the jealous type?'

'Not as far as I know.'

He gave her a wolfish smile that was surprisingly attractive.

'Perhaps I could take you for a coffee, or maybe something stronger, and we could find out?'

McKenzie felt her cheeks flush at his unexpected directness.

'That wouldn't be very appropriate. Going back to Monday, is there anyone who can confirm you were in Hull until you met with your girlfriend?'

'Not really. Is that a problem? I promise I wasn't with Fern. I really have no idea where she is.'

On the drive back to the office, McKenzie ran through the conversation with Parry. If he was Fern Marshall's mysterious boyfriend, he was doing a good job of not seeming overly concerned by her disappearance… unless, of course, he knew where she was. But if he had had anything to do with it, he couldn't have dumped the bike, as on Wednesday he was with Melissa hundreds of miles away in Hull. Nor could he have had anything to do with Bridget Forker's murder for the same reason.

So if it wasn't him, who was it?

She turned her thoughts to what they knew about Mrs Marshall and her seemingly narrow set of routines. If the boyfriend wasn't someone from Freedom Farm — and she was pretty sure Danny would have known about it if it was — then how had she met him? It was hard to know who else to ask. Could the whole boyfriend thing be a red herring? What if the baby was Mr Marshall's after all? What if she hadn't told him because she knew he didn't want children? What if she wasn't even pregnant?

She called Crawley.

'Darren, it's Cat. I've just finished at Parry's and am on my way back. How did you get on?'

'Get on with what?'

'Following up on the ultrasound scan. I left a note on your desk this morning.'

'Oh that. I haven't done it yet.'

'Darren, it's important we know if it was hers or not.'

'It might be important but is it urgent?'

'What? Darren, just do it.'

'I'm busy. You just said you're on your way back. You can do it yourself when you get in.'

'What do you mean, you're busy? What with?'

'I'm working on the serial killer angle,' he said, not bothering to disguise the glee in his voice. 'Bob had a word with Alex. Said it's more important we put everything into Forker's murder rather than searching for some woman who might have just left her husband.'

'Or might just be dead,' McKenzie snapped.

'In which case, it really could be a serial killer, so what I'm doing is even more important.'

She terminated the call and spent the remainder of the journey seething. Back in the office, the call to the clinic took less than ten minutes. After some toing and froing sending proof of her credentials, they eventually gave McKenzie what she was after.

'And…?' DI York asked after she'd tracked him down.

'Fern Marshall is definitely pregnant. Or rather, the scan was hers.'

'That puts the cat amongst the pigeons.'

'You mean with her husband not knowing?'

'That and the talk of an affair. How did you get on with the ex?'

'He didn't really tell me anything we don't already know. His whereabouts on Monday are a bit sketchy, so it's always possible he could have slipped back, abducted Fern, then driven back north, but seeing as his girlfriend joined him Monday night and they spent the rest of the week there together, it's hard to see how he could have had anything to do with the bike getting dumped or Mrs Forker's murder.'

'That's him ruled out then.'

'Looks like it.' Feeling distinctly out of ideas, she asked, 'Do you think I'm wasting my time looking for this mystery man? The baby could be Mr Marshall's after all. It could just be some random nutter saw Mrs Marshall out on her bike and took a fancy.'

'A random nutter? Really?'

'I figure you must think it's a possibility, seeing as you've given Darren the go-ahead to look into the serial killer angle.'

'I only told him he could do some digging because he told me you were out and he had nothing to do.'

'That's bullshit!' She hastily held up her hands. 'Sorry. I shouldn't have said that, but I left him things to do and from what I can tell, he's done none of them.'

York darted a look across the office. Crawley was at his desk, eyes glued to the computer screen. He shook his head.

'I'll have a word.'

'No, don't. Nobody likes a grass.'

But York batted her reply away with a wave of the hand.

'And I don't like being played. A quiet word, let him know he's been rumbled. Suffice to say, he'll be back working with you on Mrs Marshall's disappearance as soon as.'

From the firm set of his jaw, McKenzie could tell York had made his mind up.

'Just make it clear I didn't come bleating to you then... please?' Just then her mobile started to ring. She pulled it from her pocket and looked at the caller ID. 'Sorry, I need to take this. It's my neighbour. She wouldn't call unless there's a problem.' She hit reply. Soon she lifted a hand and cupped her mouth as her eyes roamed wildly. After a few muttered words, she hung up.

'I've got to go,' she said. 'Harvey's unwell… like, really unwell.'

A minute later, she passed York's office on her way out.

'Hope everything's alright,' he called after her.

'So do I,' she said, rushing from the room.

23.

McKenzie got home in record time. Entering the kitchen, she found her neighbour, a lovely woman called Rose, bent over Harvey's prone form. He was in his basket and didn't even open his eyes when McKenzie dropped to her knees and began to check him over. His breath rasped and rattled in his chest. She gently laid a blanket over him.

'I need to get him to the vets,' she said to Rose. 'Help me get him in the car. I'll call them on the way.'

They carried him to the back seat of her car still in his bed. She drove as quickly as she dared, while calling the vet's surgery. By the time she pulled into the car park, a young bespectacled man wearing a white coat and a concerned expression was there to greet her. He carried Harvey, limp and unresponsive, into an empty consulting room. McKenzie waited outside, pacing the tarmac, praying the situation wasn't as bleak as it appeared. After an excruciatingly long wait, the door opened. The vet peered out, a glum expression on his face.

It was gone six by the time she got home. She threw her keys onto the hall table, slung her bag over the end of the banister and slumped onto the bottom stair, where she let her head drop into her hands. Her shoulders shook as her raw howls echoed through the empty house. When her sobs grew dry and her cries fell quiet, slowly she straightened up. Exhausted, she pushed her tear-soaked hair from her face and wiped her eyes on her sleeve, while reaching into her bag for a tissue. Feeling numb, she rose from her spot on the stairs and made her way into the lounge, where she sank down onto the sofa, hugging herself. She stared blankly at the spot of floor by her feet where Harvey had so often slept. The realisation that he would never be there again started a fresh bout of tears. When she finally had no more to give, she climbed unsteadily to her feet and padded through to the kitchen, where she freshened her face with a sluice of cold water. With a clean towel pressed to her face, she stood regarding the room. It seemed so ridiculously empty. Two stainless steel bowls sat by the back door, full of food and water that Harvey would never now enjoy. A dog chew lay on the floor under the breakfast bar; another of his favourite haunts. She knew she'd have to pick them all up and clear them away. But not yet. She didn't have it in her. Not right now.

She returned to the hallway and grabbed her phone from her bag. Walking through to the living room, she thumbed through her contacts then hit dial.

A female voice answered, 'Hello?'

McKenzie cleared her throat.

'This is Cat. I was hoping to speak to Phil.' She sniffed a couple of times. 'Is this Lolly?'

'Hi. Yes. Phil's just nipped to the bathroom. I can get him to call you back as soon as he comes down. We are working, by the way, just in case, well....'

McKenzie had called hoping to find a sympathetic ear and someone able to take her mind off the fact that the only soul who had been her constant companion since her return to the UK from the Maldives was now gone.

183

'You know what, don't bother. I'm not in the mood for a fight. Just tell him to forget it. Forget me, forget us… just forget it.' She ended the call and slung the phone down onto the table. It slid across the surface and dropped onto the floor. In the past she would have had to race around to pick it up before Harvey decided it was his most recent chew toy, but not today. Today, she left it where it fell.

Why did everybody and everything she cared for have to die? And why, when she most needed someone to talk to, was there no one?

Her mobile started to ring. It'll be Phil. Perhaps Lolly had told him she sounded like she'd been crying. She heaved herself up and grabbed the phone before flopping back in her seat and pressing it to her ear.

'Look Phil, I know you probably—'

'Cat, it's Alex.'

'Alex?'

'I called to see how Harvey is. Are you okay? You sound like you've been crying.'

And so it started all over again.

By the time he got to the house, though her face was still puffy and her skin blotchy, she had at least managed to stem the tears.

'Something to dull the senses,' he said, brandishing a bottle of red wine on entering. He put the bottle on the hallway table and held his arms wide. 'Come here. You look like you could do with a hug.'

She stepped forward and let his arms wrap around her. Nestling into his chest she took a deep breath in and felt the tension ease from her bones. They stood there, saying nothing, for what felt like forever, until eventually he released her.

'I take it you haven't eaten?'

She shook her head.

'I don't know if I can face anything.'

'You need to eat. I bet you haven't had anything since breakfast?'

Another shake of the head. He ushered her towards the kitchen.

'Come on, sit down. I'll knock something up.' He flicked a switch on the radio and turning the dial down, keeping the music as background only, made his way over to the fridge. He opened the door and peered inside.

'I'm not sure if I'm going to be able to do much with this all this healthy shit. No wonder you're so skinny.' He started to pull out a selection of vegetables. 'Got any eggs?' McKenzie pointed to a wire spiral egg holder. 'How about an omelette?' Without waiting for an answer, he quickly grabbed a chopping board and sharp knife and set to work.

After dinner, which McKenzie only really picked at, York carried the half-finished bottle of wine through to the living room and settled on one end of the sofa. McKenzie sat on the opposite end, facing him. She lifted her stockinged feet and tucked them under her.

'Thanks for coming over. I don't know what I would have done with myself if I was stuck here on my own all evening.' Her voice gave a little wobble. 'The place feels so empty now.'

'It'll get easier with time.'

'I'm not sure I want it to.'

He smiled.

'Contrary as ever.'

'I can't help thinking it was my fault,' she said. 'I shouldn't have given him so many treats… and then there was the walks. Harvey would only go as far as the end of the lane. If I wanted to go any further, I had to carry him.'

'But he was what... seven years old? And didn't you say on the phone the vet said bulldogs are susceptible to heart problems?'

'Yes, but...'

'So stop beating yourself up. You took him on after Pete died without question. I bet there weren't many other takers.'

'No, but...'

'No buts. Just try to focus on how much you got from having him around and how much you gave him.' She nodded and for a moment or two the silence sat between them like an old friend. York reached for his drink and said, 'You know, I remember when Pete got Harvey. I thought he was mad. He got him for cover as part of an undercover op we were running. Did you know that?'

'No. What sort of op is a dog cover for?'

'It was when we were both in narcotics. A guy linked to a local OCG suddenly decided to open a kennels. You know, the type where you leave your dog when you go on holiday. Word on the street was that it was a cover for a crack factory. When Pete said we needed a dog to legitimise our interest in the place I thought he was going to get one from the canine unit or borrow a neighbour's. I never dreamt he'd actually get one himself. But no. Up he trucks with Harvey in tow. He'd got him from a dog rehoming place who'd rescued him from an illegal puppy farm. It wasn't long before the two were inseparable.'

With a melancholic expression, York reached for the bottle and topped their drinks up.

'It's the anniversary of Pete's death next weekend,' McKenzie said, staring into the ruby liquid. 'Five years.'

'God, really?' He shook his head. 'That's gone fast. He was a good mate, you know.'

She nodded.

'A good brother too.'

York raised his glass.

'Here's to Harvey and Pete.'

'To Harvey and Pete.'

They touched glasses. She looked into his eyes. She'd always been drawn to their dark depths. Feeling a warm flush creep upwards towards her face, she tore her gaze away and switched her attention back to her glass.

'What happened… to us, I mean?' she asked, swirling the wine around. 'I thought we were good mates too.' She looked across at him.

His Adam's apple bobbed as he swallowed and for a moment, she thought he wasn't going to answer, or worse… make some excuse and leave, but then he said, 'It's complicated.' Another pause. McKenzie had to press her lips together to stop her from filling the silence. Eventually he went on, 'Mel was never very happy with the amount of time I used to spend on the job. And then Cody getting sick… after we'd spent so many evenings working late.' She could see the anguish in his face. 'I was afraid I was going to lose my family. I thought if I gave Mel what she wanted, then it would all be okay. Only it turns out there are other issues.' He gave a cynical snort. 'Which is why I'm currently sleeping on a sofa bed in a mate's spare room, unsure if I'll ever be going back home.' He rubbed his face. She'd never seen him look so vulnerable.

She untucked her legs from under her and slipped across the sofa, putting an arm around his shoulders. She could feel his heat; smell his aftershave. He looked up and turned to her, their faces mere inches from one another.

Just then a faint sound came from the direction of the front door. She felt York grow taut.

'What was that?' he asked.

'I don't know.' She looked towards the front window as another noise filtered through. 'That sounded like a car door closing.' She jumped up and peered through a gap in the curtains out into the dark night. 'There's a car driving away. It'll be someone visiting one of the neighbours.' She let the curtains fall back into place and returned to the sofa.

'It sounded close. You aren't expecting any deliveries?'

'No.'

He jumped out of his seat and headed for the hallway. McKenzie was right behind him when he pulled the door open. The road ahead was cast in darkness. They both looked down at the large cardboard box sitting on the front step. She took a step forward, about to reach for it, but York set out a hand.

'Don't!'

'What do you think it is?'

He bent down to take a closer look. 'No name. No address. I don't think we want to take any chances.'

'What? You think it's a bomb or something? I don't think I'm important enough in anyone's world to warrant being a target in a terrorist attack.'

'I wasn't thinking terrorists. More like someone you've pissed off.'

She stooped down, listening for any sounds emanating from the parcel. After a few seconds, 'Well, it's not ticking.' She reached out and gave it a gentle push. 'It feels quite heavy.'

'Just move away from it. It makes me nervous seeing you so close.' She stood up and took a step back. 'What about the car?' he asked. 'Any idea of the make or model?'

'The only thing I saw was the lights as it pulled away.' Suddenly her mouth opened into a wide O.

'Shit... Phil. I wonder...?'

'Phil? As in your bloke?'

'My ex-bloke. As of tonight, at least.'

'You had a row?'

'Sort of. Well, not exactly. To be honest, we didn't even speak. I told the woman who answered his phone for the second time in a week to tell him to forget it.' She looked back down at the box. 'Maybe it's an apology? There would have been just enough time for him to get here.'

'Surely he's got more sense than to leave an unmarked package on your doorstep?' He shook his head. 'That said, if he's been playing around behind your back, he's obviously an idiot.' He looked back down at the package. 'Go and call him, see if it's from him.'

'I'd rather see what's in it first,' she said. And before he could stop her, she stepped forward and started to open the box.

24.

The white-suited Crime Scene Investigator knocked at the kitchen door.

'All done,' he said, snapping off his latex gloves.

York and McKenzie looked over from their seats at the breakfast bar.

'Find anything useful?' York asked.

'Maybe. The box was clean but the tape sealing it turned up a couple of partials on the sticky side. You know what a bitch it can be trying to stop that stuff sticking to itself. Also, I'll need to get an expert opinion from the forensic vet, but I'd say whoever did it killed the animal after stunning it with a captive-bolt and then removed the head, which suggests it was done by someone in the trade. I'll run the prints against the database first thing tomorrow,' the CSI said, dropping his gloves into his bag. York gave a nod and the CSI retreated down the hallway.

They heard the front door slam shut.

'Looks like I pushed someone's buttons at the slaughterhouse,' McKenzie said. She mustered up tired smile. 'That's a good thing, right?'

The lines around York's eyes creased as he broke into an unexpectedly hearty laugh.

'Ever the Pollyanna,' he said, shaking his head.

'Why do you think they did it?' McKenzie asked, slipping out of her seat and reaching for their empty mugs. She started to load them into the dishwasher. 'I mean, it's hardly like we'll stop investigating them because of it.' She looked back over to York. 'Do you think the fact it's a sheep's head is relevant? I mean, six dead sheep were left at Freedom Farm. What if someone is trying to implicate the Skinners by doing something similar? They could be trying to send us in the wrong direction.'

'Funny way of going about it. And how would they have got hold of the head?' York stood up and reached for his jacket. 'Anyway, we'll soon find out. First thing tomorrow, I'll send someone to get the prints from everyone at Skinner's Yard.'

With nothing more he could do and with McKenzie insisting she was okay, York left for his makeshift bed at his pal's place. After he'd gone, the house felt emptier and quieter than ever. She stood in the middle of the kitchen looking around, feeling hollow. With a heavy heart, she cleared away Harvey's food and water bowls with as much detachment as she could manage, then went to bed, a trail of fresh tears tracing their way down her cheeks.

The next morning, her brain was blissfully slow to rouse and for a moment the events of the previous day seemed as unreal and elusive as her dreams. But slowly, her waking mind cleared and her stomach lurched as the memories of the previous day made themselves known. She felt her throat tighten as the tears threatened to come afresh. She pushed them aside, along with the bedclothes, and climbed out of bed, heading for the bathroom, where a set of puffy, red-rimmed eyes stared back. She quickly doused her face with water, then made her way downstairs. Five minutes later, she was hugging a mug of coffee, staring through the window at the flat, grey sky without really seeing it. She leaned back against the counter and let her gaze drift to the empty spot where Harvey's bowls usually sat. The sadness wasn't ready to let her go just yet and an unwelcome tightness gripped her chest. Determined to fight the mounting feeling of grief, she took a deep, juddering breath, took a last swig of the coffee and headed back upstairs to get ready for the day ahead.

By the time McKenzie arrived, despite the early hour, the office was already busy. She sat at her desk, trying to remember what she was supposed to be doing. So much had happened since she'd last sat there. She caught Crawley staring. Knowing she looked as lousy as she felt, she reached up and unhooked her hair from behind her ears and let it fall in front of her face. Maybe she should have tried putting some make-up on for a change?

Crawley ambled over.

'You okay?'

'Yeah. I'm fine.'

'You sure? It looks like something really shook you up.'

'I'm just tired. I had to…' She cleared her throat then swallowed, not trusting herself to tell of Harvey's sad passing without a fresh bout of tears. She shook her head. 'It doesn't matter.'

'Maybe you should take a few days to, you know, get yourself together. My dad always said policing's a tough job for a woman.'

McKenzie looked at him, incredulous.

'You do talk some shit. Do you know that? You wrap it up in 'Daddy says' and think you can get away with it. Do you have any idea how stupid you sound?'

'At least I don't burst into tears at the slightest thing.' He started to walk away, issuing a parting shot over his shoulder, 'By the way, Alex is in, if you need to go and cry on his shoulder.'

Her jaw dropped. Had she heard him right?

'Everything alright?' came a voice from over her shoulder.

She turned, ready to have a go at the next idiot to say something stupid. Seeing Wynchcombe's pinched brow and obvious concern, she sagged back in her seat.

'Not really. I had to have Harvey put to sleep yesterday,' she said, swallowing the lump that had formed in her throat.

Wynchcombe pulled over a chair.

'Oh shit, Cat. I'm so sorry. I know how much he meant to you. I'd give you a hug, but…' He darted a look around the office.

'Thanks. But it's okay. I'll be fine.'

'I know it's not the same, but when my rabbit died, I was gutted. I went to top up his food one morning and found him dead. It was horrible. I was only twelve. I was so upset but Mum insisted I went to school. But the worst thing was, when I got home, his hutch was gone. They'd already taken it to the tip. Mum said I was too old for another. For weeks I'd look at the rectangle of yellow grass where the hutch had been and feel sad all over again. Eventually the grass grew back and I didn't feel quite so sad. I guess I got used to him not being around. Funny, isn't it…?' He pulled his brow together into a pained frown. 'I didn't even know it still bothered me.'

'Thanks Spence.' She knew how hard it must have been for the twenty-two-year-old to share a story like that; no bravado, no pretence of being a tough guy. 'You're right though. The littlest things are the worst. This morning, when I went down for breakfast, I kept looking at where Harvey's bowls used to be. I…' She paused. Her brow crimped into a frown. Something had stirred up a memory. She rewound the conversation… the rabbit… the hutch… the marks on the grass… the grass! The dead grass by the chicken coop. She jumped up. 'Sorry Spence, I need to see Alex.'

Wynchcombe watched her rush off, a confused look on his face.

York was in his office. She knocked at the open door and walked straight in.

He held up a sheet of paper.

'The test results from the blood and tissue samples found in Mrs Forker's hallway. It looks like the sick bastard really did feed her kidney to the dogs. Just when you think you've seen it all.' He dropped the sheet on to the desk. 'What's up?'

'I think I might have a lead. It's just an idea, but Spence was telling me about his rabbit dying. He said something about its hutch that reminded me of a rectangular outline in the grass at the Skinners' place. I think it came from a nearby chicken coop. But why would they move it? It was virtually falling apart and nothing else looked like it had been touched in years.'

'Hang on, back it up a sec. You saw a chicken coop at the slaughterhouse?'

'No. It was in the Skinners' back garden.'

'When were you in the garden? I thought you said Don Skinner kicked you out on your arse.'

'I only had a quick look.' York hooked an eyebrow. She hurried on, 'The first time I went round they weren't in, but Mrs Forker had already mentioned seeing Fern's bike hidden by the gate to their garden. I thought... well, I thought I'd better just check she hadn't gone in for some reason and hurt herself... or worse. I was only there a minute. Two at most.'

'When will you learn?' York said, shaking his head. 'You can't just trespass whenever you feel like it.'

'I was concerned for Mrs Marshall's safety. We knew someone's been taking livestock to Freedom Farm. I thought, what if it was Fern? What if she'd gone to the Skinners' house to see if there was anything there to save? She could have been injured or locked in a shed or something.'

'And?'

'Obviously I'd have said if I'd found anything important. The garden's a mess, totally overgrown, but I noticed a patch of dead grass, or rather, an outline in the grass where something had been. I didn't think anything of it at the time. It's only after Spence mentioned his rabbit dying and its hutch being moved, I remembered there was a chicken coop nearby about the same size as the marks on the grass.'

'You're not suggesting Fern Marshall's body is hidden in the coop?'

'No. It wouldn't fit. But why move it?'

'Aren't you supposed to move chicken coops, to stop foxes digging under?'

'That would make sense if there were chickens in it, but this was an old decrepit thing and Robbie Skinner told me they haven't kept chickens for years.'

'Could it have been moved to get to something else? Or to climb on to get to something above? It's the sort of thing I'd do, if I can't be arsed to go and get a ladder.'

McKenzie took a moment to recall the scene, then shook her head.

'I don't remember anything behind it or above it. And anyway, there's a ladder nearby that goes up to the treehouse.'

'There's a treehouse? Did you take a look inside?'

'What... like climb up? No. Besides, I can't see anyone killing Mrs Marshall then dragging her body ten foot up a ladder.'

'What if they got her to climb the ladder and then killed her?'

'But why would she do that?'

York reached for his car keys.

'Let's deal with one thing at a time, shall we?'

25.

Robbie Skinner placed the leg of lamb in the pre-heated oven and gently closed the door. On the draining board the potatoes were peeled, quartered and sitting in a bowl of water, ready for roasting; the carrots and sprouts were already in pans of water on the stove top and the Yorkshire pudding batter was resting in the fridge. Confident the old man would be out for the count for another hour at least, he grabbed his jacket, picked up his keys and started for the door. Beset by a flicker of doubt, he paused and cocked his head, listening for sounds from above. Nothing. He turned the latch and slipped silently out of the house.

In the garage, he dug out his old birdwatching kit and climbed into the van. Thankfully the old man had been too drunk to manoeuvre the Range Rover onto the drive when he'd got home the previous evening, leaving it at the side of the lane instead. Robbie drove out of the garage keeping the revs as low and as quiet as possible and turned left onto the road. After turning right at the first junction he then drove on for quarter of a mile before pulling off the road and onto the grass verge. He waited, checking for traffic. After a minute, when nothing had passed, he climbed out and started to walk along the side of the drainage ditch, stopping occasionally to look at something that inevitably turned out to be nothing. There was no trace of where the bike had been, not even a flattened section of grass. Robbie returned to the van, turned it around in the road, and drove back up the lane. He ignored the turning that would take him back to the house and continued on until he was at the gate that led through to his garden. He couldn't help but glance over, half-expecting to see his father standing there wearing a scowl as deep as raked ground. But of course, there was no one there. A little way on, he slowed the car to a crawl and pulled to a stop in front of a picket fence. Blue and white tape hung like bunting across the front door to the house. Curtain-shrouded windows stared back at him, dead-eyed. He thought of the headlines, words like grisly murder and macabre scene, and the comments that the police had yet to rule out a link between the death of the 63-year-old dog-walker and the disappearance of Fern Marshall.

What did that mean? Had they found something, or hadn't they?

Still staring at the house, he grabbed his jacket from the passenger seat and, with shaking fingers, pulled out two photographs from the wallet in his pocket. The first, a dog-eared snapshot, showed mother and son posing for the camera. The memories came flooding back. He had been so happy, so untroubled, back then when it had been just the two of them. Both blissfully unaware that, before the year was out, she would be dead and he would be back living with his father, a man who could suck the joy out of a room just by walking in.

God, how he hated him.

He shook the thought from his mind and turned to the second photograph, to her beautiful face with its beautiful smile; how lovingly she held the tiny lamb cradled in her embrace. The image became blurry and he wiped his eyes with the heel of his hand. Returning the photos to his pocket, he started the engine. A quick glance at the clock told him he was running out of time. Soon, his father would be up and demanding his breakfast, despite the fact there'd be a roast dinner on the table in a couple of hours. Yet, instead of rounding the corner and completing the loop back to the house, he executed a messy three-point turn and set off in the opposite direction. Three-quarters of a mile and a few turns later, he pulled the van to a stop outside a wide set of gates. His eyes swept up the drive, past the triple garage to the house beyond. He couldn't imagine her living in such a place, with its striped lawn and pristine borders. Just then, he sensed something move at an upstairs window. He reached for his binoculars. After a couple of minutes and having seen no further sign of movement, he was wondering if he'd been mistaken, when the front door opened and Karl Marshall stepped out. He threw the binoculars down, rammed the car into gear and pulled away, leaving a plume of blue exhaust fumes shimmering in the air like a memory.

26.

'Hold your horses,' came a shout in response to York's insistent hammering. The front door swung open to reveal Don Skinner, half-dressed and struggling to do up the buttons on his shirt that was straining to meet over his expansive gut. An aura of stale alcohol radiated from him like a hazardous material. He barely glanced at the detectives on the door step. 'We don't want any,' he said and started to close the door.

'Police! Don't close the door Mr Skinner. We're coming in.' York recited the relevant part of the Police and Crime Act that entitled them to enter and search and led the team inside.

'This is bloody harassment, this is,' Skinner bellowed, before issuing a stream of profanities at the detectives as they set about searching the premises.

York made straight for the back door, McKenzie at his side. He nodded in the direction of the garden.

'Lead on McDuff.'

They started down a stone path that wound down the garden's two-hundred-foot length, passing through an unkempt wilderness of overgrown greenery littered with decrepit, rusting junk. Half-way down, McKenzie pointed to a large oak tree that towered majestically over the garden. They walked over and peered up, craning their necks to get a better look at the treehouse nestled high in the leaf canopy above. A ladder led from the ground to a hole in the bottom of the substantial wooden structure.

'How are you with heights?' York asked.

McKenzie's gaze slid skyward. It looked a hell of a long way up. She grabbed the ladder and pulled on it gently. It felt sturdy enough. She put a foot on the first rung

'I was only joking,' York said. 'Move out of the way. I'll do it.'

'It's alright. I don't mind. Besides, I'm not sure it'll be able to take your weight,' she said, giving a wink.

'Cheeky mare. I'm serious. I'll do it.'

'So am I.' She started to climb.

'Be careful. Test each rung as you go. And you hear anything remotely like wood splintering you get back down here.'

'I won't be able to hear anything if you keep yammering on.' Six rungs up now.

At the top of the ladder, she poked her head through the hole and peered into the surprisingly large accommodation.

'It looks like someone's been here recently,' she shouted down. 'There's a couple of blankets, a rug and a few other bits and pieces.' She started to make her way down, adding, 'No missing woman though.' At the bottom, she dusted the dirt off her hands and from the front of her jacket.

'Okay. Let's take a look at this chicken coop.'

McKenzie led him back to the path. A little further on, she crossed onto a rough patch of grass, home to a collection of disused wooden constructions. She stopped and pointed to a weathered, rickety wooden ark. 'There. That's the coop I was telling you about. And that's where I think it used to be.' She pointed out a rectangular outline of flat and yellow grass that stood out on the weed-ridden lawn. 'See what I mean?'

'Yes. And see how the grass between the two has been flattened. It looks like someone dragged it rather than carried it over.' He approached the coop and, plucking at the knees of his trousers, bent down to peer through the mesh of the run. 'There's something under here.'

McKenzie came to stand next to him and followed his gaze. Half-buried in the ground was a large concrete disc with a metal ring projecting from its centre.

'What is that?' she asked.

'I don't know. Give me a hand, will you?'

York took hold of one end of the coop while McKenzie grabbed the other. They moved it a few feet away before returning to study the concrete disc.

'I'd say that's a lid to a cesspit,' York said.

Now he'd said it, she could see it was clearly a lid. And judging by the flattened grass around it, it was clear that it was a lid that had recently been accessed. More importantly it was a lid that was big enough to fit a person through, especially one as slim as Fern Marshall.

McKenzie felt the blood drain and the bile rise.

'You don't think…?'

'There's only one way to find out.' York slipped on a pair of gloves, straddled the lid and bent down.

McKenzie watched, mouth dry, heart clamouring, as he grasped the handle and pulled. It moved with surprising ease, releasing a surge of fetid air that smelled of drains and dankness and death. She pulled out her flashlight and cast the LED beam down into the abyss.

27.

The foul stench hit McKenzie face on. She recoiled, grateful there was no food in her stomach to force its way back up, then steeled herself before bending down for a closer look.

'Shit,' she said, the word escaping on a breath.

There, cast in a disc of torchlight, lay the pale and twisted body of a woman looking like the principal in some macabre stage show.

McKenzie dropped to her knees and called, 'Fern, can you hear me?' No reply. She turned to York. 'We need to do something. She might still be alive.'

'Surely she's dead?' he said.

McKenzie looked back down at the still form, taking in the unnatural angle of her limbs.

'It's impossible to know. Her systems might have slowed down with lack of oxygen. She could just be unconscious. We've got to make sure.'

'How?'

'I'll go down.'

York shot her a shocked look. 'Are you serious?'

'What else can we do?' Her heart was banging in her chest at the thought of the woman beneath their feet taking her last breath. 'I've got some rope in my car. I'll go and get that while you grab some of the others, they can help take my weight when I go down.' Without waiting for him to reply she started to sprint back towards the house.

York was back first, with Crawley and Wynchcombe in tow. Bells remained back in the house, keeping an eye on Don Skinner. They watched as McKenzie hurried towards them, carrying an armful of supplies. She dropped the rope by the black hole, which sat in the unkempt grass like a festering sore, then started to climb into a blue scene suit.

'I've called for an ambulance,' York said. 'In the event, against million-to-one odds, you're right and she's still alive.'

'How far down does it go?' Wynchcombe asked, walking over to the hole and peering down. He quickly stepped away, putting a hand to his mouth, his face now a sickly shade of green.

'Far enough,' McKenzie said, wondering what the hell she'd volunteered for. Five minutes later, enveloped in a double layer of protective Tyvek and with a rope looped around her waist, she was sitting on the lip of the stinking cesspit, legs dangling.

From what they could tell, the drop was between ten and fifteen feet. Thankfully it looked like it had long been decommissioned as the water level only came half-way up Fern Marshall's body.

'Cat, are you sure you want to do this?' York asked.

'Not particularly… but, well, does anyone else want to try?'

'You know I would but…' York said. They'd already agreed he was too broad to fit through.

'How about Spence?' Crawley said. 'He's not called Pencil for nothing.'

Wynchcombe sent a scathing glare in his direction, before turning to McKenzie, his face pinched with anguish.

'I'm really sorry. I just can't,' he said, swallowing heavily. 'Just looking into it makes me want to throw up. You know I'm no good with dead bodies and stuff at the best of times.'

'What about you Darren?' York asked. 'You were quick enough to nominate Spencer. How about you giving it a go?'

Crawley had a boyish stature to go with his boyish looks. There was no doubt he'd fit. McKenzie wondered what excuse the pretty boy would use to get out of sullying his on-trend clothes.

'I would boss, but I'm not very good with tight spaces. I wouldn't want to have a panic attack or something like that down there. Then you'd have two bodies to deal with,' he said with an apologetic shrug that looked as genuine as the Rolex on his wrist.

McKenzie took a deep breath, shook her head and said, 'Right. Come on then, let's get on with it. It can't be any worse than the stench a pod of orcas generates and I used to deal with that okay.'

York reached for the rope tailing behind her and took hold. 'You two grab the rope behind me. And do not let go!'

McKenzie shuffled forward and felt the loop strain against her waist.

'Here goes. You got me, yeah?'

'Yes. We've got you, don't worry,' York said and they began to lower her into the chasm.

A graceful entry it wasn't, but at least she landed in one piece, even managing to avoid treading on the woman lying directly below the hole.

'I'm down,' she yelled up to the dot of blue above.

Moving quickly, she pressed her fingers to the other woman's neck, feeling for a pulse, whilst trying to ignore the clamouring in her chest. A minute later she switched sides. Still nothing. She reached into her pocket and pulled out a small cosmetic mirror she'd taken from her handbag. 'It always works in films,' she murmured, then held her breath and watched for the tell-tale misting of breath from Mrs Marshall's delicate nose. Two minutes later, when the mirror remained clear, she lifted it to her own face and gently breathed out. Condensation beaded on the glass surface. Her shoulders slumped.

'Too late,' she called, her voice sounding flat.

'What?' Alex shouted down.

'I said we're too fucking late. She's dead!'

They heaved her back out of the pit; an inelegant affair. She emerged pale and ripe with the odour of death and decay. She started to peel off her protective clothing, dropping each item into the plastic bag Wynchcombe was holding open for her.

'Where's Alex gone?'

Wynchcombe pointed in the direction of the oak tree. She looked over and saw York pacing back and forth, phone pressed to his ear.

By the time she had divested herself of her PPE, York was on his way back.

'Right. We're all set. Everyone's on their way.' He turned to McKenzie. 'How are you doing Cat?'

'I'm fine. I just wish I could say the same for her...' She glanced towards the hole. 'We should have done something sooner. Maybe if we'd taken her husband's concerns more seriously at the start, we'd have found her in time.'

'You don't know that. She might have been dead before she was put in there. And even if she wasn't, you were down there, how long would anyone last in a place like that?' Feeling a sudden chill, McKenzie wrapped her arms around her chest, an action that York clearly spotted as he said, 'Why don't you go and get your fleece from the car and take a few minutes, then meet us back in the house?'

'It's alright. I'd rather carry on.'

'You sure?'

'Honestly, I'm fine.'

'Good. I need you firing on all cylinders if you're going to interview Don Skinner with me.'

'Boss... What about me?' Crawley said. 'Mrs Marshall was my case too.'

York looked at him and hooked an eyebrow.

'I thought you wanted to run with the serial killer angle... focus on the statistics and the database searches?'

'I did... I mean, I do, but, well...' He could barely contain his excitement. 'I'd rather interview a serial killer.'

'And I'm sure Cat would rather someone else had volunteered to take a dive into that cesspit.'

York started towards the house. Crawley shot McKenzie a peevish look before stalking off up the path. All four entered the kitchen together.

Don Skinner regarded them warily. As York recited his rights, the slaughter man's jaw slowly dropped.

'It's nothing to do with me. I told you, I didn't even know the woman. And what sort of idiot would hide a body in his own garden?'

'One who thought no one would think of looking in a cesspit,' McKenzie said.

'If I was going to get rid of a body, love, I can think of better ways of doing it, believe me.'

'Where's your son, Mr Skinner?' York asked.

'No idea. He was out when I got up.'

'Been using him as a punchbag again?' McKenzie asked.

Skinner looked at her through hooded eyes.

'Don't you have to have evidence before you accuse me of doing something like that?'

'Evidence like a face full of bruises?' she parried. Skinner glowered at her. She went on, 'If you didn't inflict those bruises, who did?'

Skinner crossed his arms and pinched his flabby lips together. 'I'm saying nothing without my lawyer.'

York gave him a hard stare and looked like he was about to say something when a knock at the door interrupted him. Two crime scene investigators, carrying an assortment of boxes, entered. Behind them came the towering form of Fitzwilliam, clutching his medical case, its leather looking as worn and wrinkled as the man himself.

'Morning folks. I'll be with you all in a second,' York said, before turning to DS Bells, who was lounging on the arm of a tatty looking sofa. 'Bob, would you take Mr Skinner to the station and get him booked in, please?' He looked back at the waiting figures. 'If you'd like to follow me, the victim's this way...' He started towards the back door just as his mobile began to ring. He shook his head and pulled the phone from his pocket. 'Cat, perhaps you could do the honours?'

28.

Robbie Skinner put his foot down, navigating the twisting, turning lanes with ease. He'd been out longer than anticipated. The old man would be doing his nut, having woken to an empty house, with no one there to make his tea or cook his breakfast. What the hell was he going to say? He could hardly tell him where he'd been and the problem with the old man is, he can always tell when he's sidestepping the truth.

Turning into his lane, Robbie was so busy dreaming up excuses, he was almost at the house by the time he noticed the line of vehicles parked outside. A puzzled frown slunk down over his brow. His father never had visitors. He stopped to let an approaching van pass — a rare occurrence on their quiet lane that was a rat-run to nowhere — and flashed his lights, but the van pulled in, joining the line of cars. Robbie's stomach lurched on seeing the words Forensic Investigation emblazoned along the side of the blue and yellow liveried van. He cruised slowly by. As he was passing, the door to the house opened. He saw his old man step out, hands behind his back. A man in a scruffy suit walking behind him ushered him into a black saloon waiting at the roadside.

At the end of the lane Robbie turned the corner and pulled over, safely out of view of the house. He sat drumming his fingers on the steering wheel, wondering what to do. As the seconds ticked by, dread nagged at his gut. He knew he couldn't sit there all day. Seized with an idea, he restarted the car and continued down the lane, passing the house where Mrs Forker used to live. He took the next few hundred metres slowly before coming to a stop a little distance away from the large holly bush that was next to the gate at the bottom of his garden. Desperate to know what was happening, yet not wanting to know at the same time, he cut the engine and sat there. After a minute, he finally plucked up enough courage to climb out of the car. He slipped the hood of his jacket up and jogged lightly towards the holly bush. As he drew close, a man's voice, loud and sonorous, filtered through the greenery. It sounded close by. Then more voices. Robbie strained his ears, trying to make out what was being said but it was impossible. Crouching down, he crept towards the gate, but it was no good, there were too many bushes blocking his line of sight. He eased up, until the ramshackle garden came into view and watched, mesmerised, as people in white suits gravitated around a black crater-like hole in the ground. It looked like a scene from an outlandish sci-fi movie. One of the white-suits moved and he saw her — the female detective who'd spoken to him earlier in the week. She was also staring into the hole. Robbie's gaze roamed the area. He noticed the flat, grey disc lying a short distance away and his heart lurched in his chest.

Just then, one of the men in white-suits squatted down and sat at the edge of the hole, before slowly lowering himself into the cesspit. Someone passed down a sturdy black camera. Shortly, the camera was traded for a stretcher fashioned from a flexible blue plastic sheet. Minutes passed with nothing obvious happening. Then everyone gathered around the hole. Robbie watched, spellbound, as they started to hoist the stretcher up.

He held his breath.

A tousled mess of black hair appeared first. Her head lolled like a rag doll in his direction; her face was hollow and full of shadows; and her once-beautiful eyes, now dull pebbles, stared back blankly.

Robbie groaned. Fighting a rising tide of bile, he staggered forward and clung onto the gate, trying to chase away the swimming sensation that had overtaken him. Unable to stop himself, he glanced back over to the scene just as the female detective stepped to one side as a white-suited scientist bent over the body. When she looked up it happened to be in his direction. They locked eyes. She broke away from the others and started to sprint towards him, calling his name.

Fear coursed through him like the charge from a taser, fuelling his race back to the van. He threw himself inside, turned the key he'd left in the ignition and put his foot down. He glanced into his rear-view mirror as the detective leapt into the road. He saw her shoulders slump as she gave up the chase.

***

'Shit!' McKenzie watched the white van disappear from view as it rounded the corner. She tipped her head skyward and blew out a sigh.

Why the hell had she yelled his name? He might not have scarpered if she hadn't. Instead, he'd got a good head start.

She turned, about to make her way back to the garden and was surprised to see Crawley leaning over the gate, staring down the empty road.

'Who was that?'

'Robbie Skinner,' she replied. Shooing him away from the gate, she set a foot on the bottom bar and vaulted over. 'He was watching us lift the body out.'

210

'So it's true then… murderers really do revisit the crime scene.'

'I think it's more likely he came home, saw all the cars parked up and came round this way to see what was happening.'

'Or he's the murderer revisiting the scene but you can't bear for me to be right,' Crawley grumbled, before turning and starting up the path. 'By the way, Alex wants you,' he called over his shoulder.

Back in the house, York wasted no time getting an ANPR alert out for Robbie's van. He hung up just as Fitzwilliam came in from the garden.

He set his bag down on the dining table.

'Damn sorry state of affairs.'

'What have we got?' York said.

'Notwithstanding the usual caveats about needing to wait for the PM, we have one leg with a rather nasty compound fracture, possible fractures on the other leg, bruising around the neck consistent with strangulation and a number of deep incisions to her abdomen.'

'More post-mortem butchery?' York said.

'Uh-hu.'

'Someone took her kidney too?' McKenzie said.

'Who said anything about her kidney?' McKenzie felt a shiver creep up her spine at the thought that Crawley might be right about the serial killer angle after all. 'Not a kidney. Not this time. Judging from the location of the incision, I suspect it was—' Fitzwilliam paused, his attention caught by something outside the kitchen window. McKenzie and York followed his gaze. Two men from the coroner's office were advancing up the path wheeling a stretcher on which rested a blue body bag.

Once they had passed, Fitzwilliam turned to them and with a grim set to his jaw continued, 'As I was saying, I can't be a hundred per cent sure until I open her up, but from the size and position of the opening, it looks like it was a rather crude attempt at a hysterectomy. I've told the CSIs to be on the lookout for any discarded body parts, though it's likely if anything was disposed of nearby, the magpies would have scavenged it by now.'

Cat thought about the ultrasound with its grainy black and white image of a tiny life and felt the blood drain from face.

'The baby...' she said in a hushed whisper.

Fitzwilliam looked at her, the wrinkles on his brow deepening.

'She was pregnant?'

McKenzie nodded.

'Eight weeks. As far as we're aware, no one knew.'

'It's possible her assailant didn't either. If he isn't a trained medical practitioner, it's likely he had no idea hers wasn't only the one life he was bringing to an untimely end.'

'He?' York said.

'He... she... I simply meant the culprit. Who that might be is your domain.' Fitzwilliam reached for his bag. 'I'll let you know the full extent of her injuries after the PM. Suffice to say I'll do what I can to prioritise it. Whoever is responsible needs to be stopped and soon.'

'Mr Fitzwilliam...' McKenzie called as he started for the door.

He turned around. 'Yes?'

'I just wondered, the knife work on the victims — does it look like it was done by someone who knew what they're doing?'

'The cuts were made by an exceptionally sharp instrument, such as a scalpel. And while they're not the standard of an experienced surgeon, or inexperienced surgeon for that matter, I would say they were done by someone who is happy wielding a knife and has a rudimentary understanding of anatomy.'

'Such as a butcher... or slaughterman?' York said.

'Possibly, yes. I dare say with a little reading up on the subject it wouldn't be too difficult for them to navigate their way around the human body. Though that could be said of anyone with a modicum of intellect and a strong stomach.'

29.

While Fitzwilliam followed the mortuary van back to the morgue, York called the team together.

'I need to get back to the station now the clock is ticking with Don Skinner. Cat, you're coming with me, yeah?' McKenzie nodded. 'Good. Darren, you can go and see Mr Marshall and break the bad news.'

Crawley stood there blinking for a moment, then said, 'Why me? Why can't Cat do it? Women are better at that sort of thing.'

'That's true of most things but it's never stopped you before,' McKenzie said.

York pulled his keys from his pocket.

Crawley said quickly, 'Actually sir, I think Mr Marshall would probably appreciate it if you took the time to give him the news. Having a senior officer do it might make him feel like he's getting some respect. Also, he'll be less angry at you than at Cat.'

'Why should he be angry at me?' McKenzie said.

'You didn't exactly go rushing out to find her.'

'That's because I wanted to be sure she hadn't done a runner and didn't want to be found. And you can talk, you were the one who thought she'd accidentally rolled on her phone while she was busy banging someone and wanted to pass the case to missing persons.'

A small smirk slipped across his lips, which he quickly erased.

'That was a joke. I said from the start we should do more.'

McKenzie's jaw dropped.

'No you didn't.'

'Now, now, children. You can argue about it in your own time. But I think Darren's right. I think it would be better if I broke the news. We can stop off and tell him on the way to the station. Spence, Darren, you stay here and take a look around. Just try to keep out of the way of the CSIs.'

'Right, let's get this over with,' York said, firing up the engine. He glanced at McKenzie and paused. 'Something wrong?'

'No.'

'So why do you look like a bulldog chewing a wasp?' He quickly held a hand up. 'Sorry. Just an expression. I forgot about Harvey. So, what is it? You're not worried about Marshall, are you?'

'It's nothing.'

'Cat…'

'I'm…' Totally pissed off at Darren getting out of doing virtually everything, was what she wanted to say. Instead, she shook her head. 'It's nothing. I'll get over it. So are you going to tell Mr Marshall his wife was pregnant?'

'Not at this stage. I'd rather leave details like that until after the post-mortem. We'll know then whether she was definitely pregnant. If we tell him about the scan and for some bizarre reason it turns out she let someone else use her name, how much extra upset will we have laid at his door?'

'Who else's could it be?'

'I don't know. Maybe someone at Freedom Farm didn't want anyone to know they were pregnant and Mrs Marshall said they could use her name and keep the scan in her locker. You should know by now; the obvious answer isn't always the right answer.'

She nodded, despite disagreeing with him. This time she thought the facts spoke for themselves. Though as soon as she saw Karl Marshall when he answered the door — unshaven and with his usually slick, dark hair in an unruly mop above a tired face — she knew York was right. Now wasn't the time.

'Any news?' Marshall asked, sounding despondent.

'Can we go inside?' York gestured towards the door, sending panic skittering across Marshall's face. After a second, he regained his composure and led them through to the immaculate kitchen. He walked over to the window and turned to face them.

'Well?'

'You might want to sit down.'

'Please, just tell me.'

York looked down at his shoes for a brief moment, then raised his gaze to meet the other man's stare.

'I'm very sorry Mr Marshall, but the body of a woman believed to be your wife was discovered earlier today. We don't yet know the exact cause of death but we have already taken one person into custody to help with our enquiries and expect to arrest another shortly. I will—'

Marshall started to shake his head.

'No. You've made a mistake. I don't believe it.'

York held his gaze.

'I'm so sorry.'

Marshall gave an anguished cry and stumbled over to a barstool, where he slumped down. burying his head in his hands. McKenzie found a box of tissues nearby and passed it to him. They waited for the tears to ease. He blew his nose noisily and asked, 'Where did you find her?'

'At an address on Green Lane,' York replied.

Marshall looked at him, deep furrows on his brow.

'The same place the other woman was killed?'

'Not exactly. A nearby property.'

'A nearby property?' Marshall repeated. 'Don't tell me... the man from the slaughterhouse?' His face contorted with anger. 'I swear to God, I'll kill him!'

York set out a hand.

'Mr Marshall, I understand you're angry, but—'

'I was told you were going to check them out. If that's the case then why didn't you find her sooner?' He started to pace up and down. 'I told you something had happened to her. The phone call made that blindingly obvious. If you'd have taken it more seriously from the start my wife might still be alive.'

'Mr Marshall, that's not true,' York said. 'We had no way of knowing where to find your wife. There was nothing we could have done that would have prevented what happened.'

'You could have traced the call.'

'We tried,' McKenzie replied. 'There aren't enough masts in the area for an accurate location.'

'Then you should have organised a search party and gone looking for her. Instead, you fobbed me off just to save yourself the effort and cost.'

As the accusations flew, McKenzie's mind went into overdrive. What if they had put an urgent appeal out over the media? What if they'd initiated a search straightaway? It might have been enough. Guilt slunk through her like a cold-skinned snake. Right from the start, she'd sensed there was more to it than a woman having simply left her husband. She should have been more insistent, tried harder to persuade York to take it more seriously. Now it was too late.

'You did the best you could,' York said, as they walked to the cars, the crunch of their footsteps on the gravel sounding unnaturally loud.

She shook her head but said nothing. There was no point arguing.

As they drove away, McKenzie glanced in the wing mirror. A ghost of a figure stood at the kitchen window watching them. She felt guilt grip her gut once more. On the journey back to the station, the image of Fern Marshall's broken body played heavily on her mind. The cruelty of the scene: the shattered limbs and defiled womanhood. She thought about the screams captured on the phone call, begging her husband to help. Where was her phone now? It hadn't been found by the body. Once again it came back to that same question — where the hell had she been between midday and four? And what had made her go to the Skinners' house in the first place?

She thought about the tyrannical Don Skinner. If the initial altercation had taken place on the lane, how had he got her over the gate and into the garden? Had Mrs Forker seen something when she was walking by and not realised its significance at the time? Was that why she became the next victim? Yet she never mentioned having seen anyone near the gate; not even Fern Marshall, who had been riding her bike further up the lane when their paths had crossed.

It made more sense if Fern was already over the gate, her bike behind the bush, when her attacker struck... the bike that was later moved. But if one of the Skinners had moved it, why bring it back a couple of days later and leave it a short distance down the lane? Why not dump it miles away? Perhaps the original plan hadn't been to kill her? Don Skinner could have simply intended to frighten her, confining her somewhere for a few hours to deter any future attempts to relieve him of his livestock. Had Robbie discovered her when he got home? McKenzie recalled how fondly he'd spoken of her. It wouldn't be the first time an infatuation had led to murder. But why take the women's womb? A curious choice of MO for someone who spends their days amongst so much death and bloodshed, though his knife skills were probably up to the job.

By the time they reached the station, her head was full of questions. She strode across the car park, matching York's long gait step for step, keen to see what Don Skinner had to say for himself.

Despite hoping Skinner senior would prove more cooperative in the light of the morning's gruesome discovery, they found him as recalcitrant as ever. Leaning back in his seat, he laced his fat fingers across his ample midriff, observing them through hooded eyes. Hostility radiated off him like steam from a compost heap. His brief, a solicitor by the name of Howard Fray, was a silver-haired man with flint grey eyes and a face full of angles as sharp as his tailored suit.

'I don't care where you found her,' Skinner said after York ran through the facts. 'I don't know nothing about any murder.'

'She was last seen on the road that runs down to the rear of your property around midday on Monday. Where were you then?'

'Ask her.' He gave a disparaging nod in McKenzie's direction.

'I'm asking you,' York said.

Skinner looked to his brief who shrugged.

'This is ridiculous.' When neither detective responded, Skinner said, 'I was in the pub with a mate. I left the yard at twelve, got back about two. I was there until we closed at half-five.'

McKenzie reached for her pad and, guarding the page with her hand, scribbled: *not yet spoken to frien*. She slipped the pad along the table. York scanned the note and nodded.

'What do you know about the disappearance of Mrs Fern Marshall?'

'Nothing. I didn't know the woman.'

'But you had met her before,' McKenzie said. Skinner's face grew a shade redder. 'She was at Freedom Farm when you confronted the staff there about some stolen lambs.'

'So I might have seen her there, what of it? The place was full of meddlesome women. Are any of them dead?'

'Good question and one that we'll be following up.' York looked at McKenzie, who scribbled a note in her pad for effect.

'Is this a wind up?' Skinner turned to his brief, threw his hands wide and shook his head.

York, with a stern set to his jaw, said, 'I don't joke about murder, Mr Skinner. You made quite a few threats while you were at Freedom Farm. Carried some out too. Like cutting the throats of half a dozen sheep and leaving them for dead on the driveway.'

Skinner leaned back and crossed his arms.

'No comment.'

'What does you son think about recent events?' McKenzie asked.

'What do you mean recent events?'

'A woman going missing, another murdered, right on your doorstep.'

'I have no idea.'

'A woman goes missing, last seen virtually outside your house and then your neighbour's found butchered in her own home, and you haven't talked about it?'

'No.'

'I take it then he didn't mention that he knew Mrs Marshall from school?'

A flicker of something — surprise or anger — crossed Don Skinner's hardened face.

'You didn't know?' McKenzie said.

'I'm not the lad's keeper.'

'But I think you are.' She held his gaze for a moment, then said, 'How did Robbie get the bruises on his face?'

Skinner shifted in his seat, but said nothing

'Mr Skinner...?' York prompted.

'He tripped on something.'

'Are you sure about that?' McKenzie said. 'Did you hit your son, Mr Skinner?'

Skinner turned to his solicitor. 'Are they allowed to ask questions that aren't anything to do with this dead woman? Surely, what goes on between me and my lad is none of their business.'

Fray set his manicured fingers down on top of the briefcase resting on the table in front of him.

'My client has a point. I fail to see the relevance of your question.'

'I would have thought it was obvious. If your client wasn't responsible for the bruises on his son, who was? A woman fighting for her life, perhaps? The post-mortem will examine the murdered woman for signs that she put up a struggle. Do you think they'll find traces of your son's DNA?'

'No comment.'

'Perhaps you were punishing your son for something, Mr Skinner?' McKenzie said. 'Had he gone off plan and taken things into his own hands with Mrs Marshall?'

Skinner turned to his solicitor and leaned in. The pair consulted in a close huddle for a few seconds.

Mr Fray cleared his throat and said, 'My client has been more than willing to answer questions relating to the unfortunate deaths of the two women. He doesn't however think it appropriate that he is asked to speculate on where his son might have got his injuries.'

221

'We're more than happy to ask Robbie directly, if we knew where he was. Do you know where he is, Mr Skinner?'

'No comment.'

'It might interest you to know that Robbie went around to the back of the house and watched us pull Mrs Marshall's body out of the cesspit. He ran away as soon as he realised he'd been spotted.' Another flicker of surprise shot across Skinner's ruddy features. 'You'll be doing him a favour if you tell us where he is. If he's got nothing to do with it, he's got nothing to be afraid of. We just need to hear his side of things.'

Don Skinner coughed the word 'bullshit' into his balled-up hand. His solicitor darted him a look of disapproval. Skinner curled his lip into a sneer and said, 'No comment.'

'That's your prerogative Mr Skinner. Not that it will help your son any,' York said. 'I think we're done… for now.' As soon as they left the interview room, he turned to McKenzie. 'We need to find out whether Skinner's alibis hold water. I want you and Darren to go and talk to this mate of his, find out if he really was where he says he was and while you're at it, do some timed runs from Skinner's Yard to the pub and then on to his house. Let's see if we can find some wriggle room in his alibi to keep him in the game.'

30.

'How long were you in the Maldives for?' Crawley asked.

'Couple of years.'

'Must have been awesome.'

McKenzie thought back to the countless hours she'd spent in a boat on the Indian Ocean, getting up close to some of the world's most majestic creatures. And then there were the evenings, spent with friends under skies flush with stars, listening to the susurration of the sea, as they all shared stories of their day's encounters.

'You could say that.'

'How come you gave it all up to do this?'

She shrugged.

'It just sort of happened. I came back for my brother's funeral and never went back.' She didn't feel inclined to mention she never went back because she'd decided to become a detective, driven by the desire to avenge her brother's death. 'How about you? Did you always want to follow in your father's footsteps?'

'Yeah. He used to tell us these stories about the good old days. Made it sound real exciting. I always liked the idea of a job where I got to kick arse. But it's not like that no more, is it? The badge doesn't get the respect it used to.' He turned and gazed out of the passenger window. 'Still, some things are the same, like how it comes down to who you know and how well you know them, when it comes to promotion.'

'Do you think?' McKenzie replied, sounding surprised. 'That's not been my experience. These days it's all targets and role maps. I don't even think being part of a masonic lodge gets you anywhere.'

'But I bet being on the right side of the boss does, eh? You must be confident about making sergeant soon, eh?'

McKenzie frowned.

'What do you mean?'

'Just saying you and Alex seem close, is all.'

'We're not that close. If it appears that way, it's because we've known each other for years. He used to hang out with my brother long before I joined the force.'

'Sure.' After a beat, he said, 'You have to admit though, it's a lot easier for a woman to get noticed, when the boss is a bloke. Especially if she's an attractive woman who's prepared to...' His head gave a little jerk. 'You know.'

'No, I don't know. Prepared to do what?' She looked at him, eyes narrowed, lips pinched.

'Whatever it takes, I suppose.'

'If for one second you're suggesting that I've—'

Crawley lifted his hand, palm out towards her face. In the close confines of the car, he was almost touching her. She batted his hand away.

'Easy tiger,' he said, laughing. 'No need to get violent. I wasn't suggesting anything.' McKenzie relaxed in her seat. He went on '...but if you want to include yourself in that category, that's your business.'

'You know what, Darren? I am sick of all your snidey little comments you make when no one else is around.' She glanced over and was surprised to see him smirking. 'I don't know what your game is, but you can stop it now.'

They spent the rest of the fifteen-minute journey in silence. McKenzie pulled into Skinner's Yard and parked alongside a pair of marked police cars.

'Why are we stopping?' Crawley asked. 'I thought the idea was to time the journey to the pub.'

She climbed out without replying and waved at a uniformed constable standing at the entrance to the slaughterhouse. The officer, a plump blond man with a round, pleasant face, started to walk over. By the time he'd reached her, Crawley was out of the car and leaning against the bonnet.

McKenzie introduced herself, then asked, 'How's it going?'

'It's like looking for a needle in a needle factory. I watched the CSIs spray some luminol in the office. Place lit up like the inside of a sunbed under the UV light. There's blood everywhere. I don't fancy their chances of finding any DNA relating to the murdered woman.'

'I take it there's been no sign of the wanted guy, Robbie Skinner?' she asked.

'Is he the driver of the white Escort van?'

'That's right.'

'He hasn't shown his face here. Don't worry, we'll grab him if he does.'

'Good.' McKenzie craned her neck and scanned the area. 'Are any of the abattoir's employees around? I was hoping to talk to someone who works here.'

'The foreman's around somewhere,' the PC said. 'I can go and find him, if you want?'

'That'd be a great help, thanks.'

As the officer walked away, Crawley asked, 'Why do you want to talk to the foreman?'

'I thought it might be a good idea to have a chat without Don Skinner breathing down his neck.'

'Why? Robbie's the one we should be focussing on.'

'What if Skinner senior snatched Fern at lunchtime, kept her locked up somewhere, then Robbie took over after he'd finished work?'

'Why would the old guy take her?'

'Maybe he thought she was the one taking the lambs and planned on teaching her a lesson.'

After a short pause, Crawley said, 'I still don't get why she couldn't have been someplace else in the afternoon and Robbie saw her when she came back for her bike. You know, like a rape-turned-murder.'

'If it was, we'll soon find out once the PM's been done. But if she was somewhere else all afternoon, where was she and who was she with? You'd have thought somebody would have come forward by now.'

'Not necessarily. Not if they're married.'

He was right.

'Whatever. I still want a word with the foreman. You can wait in the car if you want.'

'No. I'm fine here.'

The foreman, a man named Ted Bagley, was rake-thin with a long, horse-like face and greying hair pasted into a thin comb over.

'Mr Skinner went out at midday, came back around two and was here all afternoon until...' He sucked air through his teeth as he gave it some thought. 'At least half-five. Might have even been later, seeing as Robbie left early.'

'I understand Mondays are usually Robbie's day to go out for lunch.'

'That's right.'

'Why did they swap?' Bagley shrugged his skinny shoulders. 'What about Wednesday?' she went on. 'Were they both here same as usual?'

'Robbie had to go out. Something about his van needing work doing. The boss spent the afternoon whinging about it.'

'Why was he whinging? Doesn't he like Robbie to have time off?'

'It wasn't that. There was a problem with the incinerator. Robbie usually deals with all the equipment. Wednesday, the boss had to do it himself. It was gone half-six by the time he left. I remember 'cos he was complaining how he didn't have time to go to the boozer.'

'He didn't go to the pub on Wednesday?' McKenzie asked. Another lie?

'Not as far as I know.'

'Okay. Going back to Monday. Do you know which vehicle Mr Skinner went to the pub in?'

'The Range Rover. Ain't never seen him in anything else. Not since he gave Robbie the van.'

'Did you actually see him drive off in it? He couldn't have taken a different vehicle without you knowing?'

'Aye, I suppose he could have. I was busy when he left.' McKenzie felt her optimism grow, until he added, 'Only he was definitely driving the Range Rover when he came back. He'd have had to come back and swap over. Why would he bother to do that?'

McKenzie ignored the question and said, 'I understand Robbie left early Monday. Do you know what time he went?'

''round four.'

'Before four? After four?'

'All I know is he was there for the half-three tea break and gone by the time I went out for a fag at half-four.' Bagley looked

227

at her and waited for the next question. When one wasn't forthcoming, he said, 'Is that everything?'

'Sorry. I was thinking,' McKenzie said. 'Apart from the office, is there anywhere on-site that's used for storage? Maybe some place not generally accessed by the staff.'

'Depends what you want to store. There's the tool cupboard in the incinerator shed. Robbie's the only one with keys to that. Or he was. That was why the gaffer got so angry when the incinerator went on the blink. All the tools were in there. Won't happen again though. The boss got himself a key cut. Got me one too.'

'Have you got it on you now?'

He shook his head.

'I gave it to the copper who asked me to open up. She took all my keys.'

Shortly, McKenzie watched as a uniformed sergeant, a smiling, blonde-haired woman, twisted the key in the lock to the tool cupboard. The door swung open to reveal a room about half the size of a single garage. A handful of tools and bottles of machine oil sat on a largely empty shelving unit.

'It's bigger than I was expecting,' McKenzie said.

'You don't need to bother with gloves. The CSIs are all done in here,' the sergeant said.

'I take it they didn't find anything out of the ordinary in here?' McKenzie asked.

'You mean like evidence someone was held here?'

'Someone or something. I was actually thinking of a push bike.'

'Nobody's mentioned anything, but let me go find out.' A few minutes later, she returned, beaming. 'You could be right, about the bike. Apparently there's a mark on the floor that could be from a bicycle tyre.' They all started to scan the concrete. 'The CSI reckons the bike rolled over a patch of oil... Here!' She bent over and pointed to the ground at her feet.

Sure enough, there was a partial tyre track about an inch long.

After explaining to the CSIs the potential significance of the mark and asking them to compare it to the tyres on Mrs Marshall's bike, McKenzie and Crawley left the yard, heading for the pub Don Skinner claimed to have patronised on Monday and Wednesday. He had also furnished them with his mate's address, but given he'd remarked that they'd more likely find his mate propping up the bar in The Bull once the sun was past the yardarm, McKenzie was hoping a visit to the pub would kill two birds with one stone.

Traffic was light, as was the cloud cover, which resulted in the afternoon being unseasonably cold and probably accounted for why so few people appeared to have ventured out. Their destination was a small village a short distance from where the fortnightly livestock market was held. The Bull, Don Skinner's hostelry of choice, was a whitewashed brick building right in the heart of the village.

'Twelve minutes and twenty seconds,' Crawley said, duly recording it in his notepad.

'It could easily be double that on market day,' McKenzie commented, flicking the indicator wand and pulling into an alarmingly small courtyard car park. Eyeing the scarred and scraped walls with trepidation, she deftly manoeuvred the Skoda between a grey Honda and a rust-riddled Mondeo that looked like it had seen better days.

'Could you have parked any closer?' Crawley said, pushing the door open and trying to squeeze through a gap not much larger than his head.

'Maybe I should have chosen one of the other spaces?' McKenzie said, looking around in an exaggerated manner. 'Oh, that's right. There aren't any.'

Crawley cast her a catty look and started to stalk away.

'I'll lead on this,' he said, then stopped outside the entrance to the public bar and waited for McKenzie. 'What's the guy's name?'

She rolled her eyes and sidestepped around him.

Inside, the place was empty apart from three men sitting at a bar of dark polished oak. Pints of ale in various degrees of consumption rested in front of them. They all turned and cast a casual glance at the new arrivals.

'Grace… customer!' one of them cried before all three turned back to ponder their pints.

Moments later came the clip-clop of heels on the grey slate floor. A slip of a girl, wearing tight black trousers and an even tighter white shirt appeared behind the bar. She set down the wicker basket of knives and forks she was carrying.

'What can I get you?'

'Nothing. Thank you. Kent Police. We're looking for Sean Campbell.'

Two of the men, those on the end stools, straightened in their seats. Only the man in the middle remained bent over his drink. He reached for his pint, swiftly downing it before returning the glass to the counter with a thump. He clambered to his feet. 'I'm off. See you later, lads.'

McKenzie stepped forward, blocking the barrel-shaped man's exit. He attempted to look down at his boots though a beer-belly that would rival any nine-month pregnancy bump interrupted the view.

'Mr Campbell?'

'Can't stop. I've got someplace I've got to be.' He went to walk around McKenzie.

She stepped sideways and blocked him for a second time.

'It won't take more than a few minutes.'

'Been a naughty boy, have we?' one of the other men said over his shoulder. 'Hey, before you lock him up and throw away the key, make sure you get some cash off him, will you? Next round's his.'

The third man chuckled into his beer.

'Can't we do this later?' Campbell said. 'I really have to go.'

'I'm sure you can spare five minutes for a friend?' McKenzie set out a hand and gestured to the front door. 'Shall we?'

Campbell acquiesced and as soon as they reached the car park he asked, 'What friend?'

'Don Skinner. I understand the pair of you are drinking buddies.'

He eyed her suspiciously.

'That's right.'

'We're hoping you might know where he was Monday lunchtime.'

'What's he supposed to have done?'

'Can you help or can't you Mr Campbell? Monday lunchtime.'

'He was here with me.'

'From when, until when?' McKenzie pushed.

'Now you're asking.' He stretched up a veiny hand and scratched his head. 'It must have been about quarter past twelve by the time he got here and he was here, what… about an hour, hour and a half? Which means he must have left about half one. So are you going to tell me what's he supposed to have done then?'

'A woman went missing near to where he lives. She was found dead this morning on Mr Skinner's property.' McKenzie fixed her hazel eyes on him, watching his reaction.

Campbell blinked a couple of times then said, 'Bet Don's well pissed off, isn't he? Someone dumping a body on his land. Drops him right in it.'

Crawley stepped forward.

'What about Wednesday evening?' he asked. 'Did you see Mr Skinner then too?'

Campbell's rheumy eyes scoured the ground at his feet.

'Wednesday? I'm not sure, I... Actually, yes. That was the day he thought he wasn't going to be able to make it. He called me from the yard, said there was some problem or other and he wouldn't be finishing till six. Said he'd go straight home. I told him not to be so daft. I was happy to have myself another pint while I waited.'

'And what time did he leave on Wednesday?'

'Ahh. Well, you see, I'd had a few jars by then. I couldn't tell you what time I left, let alone when Don went.'

'Did Mr Skinner mention the missing woman at all... Mrs Fern Marshall?'

'No. Did he know her then?'

'That's what we're trying to ascertain.'

'You know, Don's not much of a ladies' man. Doesn't hold much with women, not since he got divorced.'

'What about his son, Robbie? Does he say much about him? Maybe he's been worried about him recently?'

'Don? Worry about Robbie?' He gave a crooked smile, revealing a mouth full of yellow teeth, and shook his head.

'They're not close?'

'Nah. Robbie's always been a mummy's boy. Don reckons he's a bit soft in the head.'

'Yet they live and work together.'

Campbell looked at her, surprised.

232

'He's flesh and blood, ain't he? Don could hardly leave him homeless, what with social services breathing down his neck after his missus got killed. Worked out alright in any case. I hear Robbie's a bit nifty at the old cooking and cleaning and he can hardly complain about getting minimum wage at the yard when he gets a roof over his head for gratis.' Campbell looked from McKenzie to Crawley. 'So, if that's everything…?'

McKenzie nodded. 'Thank you for your time, Mr Campbell.'

Campbell thrust his hands in his pocket and scurried off, crossing the road and disappearing down the lane.

'Right,' McKenzie said. 'We'll have a quick word with the barmaid, then do the timed drive to Skinner's house. Though if we can't get a better handle on what time he left here, that's not going to be of much help.'

They returned to the bar.

'Grace, isn't it?' McKenzie said to the barmaid. The girl nodded, dark hair bobbing. 'Have you got five minutes?'

'Sure.'

McKenzie led her over to a table in the window, where they could talk in private.

'Do you know a Mr Don Skinner?'

'Don, sure. He comes in most days.'

'Was he here on Wednesday?'

The girl's thick, drawn-on brows huddled together. She started to nod.

'Yes. He came in during the evening rush. He was a bit later than usual.'

'What time did he leave?'

'I'm not sure. I was in and out, what with serving at the bar and taking food through to the dining room.'

'What about Monday lunchtime?'

'No.' She shook her head. 'Don only comes in lunchtimes on market day.' Quickly adding, 'Fridays.'

'Ah, that's awkward. You see, Mr Campbell told us he was here with Don from around midday on Monday.'

'Sean was here. I remember serving him. Thinking about it, he sat outside and ordered two ploughman's and a couple of pints. I suppose Don could have been with him. I can't be a hundred per cent sure. I was covering the bar and didn't go into the beer garden that day.'

Only half-satisfied, McKenzie thanked the barmaid and they left the pub. After a timed run to the Skinners' home, they returned to the station. Crawley got her to drop him next to his car, muttering something about a family gathering. McKenzie watched him speed away. With nothing but an empty house waiting for her, she climbed out and headed into the station. The office was in darkness. She flipped on the lights and settled at her desk. She had just hit the on switch to her computer when the door opened and York entered. He gave a wave and headed over, hitched himself onto the edge of her desk and opened the brown paper bag he was carrying, unleashing a medley of bready, salty, fried aromas.

'Oh, not fair,' McKenzie said. 'That smells too good.'

'Have a chip…' He ripped open the bag and shuffled a handful of anaemic fries out of their cardboard carton. After popping a couple in his mouth, he picked up the burger and started to peel off its greaseproof wrapping. 'I'd offer you some of this, but I don't think a quarter-pounder's your sort of thing. So, how did you get on?' he asked, taking a bite of his burger.

'We tracked down Don Skinner's mate. Looks like his alibi for Monday stacks up. He didn't have time to go from the pub, drop by his house and still get back to the abattoir for when he did.

Wednesday night's less clear cut. But if he's in the clear for Mrs Marshall, how likely is it he killed Mrs Forker?'

York pulled a minuscule paper napkin out of the bag and wiped his fingers.

'We really need to get hold of Robbie,' he said, reaching for McKenzie's desk phone and punching in a number. 'Maybe now Skinner senior has had time to sit and sweat, he might be more willing to talk.'

Half an hour later, they were back in the small interview room sitting opposite the slaughterman. Don Skinner stared at them with a bored expression. He looked disparagingly at the plastic cup of vending machine coffee McKenzie placed in front of him. The door opened and his sharp-suited solicitor entered and took the empty seat next to his client.

York once again ran through the formalities and set the equipment to record.

'I trust you've had time to confirm my client's alibis, detective?' the legal man asked.

'We'll come to that in a minute.' York faced Skinner. 'We're still trying to get hold of Robbie, Mr Skinner. We need him to confirm the time you arrived home on Wednesday.' York set his hands down on the desk in front of him and waited.

The slaughterhouse man leaned over and whispered something to his solicitor.

'My client has already told you that he took longer than required to travel home that evening, having taken a scenic route and stopped to relieve himself. He believes any information his son might be able to provide will only confirm that he did not drive home directly.'

'I appreciate that fact, Mr Skinner,' York replied. 'But this is a murder investigation and the times you've given in your statement need to be corroborated.'

'You must think I was born yesterday,' Skinner sneered. 'Don't give me that bollocks about confirming my alibi. You just want to get hold of Robbie, because you think he murdered that woman.'

'And did he?' McKenzie said. 'Do you think your son killed those women, Mr Skinner?'

'Pshh… Robbie? Kill someone? The boy couldn't kill a fly. He's a wimp. You should have seen him on his first day at the yard. Bloody cried, he did. That was his mother's doing. Spoiled him. He's too soft by half.'

'All the same, we still need to talk to him,' York said. 'Where is he, Mr Skinner?'

Skinner shrugged before leaning his sizeable frame back in his seat, the chair squeaking in complaint. He settled his gaze on the wall above the detectives' heads and crossed his arms.

That was the last they got out of him.

31.

Monday morning, Robbie woke, muscles stiff and aching from the van's cold, hard surface; his left arm was numb from where he'd lain on it. After pushing himself upright, he sat for a few minutes bringing it back to life with a strong hand, pondering what to do next.

The truth was he had no idea. Not of what to do, nor where to go. Not now, not in the future. If indeed he had a future. He took the fawn cable knit jumper he'd rolled into a makeshift pillow and buried his face in the soft wool, inhaling deeply. The aroma — her aroma — caused the breath to catch in his chest and he was seized with a compulsion to cry. Five minutes later he rubbed his mottled face, his rough hands rasping over the day-old growth on his jaw and groaned as the hopelessness of his situation hit him. He thought of the animals in the abattoir whose days were numbered, brought to an end with a bolt to the brain. How he wished he were one of them.

But then something inside him railed against his despair. It wasn't over yet.

He needed to get his head together. He'd seen enough cop shows to know about automatic number plate recognition; knew if his plate got caught by a patrol car that would be the end of it. Which is why, so far, he'd kept to country lanes and roads through small villages where a police presence was about as common as Halley's comet, finally resting up in a layby on the outskirts of an industrial unit, hidden in the embrace of a long line of lorries. But from here he knew it was going to be tricky. He needed a plan. But first... food. He was ravenous, thanks to the smell of fried bacon and onion that had permeated the back of the van, courtesy of Tony's Snack Van parked nearby. He wriggled out of his sleeping bag fully dressed, slipped his trainers on and pushed open the rear doors.

***

At the same time that Robbie was stirring, McKenzie opened her eyes. The radio alarm played quietly in the background. She indulged in a long stretch, her legs slipping easily under the warm quilt towards the bottom of the bed. And then she froze. The emptiness there a new sensation. No Harvey. She threw off the bedclothes. Forty minutes later, she zipped up her boots, grabbed her keys and jacket, and disappeared through the front door.

When she arrived at the station, DI York was in his office, talking on his phone. They exchanged nods as she passed. All around her talk was on finding Robbie Skinner. She sat down and thought back to the previous evening's interview with Don Skinner. It sounded like Robbie's mother had been a big influence on him. Had her death been a defining point in his life? The original police report hadn't said much about him, other than the thirteen-year-old had been at home, waiting for his mother to return from her evening cleaning job, when they'd gone to give him the tragic news. Not exactly an ideal upbringing, left home alone with a microwave meal, but there were kids who'd had it considerably worse and hadn't turned into a murderer. Was the fact Robbie and Fern Marshall were at school together when his mother died relevant? Seized with an idea, McKenzie logged into her computer and went to Fern's Facebook account. Its contents might have been scant and woefully out of date, but there, amongst the meagre collection of personal information, was exactly what she was looking for: Fern Marshall's school history.

'I couldn't believe it when I heard the news last night,' the headmaster said, after McKenzie explained the reason for her call. 'So, how can I help?'

'We're trying to find a fellow pupil of Fern's — a Robbie Skinner. It's possible he may have some information that could help us.'

'Robbie Skinner. Now that's a name I haven't heard in a long time. I don't think I've seen him since he left. Were he and Fern in the same year? I don't recall him graduating at the same time.' There was a small pause, then he said, 'Yes, I remember now. They were. The fact that Robbie left early, as soon as he was legally able to, threw me for a minute.'

'Do you know if they were friends?'

'I don't, I'm afraid, but I would have thought it unlikely. They might have started in the same class, but Robbie's performance dropped after his mother died and he ended up slipping down to the bottom grade. Fern, on the other hand was a straight A student and stayed on for sixth form.'

'It sounds like Robbie changed a lot after his mother's death.'

'Oh yes, it affected him profoundly.'

'Do you know if he ever received any counselling?'

'We tried, but he wasn't interested.'

'Was he angry, about her dying?'

'If he was, he kept it to himself. It was more like it had sucked the life out of him. I called his father to discuss it once. To say the conversation was a disaster would be an understatement. The man was rude, arrogant and self-serving. He had no interest in his son's welfare. I wouldn't be surprised if it was his deleterious attitude that was responsible for Robbie's drop in performance. He told me he saw no benefit in Robbie continuing with his education as he expected him to start work for him — I don't know if he still does, but he used to own an abattoir. I tried explaining that he had a statutory responsibility with regard to Robbie's schooling and... well, let's just say his reply doesn't bear repeating. The long and the short of it was Robbie continued to show up, at least most of the time, but stopped engaging. He left at fifteen, with no qualifications to show for it. A tragedy really.'

'It sounds it. Was there anyone he was particularly close to at school? Friends, I mean.'

Maybe someone was harbouring him? It wouldn't be the first time.

'I'm sorry, nobody springs to mind.'

Another brick wall.

McKenzie thanked the headmaster for his time. Afterwards, she sat wondering what Robbie's childhood was like in the days before his parents separated. In the garden were relics of what might have been a happy childhood: the rusting frame of a swing and two empty chains hanging from it and that treehouse — every child's dream. But she knew it took more than toys to make a happy child. A mother's love surely was the bedrock. How must he have felt when his mother died, to have to move back in with a man whose only reason for wanting him there was to cook and clean and work for a pittance in a place synonymous with death and dying? Were the brutal attacks on innocent women a consequence of him feeling that his mother had deserted him?

She leaned back in her seat, looked up at the ceiling and gave the idea some thought. Shortly, she sat back up and shook her head. Robbie's mother died almost twenty years ago. Why would he start killing now? She could understand it if they'd found Don

Skinner dead with a knife through the heart, but a neighbour Robbie had hardly known and an old school friend? It didn't make sense. So far, the Robbie everyone talked about was a kind and gentle soul. She remembered boys like him at school. Shy types who watched from afar, never daring to make a move or chance a clumsy chat-up line, crippled by self-doubt. Poles apart from cocky, brazen types like Simon Parry, who fancied themselves as well as fancying their chances.

If, for a second, she accepted that Robbie didn't murder Fern Marshall, then it meant someone must have gone out of their way to make it look like he did; hiding her body in his garden and parking a van like his on the road at the back of his house the same time that she was passing. All at a time when Robbie would ordinarily have been enjoying a lunch break away from the abattoir.

Perhaps the killer knew about the altercation with the Skinners at Freedom Farm earlier in the year and thought Robbie a suitable scapegoat.

She walked over to Crawley, who was staring intently at his computer screen.

'Darren, have you done the ANPR checks on Simon Parry's car?'

He leaned back in his chair and looked up at her.

'What?'

'You were going to see if Parry had been in the area when he was supposed to be in Hull.'

'Forget that. I've found something much more important.'

'What?'

A smug smile curled on his lips.

'More evidence to nail Robbie Skinner with.'

'What've you found?'

'You know how his mother was killed in a hit and run. At first, I thought maybe he'd done it, but he was only a kid at the time, so I figure that's unlikely. So then I thought maybe her dying somehow turned him into a psycho. You know, like in the film, that Bates bloke went loopy after his mother died.'

'I had a similar thought but ruled it out. His mother died years ago, why would he become violent now?'

'How do we know he hasn't killed before? Maybe he usually disposes of them at the abattoir but for some reason couldn't this time. I mean talk about the perfect place for a serial killer to work.'

'Have there been many women go missing in the area over the last twenty years?'

'I don't know. People go missing all the time. But there's something else… his mother was an organ donor.'

'So?'

'It explains the missing kidney and other thing. He's got to have some sort of hang up on the fact they cut his mum open and took everything out.' He looked at her with a triumphant glint in his eye. 'I'm going to go tell Alex. I reckon he'll be stoked.'

'You think?' she said, shaking her head. 'You know what he'll say?'

Crawley frowned.

'What?'

'That you haven't got any evidence. Everything you just said is pure supposition.'

'Maybe. But I bet Robbie Skinner will cry like a baby when we confront him with it. Wouldn't be surprised if we get a full confession out of him, if we push the right buttons.'

Crawley got up and started to walk away.

'So, just to be clear…' McKenzie said to his retreating back. 'You haven't done the ANPR check on Parry. Is that right?'

He stopped walking and turned, glaring at her.

'No. I haven't done it. And before you go whining to Alex *again*, it's not my fault. There's been a problem with the system. Anyway, it's not important now. Not with everything we've got on Robbie Skinner.'

A problem with the system… how easily the lies tripped off his tongue. She was about to challenge him, but… what was the point?

She crossed back to her own desk and sat, drumming her fingers. So, Simon Parry could still be in the running. By his own admission he couldn't prove where he was for most of Monday. And while he had supposedly spent the rest of the week with his girlfriend, she hadn't actually asked them whether they'd been together the whole time. Given it sounded like they'd had some sort of argument, maybe they hadn't.

She thought back to Saturday morning — no washing machine rumbling away in the background, no half-unpacked bags at the bottom of the stairs. And then there was Melissa, returning with freshly painted nails, laden with shopping. None of it consistent with a couple having just returned from a few days away. Had she made a mistake assuming they'd been in Hull the whole week?

She reached for her phone. Melissa answered.

'Hi. It's DC McKenzie. We met the other day when I came to talk to Mr Parry.'

'He's not in.'

'Wait!' McKenzie said urgently, sensing the phone was about to be put down. 'I just need to know when you and Mr Parry returned from Hull.'

'Wednesday. Why?'

McKenzie felt her stomach churn.

'What time did you get back?'

'Around five.'

'I thought you were supposed to be there until the weekend.'

'We were, but we had a row and came back early. Look, what's with all the questions? I thought you said it was just routine.'

'It is. It's just—'

'Then I guess we're done then. Bye.' The phone went dead.

McKenzie hit redial. The dull tone of an engaged signal droned in her ear. She gave it a couple of minutes then tried again. Still nothing. She snatched up her bag, grabbed her car keys and coat and stalked out of the office, full of self-reproach.

Half an hour later, she was back outside the oast, knocking at the solid wood door. She peered through the long, tall window at the side, looking for signs of movement. Nothing. She glanced back at the pale blue Audi convertible sitting on the drive, at the scarf and sunglasses draped on the passenger seat, and resumed knocking, harder this time. With her fist growing sore, she stopped and was considering trying to gain access to the back, when she heard the sound of a car crunching down the drive towards her. Parry's silver BMW drew to a stop next to the Audi. He hopped out, threw his keys up and snatched them from the air.

'Twice in one week,' he said, grinning affably. 'You'll have the neighbours talking.' He must have noticed McKenzie's serious countenance as his expression grew suddenly sombre. 'Terrible news, about Fern. I still can't believe it. I mean who in their right mind…?'

'That's what we're trying to find out. I'm sorry to disturb you again but I need more information on your movements earlier this week.'

He looked at her a long second, then nodded, before walking over to the front door and slipping in the key.

'Come in.'

She followed him inside. Loud dance music thumped out from behind the kitchen door. Parry threw his jacket in the direction of an overloaded coat rack. It slipped off, landing on top of the golf bag underneath and knocking a red baseball cap to the floor in the process. McKenzie stepped forward and picked the cap up, setting it to hang from one of the clubs.

Parry pushed through the door into the kitchen. Over his shoulder, McKenzie could see Melissa sitting at the breakfast bar, reading a magazine.

'Lissy! Turn that down,' Parry yelled. 'We've got company.' But Melissa didn't even bother to acknowledge his presence and continued to read. 'For Christ's sake… Lissy!' Parry marched across the room, snatched up the remote and snuffed out the racket. 'Didn't you hear me calling?'

Melissa's response was to fling the magazine across the counter. She stood up and started to flounce across the room.

'Sorry, could you sit back down please?' McKenzie said. 'I need to speak with you both.'

Melissa flashed her a fiery look, which McKenzie met with a cool glare. The impasse only lasted a few seconds before Melissa rolled her eyes and stalked back to the breakfast bar. She stood with her back leaning against it, arms crossed, glowering at McKenzie.

'I'm sorry to trouble you both again,' McKenzie said, taking a step into the room. 'As I'm sure you're aware, since we last spoke, Mrs Marshall has been found, murdered. As a result, I'm going to need to go over the timings of your Hull visit again.'

'It's pretty straightforward,' Parry started. 'I—'

'Wait a minute!' Melissa interrupted. 'Did you say murdered?' Wide-eyed, she suddenly looked much younger.

'You haven't seen the news?' McKenzie replied.

'I don't like watching it. It's always so negative.'

'You didn't think to mention it to her, Mr Parry?'

Melissa looked at him accusingly.

'Yes Simon. Why didn't you say anything?'

His eyes darted from Melissa to McKenzie. He gave a shrug.

'I don't know. It didn't seem appropriate.'

McKenzie tipped her head and looked at him for a long moment, then pulled out her notepad. 'Let's talk about those timings, shall we?'

Parry took a deep breath and regained some his composure, then began, 'I arrived in Hull Friday morning at about nine. I worked at the festival all weekend, until late Monday morning. Lissy took the train up and joined me on Monday night and we left together on Wednesday, shortly after lunch.'

'When we spoke before, you said you spent Monday mostly on your own.'

'Yes. Sunday was the last day of the festival. I was there until the early hours and went back again about eight Monday morning to help dismantle the last of the rigs. We finished around twelve then I went with some of the other organisers for a bite to eat. That was until about two. After that I crashed in my hotel room for the rest of the day, until Lissy arrived.'

McKenzie looked at Melissa.

'Which was when?'

'I got to the hotel at eight.'

'And what time did you return to the hotel, Mr Parry?'

'I'm sorry?'

'Last time I was here, you said you'd nipped out for a coffee. What time did you get back from having your coffee?'

'I, err... It must have been ten past?'

'Half past,' Melissa corrected, wearing a stern expression.

Parry turned to McKenzie. 'Look, I'd slept all afternoon. When I woke up it was an hour before Lissy's train was due in. I was still really knackered and figured some fresh air wouldn't hurt, so I left the hotel, grabbed a coffee from a place on the corner and went for a walk. I must have taken a wrong turning as I got lost and took ages to find my way back.'

McKenzie scribbled down the details, then looked back at Parry.

'You said you came back on Wednesday... I thought you were due to stay until the weekend?'

'We were. Only someone decided they weren't in the mood so we came back early.' Now it was Parry's turn to shoot an irritated glance in Melissa's direction.

'What time did you get back?'

'Around five.'

'And what did you do when got back?'

'I booked a table at our favourite restaurant, where we spent a very nice evening together.'

'What time was that?'

'The table was booked for half-eight.'

'What did you do in the intervening three and half-hours?'

Parry shrugged.

'Nothing. I don't think.'

Melissa cast him a suspicious look.

'That's not true. You went out.'

Parry gave a nervous smile.

'You're right. I'd forgotten. I went to the driving range, hit a few balls.'

Pen poised over her pad, McKenzie asked, 'When was that?'

'Half-six to half-seven.'

'And what time did you get back here?'

'It would have been around quarter to eight. Something like that.'

Bridget Forker was alive at seven. Could he have done it? There might have just been enough time. McKenzie turned to Melissa.

'Were you here when he got back?'

'Of course. I was getting ready to go out.'

'Mr Parry, apart from your car, do you have a business vehicle?'

'Yeah. A Merc long-wheelbase Transit. Big company logo on the side.'

'Colour?'

'Black.'

'Have you driven a white van recently? A small, Escort panel van.'

'No.'

'What is this really about?' Melissa asked. 'There's no way you're asking everyone who used to know that dead woman where they've been and what they've been doing.'

Parry looked at McKenzie who looked straight back at him. He wiped his face with his hands, then turned to Melissa.

'You know I said I hadn't seen Fern for years?'

She looked at him through narrowed eyes.

'Yes.'

'Well I hadn't... Until recently. I promise I only saw her the once. Well twice, if you include the time we bumped into each other in town and agreed to meet up... only so I could return her things that she'd left when she moved out.' He added hastily, 'I swear, we only had lunch.'

Melissa's face contorted into an ugly scowl. She walked over to Parry and slapped his face before storming out.

'I guess I deserved that,' he said, rubbing his cheek on which a broad patch of pink was blossoming. McKenzie said nothing. 'Seriously though, you can't think I had anything to do with Fern's murder? Why would I? I have no reason to want Fern dead.'

McKenzie slipped her pad back into her bag.

'Unfortunately, Mr Parry, you also have no alibi. It's a shame you spent the afternoon alone, asleep in your hotel room.'

'Actually...' He crossed to the door and gently pushed it closed. Dropping his voice to a whisper, he said, 'The truth is, I wasn't in my hotel room, and I wasn't alone. There was this woman. A music journalist. We sort of got together on the Sunday night. I bumped into her again the following morning and invited her out to lunch. You know what it's like. One thing led to another. I couldn't take her to my hotel room, so we went back to hers. I kind of lost track of time, which is why I was late meeting Lissy. I'm sorry I didn't say anything before, it's just... you have no idea. When Lissy gets jealous she can make life hell. There's no telling what she'd do if she found out there was good reason for her to be jealous. It wouldn't be pretty, that's for sure.'

McKenzie pulled her pad back out of her bag.

'This journalist's name?'

32.

McKenzie let herself out, Parry having rushed after his girlfriend, trying to convince her of his unwavering adoration. As she started the car, she reflected on what he had just told her. She thought about Melissa's outburst, wondered why she was still with Parry, if she really thought he was cheating on her. Then thought of her and Phil's relationship — as challenging as it was, she couldn't help but cling onto the idea that it would somehow get better. Most people, it seemed, would put up with a lot less than perfect if the alternative was being alone. Most people... but not all. After all, Fern Marshall had walked out on Parry. A strong independent woman was one of the many personas the dead woman appeared to have had. Along with fun-loving friend, devoted wife and animal liberator. What else had she been? Secret lover, excited mother-to-be? Yet, if she'd been the doting wife, why hadn't she shared the news of her pregnancy with her husband? And if she'd had a lover, then why hadn't they come forward? None of it stacked up.

She reached for her phone.

A female voice answered after only two rings, 'Sound Bites Magazine. Anika Mostue speaking.'

'Hi. This is Detective Constable McKenzie of the Kent Police. I've been given your name by Mr Simon Parry in connection to a case I'm working. I understand you and Mr Parry spent Monday afternoon together. I wondered if you could confirm that for me?'

'Who?'

'Mr Simon Parry.'

'Never heard of him.'

Maybe he hadn't given her his real name?

'Did you spend Monday in the company of any man?'

The phone went dead.

Interesting.

***

DI York stuck his head around the door to his office and scanned the room looking for McKenzie. Her chair was empty and there was no jacket on its back. He started across the room. Crawley was also nowhere to be seen, though from the fact that his mobile phone and car keys were on his desk, York surmised that he couldn't be too far away.

He stopped at Wynchcombe's desk.

'Spence, any idea where Cat is?'

'She's gone out. Said something about checking out an alibi.'

Crawley entered the room and walked over to them.

'Hey. Sorry to interrupt. Sir...' he said. 'I found something interesting about Robbie Skinner's mum when I—'

'Not now Darren. A patrol car has spotted Robbie Skinner's van parked up in a layby on an industrial estate. I came to see if you and Cat wanted to come with me and check it out, only it looks like Cat's out.'

'I'll get my things.' Crawley hurried over to his desk and grabbed his jacket and phone.

York turned and said to Wynchcombe. 'There's room in the car if you want to come?'

***

It was a beautiful autumn day. Sunny and dry and warm enough even to have the windows open. Perfect for enjoying a drive in the country. Not that McKenzie was in the mood to enjoy anything. She was too busy thinking about Bridget Forker's murder. Even if Parry had time to go from his place to hers on Wednesday evening — and she'd know soon enough — if he'd been in Hull since Monday night how did he even know she was a threat?

She was pondering this and a multitude of other questions when the familiar voice of her SatNav cut through her thoughts with an instruction to take the next right. She took the turning and found herself on Karl Marshall's lane. As she passed the house, she instinctively slowed the car and glanced up the drive. Marshall's Range Rover was there, parked in front of the house, boot open. Marshall appeared from the side of the garage, wheeling a golf trolley. He paused and raised a hand. But McKenzie couldn't stop. Not in the middle of a timed run. She continued on down the lane to where a T-junction took her onto the road that Mrs Forker had called home. Turning right, she passed the end of the Skinners' garden and continued on to the dead woman's weatherboarded cottage, where she pulled onto the verge. She reached for her pad and made a note of the time it had taken from Parry's. As she suspected, it was certainly possible. She threw the pad onto the passenger seat and, with her hand poised on the gear stick, took one last look at the house. Already it was beginning to look unkempt and unloved. The lawn needed mowing and weeds ran rife amongst the flower beds Mrs Forker had painstakingly planted; the blue and white barrier tape strung across the door flapped feebly in the breeze. Suddenly an image of the grey-haired woman, lying lifeless on the kitchen floor accosted her, bringing with it a fresh surge of guilt. There had been so much death recently, it was impossible to be so close to it and for it not to leave its mark.

With tears pricking at her eyes, she turned her gaze away from the house, heaved in a deep breath and once again, resolved to catch whoever was responsible and deliver justice to the two dead women.

***

In the car, Crawley fidgeted like a five-year-old on his way to see Santa. He was sitting in the back of York's black BMW. Wynchcombe was in the passenger seat. They were racing along the A road leading east, to where the white van had been sighted.

'Do you reckon he'll make a run for it?' Crawley asked, leaning forward, his head poking between the front seats.

'Darren, sit back,' York said.

Crawley did as he was told. His leg started to jiggle.

'Do you think he'll be armed? He might have a knife. They use some serious blades in the trade.'

York ignored him. Fifteen minutes later, they pulled up behind a police car.

'I'll be back in a second.' York climbed out and made straight for two uniformed officers standing next to the marked car.

'Cat's going to be well pissed off when she finds out she's missed all the excitement,' Crawley said. 'Probably best she's out of the way. Might get physical.'

'Cat can handle herself,' Wynchcombe said.

Crawley gave a lewd smirk.

'I bet she can… and I bet it's not only herself that she handles.' Leaning in, he kept his voice low, 'I heard she and the boss are, you know, close.'

Wynchcombe shot him a distasteful glare.

'I don't know who you've been talking to but you want to be careful who you say that sort of thing to.'

'Yeah? They're the ones who should be more careful. I—' Crawley stopped. York was leaning in through the open driver's door. Crawley looked at him keenly. 'All set are we, sir?'

All three of them walked down the road towards the junction. A tall wall on their left blocked their view of the adjoining road where the white van was parked, according to the uniformed patrol. York brought them to a stop just before the corner and walked the last couple of metres on his own to steal a look around the wall.

He beckoned them over.

'The van's only a few hundred metres away. We'll walk over together. I'll go to the driver's door. Darren, you take the passenger side and Spence, you cover the back. If Skinner gets out as we approach then you'll need to sprint like whippets and get after him.'

'I'll do my best, boss. Only I picked up a bit of a dodgy knee at football the other week,' Crawley said.

York looked down at Crawley's polished brown leather brogues then at Wynchcombe's black loafers.

'Just try. There's a pint in it for whoever gets him,' York continued, 'Obviously, there's a good chance he's not here but he could come back at any time, so keep your eyes peeled. See anyone acting nervous or suspicious, grab first and ask questions later. Got it?'

They turned the corner and started to approach the white van tucked in between a pair of HGVs. York stepped into the road and started to walk around the first lorry. Crawley and Wynchcombe continued their advance on the pavement. The only sound in the silent street was three sets of footsteps. With ten metres to go, their movements became stealthier, their tread softer. Emerging from the far side of the lorry, York gave a thumbs up as they drew level with the white van. Crawley sidled up to the passenger window, while York made his way to the driver's side. They peered in simultaneously.

33.

McKenzie slipped the car into gear. She glanced in the mirror to check the road was clear, about to turn the car around, when a flash of blue caught her eye. She squinted but, still unable to make it out, executed a hasty three-point turn and started down the lane. As she approached, the glint of blue grew until she could make out the familiar form of a mountain bike partially hidden in the glossy green leaves of the large holly bush. She pulled in front of the gate next to the bush and climbed out. The bicycle looked to be a perfectly ordinary men's mountain bike, which in itself was totally unremarkable, if it weren't for the fact it had been left in exactly the same spot as Fern Marshall used to leave hers. McKenzie looked around, but the road was deserted. Approaching the gate, she gazed into the neglected wilderness beyond. She thought fleetingly of calling for back-up, but back-up for what exactly? Instead, she called York's number, which bounced straight through to voicemail. She left a brief message, switched her phone to silent, then jumped over the gate, landing silently on the leaf-littered ground beyond.

Scanning the area, she moved slowly forward, pausing every so often to listen. The scrappy lawn and overgrown shrubs looked the same as they did the last time she was there, apart from the shiny new padlock securing the lid to the septic tank.

A robin landed on a nearby branch and warbled convivially. Not so much as a leaf stirred on the trees. Then, a creak of wood cut through the silence. McKenzie's gaze tracked over to the colossal oak looming in the middle of the garden. Another creak. She crept forward, like a cat stalking its prey. On the floor by the foot of the ladder lay a rucksack. She bent down, about to pick it up, when a guttural, animal-like sound came from above. A cold chill raced up her spine. What if Robbie Skinner had his latest victim up there? She set a foot on the bottom rung and started up. There was no time to test for rotten rungs and half-way up, a cracking sound rang out. Wood splintered under her weight, sending her jolting six inches down to the next rung. She gripped the side rails tight and heaved in a deep breath. The wailing cries from above continued unabated. She lifted her foot to the next solid rung and pressed on until the top of her head was level with the floor of the treehouse. She slowly peered into the gloom.

Robbie Skinner was alone, huddled in a corner, arms wrapped around his knees. A knitted blanket dangled from his fingers. He looked a mess, with his scruffy hair and puffy, dirty looking face, courtesy of the ageing bruises and day-old beard.

'Robbie...' McKenzie said gently, hooking an arm around the top rung of the ladder. He gave a start and looked over to the paneless window in the wall. For a moment, she feared he might jump. Surely, he'd break his legs? The image of Fern Marshall's broken limbs flashed across her mind. Was that how it had happened... jumping out of the window as she tried to escape? She shelved the thought for later and turned her attention back to the man in front of her. 'Please Robbie. I only want to talk.'

'I knew I should never have come back,' he said in a pitiful voice. 'Not after...' He thrust his head between his arms and started to cry.

'Not after what Robbie?' When after a minute he still hadn't looked up, she said, 'Come down with me and we'll find some place where we can talk.'

'No!' he said sharply. 'I know you think I did it, but I didn't... I couldn't.'

'If you didn't do it then you've nothing to worry about.'

He looked at her with red-rimmed eyes.

'My life is over and you say nothing to worry about.'

'What do you mean your life is over?' He hung his head. 'Robbie, please...' After another minute of silence, her patience was growing thin. 'Robbie you can't stay here forever. It will be a lot easier if you come with me now. You say you didn't do it, then help us find who did.'

She watched him lift the knitted blanket to his face and take a deep breath in. Shortly, he gave a reluctant nod and started to fold the blanket. McKenzie's eyes widened as he held it up revealing its shape. It was a woman's jumper he'd been clutching, not a blanket. He set the folded garment down tenderly and she made a mental note to return with an evidence bag as soon as she'd got him secured in her car.

'Ready?' she asked.

Robbie nodded and started towards her. She took in the line of his jogging bottoms and sweatshirt, looking for any tell-tale bulges. Feeling confident there were no concealed weapons, McKenzie lowered a foot, feeling for the next rung.

They were about half-way down, Robbie a couple of rungs above her, when they first heard the two-tone wailing coming through the trees.

'You lied!' Robbie shouted.

'I didn't,' McKenzie called back. 'A siren carries for miles. It's nothing to do with you. Nobody knows I'm here.' She looked across the treetops, in the direction of the road, as the noise grew steadily louder, then dropped down another step. When she looked back up, she could see he hadn't moved. 'Robbie. If I'd called for back-up, why did I bother to climb up? I'd have waited, wouldn't I?'

Her reassurances did the trick and he started down. As soon as they were both safely on the ground, McKenzie grabbed his rucksack. A hollow, metallic sound came from within. She opened the bag and spotted two cans of spray paint amongst a handful of clothes and a shabby toiletry bag.

She held up one of the cans.

'What's this for?'

'I was going to respray the van.'

She stuffed it back into the bag, next to a thick roll of twenty-pound notes, which poked out from a pair of balled-up socks. She pulled the drawstring tight and gestured towards the gate. Just then, the sound of a car fast approaching followed by a squeal of tyres came from the direction of the road. Robbie set off at a sprint towards the house. McKenzie jettisoned the bag and started after him, legs and arms pumping hard. She launched herself at his back, grabbing him around the waist and sending him toppling over. He landed with a thump, letting out a loud groan. McKenzie scrabbled onto his back, thrusting a knee between his shoulder blades as she reached for his arms. As she pulled his hands behind his back, she became aware of footsteps rushing towards them. She twisted to look behind her, expecting to see DI York rushing over to help. Robbie must have felt her weight shift as just then he pushed himself up, sending her rolling to one side. He was scrabbling to his feet when a pair of strong hands yanked him upright. McKenzie rolled over and looked up. She could do little more than watch as Karl Marshall landed a series of powerful punches to Robbie's head, sending him staggering back. She jumped up and rushed at Marshall, trying to pull him off, but he was too strong and there was nothing she could do to prevent a further volley of strikes that eventually saw Robbie slump to his knees and fall sideways onto the ground, his beaten and bloody face smeared with earth.

Marshall towered over him.

'You bastard! I should kill you for what you did to my wife.'

He pulled back his foot, about to take a shot, when McKenzie hooked his leg with her foot, sending him falling to the floor like a felled tree. She turned, drawn by the sound of car doors slamming. Seconds later, DI York and a uniformed officer appeared at the end of the path and started sprinting towards them. As they grew closer, their steps slowed and their faces widened with surprise at McKenzie, standing there with two men lying at her feet.

34.

After checking Robbie Skinner into custody and sending Karl Marshall home with a caution, York called McKenzie into his office.

'You should have called for back-up, or at least waited for me to call you back,' he said, once she'd finished briefing him on her afternoon and her thoughts on how Fern Marshall came to have two broken legs.

'I did think about it, but I was worried I'd be wasting everyone's time. At that stage I had no idea Robbie was there. I thought it made sense to take a look first.'

'You could have called it in as soon as you knew.'

'And risk him giving us the slip again?'

York's phone gave a shrill ring. He snatched it up.

'DI York.' He listened for a minute then said, 'We'll be right down.' He returned the handset to the cradle. 'Robbie Skinner's brief is here.'

Robbie was sitting slouched in his seat, arms wrapped around his chest, head down. He looked up as the two detectives entered. He looked more like an errant schoolboy than a thirty-year-old man facing a murder charge.

He leaned forward, wearing an anxious expression.

'What's happened to Shane?'

'Shane?' McKenzie said.

'My dog. Mr Fray says Dad's here too, which means there's no one at home to feed him.'

'It's alright,' she replied. 'He's in temporary kennels. He can be collected as soon as you or your father leave.'

Robbie leaned back heavily in his seat.

'If we're ready…' York made the necessary introductions, set the equipment to record, then started. 'So, Robbie, why don't you start by telling us what you were doing in the treehouse today?'

'I wanted… I thought if I…' He shook his head. 'You wouldn't understand.'

'Try us.'

After a minute's mounting silence, McKenzie asked, 'Was it to do with Mrs Marshall?'

Robbie brought his hands up and covered his face, before shaking his head.

'Please speak your reply for the tape,' York said.

The solicitor leaned over and whispered something in Robbie's ear. Dropping his hands and transferring his focus onto the table top, Robbie mumbled, 'No comment.'

McKenzie shifted forward in her seat, closing the gap between them.

'Robbie, back in the treehouse you told me you didn't do it.'

'I didn't,' he replied urgently.

'Then you must want us to catch the person who did, don't you?'

'Yes.'

'Then you need to help us.'

'I can't.'

'Why don't we talk about Mrs Marshall… Fern? You told me you were at school together.' He gave an almost imperceptible nod. 'Had you seen her since then, more recently?' Another nod.

'For the purposes of the tape, Mr Skinner has just nodded,' York said.

'When Robbie?' McKenzie urged. 'When did you last see her?'

He went to speak but it was as though the words got caught in his throat. He reached for the plastic beaker of water in front of him, took his time drinking, then said, 'Friday.'

'Last Friday?' McKenzie asked.

He nodded again.

'Could you reply, for the tape, please?' York said, sounding irritable. 'It's for your benefit that we have an accurate record of this conversation.'

'Yes,' he said in little more than a whisper.

'Where were you?' McKenzie asked.

'In the treehouse. We were just talking. That's where we used to meet.'

The solicitor suddenly came alive. Moving forward in his seat, he drew close to Robbie and muttered something in his ear. Robbie shook his head and twisted in his seat, turning his back on the legal man.

'You met there regularly?' McKenzie went on.

'Yes.'

'How long have you been meeting like that for?'

'About six months.'

'What sort of things did you talk about?'

Robbie's gaze dropped back to his knees.

'Just things. Things we wanted to do with our lives. Things we wanted to see.'

'Were you in a relationship with her?' McKenzie asked.

Robbie nodded.

'A sexual relationship?'

Again, he nodded.

York shifted in his seat.

'You're saying that you and Fern Marshall met on a regular basis for sex in the treehouse?'

Robbie shot him an angry look.

'You make it sound sordid and dirty. It wasn't like that. We were in love.'

York held a hand up and dipped his head.

'My apologies. I was just trying to understand.' He resumed his previous relaxed stance and asked, 'How did the two of you get together?'

Robbie looked back down at the table top.

'I can't tell you that.'

McKenzie frowned.

'What are you worried about?'

He shook his head, not even bothering to look up.

'Has it got something to do with how or why Fern died?' she asked.

Robbie looked at her, horrified.

'What? No!'

'Look Robbie,' York interjected. 'I'm having a hard time believing this glamorous socialite who devoted her spare time to rescuing animals was having an affair with someone who slaughters animals for a living. And the fact you can't even tell us how you got together only adds weight to the idea that the whole scenario is a complete fabrication. Isn't it true that the reason you can't tell us how you got together is because you weren't together? Nowhere other than in your imagination, at least.'

'No!'

McKenzie leaned forward until she caught Robbie's eye and said gently, 'Then tell us how it happened.'

Robbie darted a sideways glance to the solicitor before returning his gaze back to the table top. He cleared his throat and said, 'Mr Fray, I think I'm okay to manage on my own now. Thank you.'

A pair of silver-streaked eyebrows shot up in surprise.

'What do you mean, manage on your own?'

'I want to represent myself.'

'But... this is madness.' Fray smoothed down his tie. 'You're not thinking straight. Your father wants you to have the very best representation and with all due respect, you really don't know what you're doing.' Fray turned to DI York. 'I would like to convene a short break while I consult with my client.'

'I don't want a break and I don't need to consult with anyone.' Robbie turned to McKenzie. 'He can't stay here if I don't want him to, can he?'

'No, he can't, Mr Skinner.'

Robbie turned to the solicitor and said firmly, 'I would like you to go now, please.'

Fray snatched his briefcase off the floor, banged it down on the table, flipped the clasps and opened the lid. He thrust his pad and pen inside and slammed it closed.

'Your father will not be happy at your decision.'

Robbie returned to studying the table surface until the door closed with a bang.

'Why didn't you want Mr Fray to stay?' McKenzie asked.

'There's stuff I don't want my dad to know.'

'You don't need to worry,' she said. 'Solicitors have to operate under an oath of confidentiality.'

'You don't know my old man. He rewards loyalty well.'

'You mean financially?'

Robbie nodded.

'He can be very generous. When he wants to be.'

'But he isn't generous to you. Not according to his friend Mr Campbell.' Out of the corner of her eye, McKenzie saw York shoot her an irritated look, but she continued anyway, 'Why is that, do you think?'

Robbie crossed his arms and dropped his chin.

'He says I remind him too much of my mum. He never forgave her for leaving him.'

'Why was that?'

'She told me he couldn't see how he'd changed; how she didn't want to be with someone who was either at work or down the pub with his mates. After we left, I remember he came around to see her a couple of times. He'd bring presents but she refused to go back. He accused her of seeing someone else. Like she had the time to see anybody. She had two jobs plus me to look after. But he only saw what he wanted to see.'

'This is all very interesting,' York interrupted, 'But can we get back to Mrs Marshall?'

McKenzie looked at him.

'Sorry, that was my fault.' She turned to Robbie and said, 'Now we're on our own, you can speak freely. Why don't you tell us how you and Fern met?'

'Only if you promise it won't get back to my dad. He'd kill me if he knew what I'd done.'

'We can't make promises like that, Robbie, but if what you say isn't relevant to the investigation, there's no reason for him to find out.'

There was a long stretch of silence while Robbie pushed and prodded at the table's scarred surface with a thumb. Eventually he said, 'I was the one who took the lambs from the yard. I took them to the rescue place. Fern arrived just as I was unloading them from the van. I asked her not to tell anyone where they came from.'

'I'm not following. Are you saying you took the lambs there to win Fern over?' McKenzie asked.

'No. I didn't know Fern was going to be there. I took them to stop them being slaughtered. They were only babies, hadn't even weaned. I thought it was wrong. I wanted to save them.'

'You just said your father would kill you if he knew you had taken the lambs. What would he have done if he thought Fern was involved?' York asked.

'But she wasn't. All she did was take the lambs from me.'

'Your dad strikes me as the type to throw his fists around first and ask questions later,' McKenzie said.

Robbie, maybe subconsciously, touched a finger to the yellowing bruising of his left eye.

'I'm telling you he didn't know.'

After a long pause, she gave a nod.

'So it was just a coincidence that you met Mrs Marshall at the gate?'

'Yes. That was then we recognised each other from school.'

'And that was the start of your affair?' York asked, not bothering to disguise his cynicism.

'Not straight away, no. I don't have many friends. Actually, I don't know why I said that. I don't have any friends, but she was nice to me and afterwards, I kept thinking about her. I drove by the following week and waited for her by the gate.' He gave a rare smile, which made him look even more young and vulnerable. 'I asked her how the lambs were and we chatted for a while, but then she said she had to go. I told her it was good to see her and asked if we could meet some time, to catch up like. I didn't really expect her to say yes, so I was really shocked when she said, "why not?". The first time we met, we went to a coffee place in town. She seemed really nervous. At the time, I thought it was because she'd changed her mind about meeting me again, but she told me it was because she'd been worried her husband would find out. When she asked if there was somewhere else we could meet, somewhere more private, I suggested the treehouse. I used to go up there a lot on my own, to get away from the old man. It felt right to share it. That's how it started… just talking.'

'How often did you meet?' McKenzie asked.

'A couple of times a week. Usually lunchtime. On Monday Fern messaged me. She had a phone she kept secret from her husband. She asked if we could make it later, so I swapped with Dad and stayed at the yard all day so I could finish early.'

'The problem is, Robbie, no one appears to be able to confirm that,' McKenzie said. 'Besides, the first time I visited the yard, you slipped out the back like a regular Harry Houdini, which suggests you could have left at any time.'

'I was there all day, okay?'

'So what happened when you left work on Monday?'

Robbie shifted in his seat.

'Fern said she'd be there at four, only I was running late. By the time I got there it was about quarter past and there was no sign of her.'

'You went straight to the treehouse when you got home?' York asked.

Robbie nodded.

'I stayed there as long as I could get away with, before I had to go and start dinner. It was growing dark by the time I went into the house.'

'And you didn't notice anything out of the ordinary?'

'No.'

'You didn't notice the chicken coop had been moved?'

'No.'

'You didn't notice any blood on the ground or any signs of a disturbance on the grass underneath the tree? Nothing?'

'No. I just said I didn't. I…' Robbie's eyes shot wide. 'Blood? What blood? What did they do to her?' His face turned an ashen grey. He pressed a hand to his chest and started to deep breathe. 'I think I'm going to be sick.'

McKenzie pushed a plastic beaker towards him.

'Have some water.'

York shook his head.

'I've got to give you credit. That's some act you've got. You work in an abattoir yet get queasy at the mere mention of blood.' But he did look ill. 'You can forget the pretence. We know you're lying. You see Mrs Marshall called her husband at five past four as she was being attacked. Yet you show up ten minutes later and see nothing. It doesn't stack up, does it?' York leaned forward in his chair, elbows on the table, hands clasped. He fixed Robbie with a cold stare. 'You know what I think? I think you slipped out unnoticed from work and went home at lunchtime only to find her snooping around your back yard. We know you were there. Your van was seen parked down the lane at the back of the house. Did she hear you and try to hide in the treehouse, only you found her? Did she jump or did you throw her down?'

Robbie shook his head.

'No. You've got it all wrong.'

York continued, 'There you were, with a woman with two broken legs, lying in your garden unconscious. Maybe you thought she was dead and left her there, planning on dealing with her later. Did you come back later and find her awake, calling her husband for help? Is that when you finished the job?'

'No! Stop saying things like that!' Robbie shouted, then like a child he closed his eyes and pressed his fingers to his ears.

'Mr Skinner!' York's voice boomed. Robbie gave a start and opened his eyes. 'Please be adult about this. Tell us if we've got it wrong.'

'You've got it wrong,' Robbie repeated.

'You were in love with her, yes?' York said, softening his voice.

269

Robbie nodded.

'How long had you harboured your secret infatuation with her?'

An angry scowl transformed Robbie's features.

'We were in love. We were going to be together.'

'Prove it. Tell me something about her we don't know. Something we can check.'

'I can't.'

'Then I don't believe you. You can't tell us anything, because she didn't love you. I suspect she barely knew you. People in love share their innermost thoughts. You would know her deepest secrets.'

'She was pregnant!' he yelled, spittle flying out of his mouth. 'Okay? She was pregnant with my baby. Go and check that out.' He shook his head. 'Somebody killed my baby!' Big fat tears started to free-fall down his cheeks and splash onto his trousers. His whole body started to shake as he began to howl.

'We need to get a psyche evaluation organised,' York said to McKenzie. They were striding down the corridor after ending the interview. 'I can see him trying to wriggle out of a bloody murder rap by claiming some sort of delusional bullshit. Anyone who did what he did to that woman has got to have issues. You watch, there'll be some psychiatric claptrap about how he resented his mother dying, which forced him into an abusive relationship with his father, yada, yada, yada...'

'Why would he take her womb out?'

'So we can't prove he's not the father.'

'You think there's nothing in it... him and Mrs Marshall?'

York stopped walking and looked at her.

'The slaughterman and the animal rescue volunteer? Hardly a match made in heaven. He probably had the hots for her at school, saw her recently, and being a sad bastard with no life of his own, concocted a new one.'

He started down the corridor again. McKenzie continued after him, only slower now.

'How did he lure her into the treehouse if there was no relationship?'

'Who's to say he didn't force her up at knife point?'

She couldn't argue with that.

'So why did he take Mrs Forker's kidney?'

'To confuse things. Or maybe it was his screwed-up way of getting his mother back for the fact she died but donated parts of herself so that other women could live.'

'You must have been talking to Darren.'

York looked up at her.

'It's not a bad hypothesis, is it?'

'It's sounds like something out of a third-rate serial killer movie. And I don't think it fits with who Robbie is.' She followed him into his office. 'So what do you want me to do now?'

'Good question.' He walked over to his desk and picked up a large buff envelope and started to rip it open. He glanced down at its contents.

'The post-mortem report into Fern Marshall.'

York flicked forward a couple of pages and started to read from the summary page, 'Both legs broken, consistent with a drop from height — looks like you could be right about the treehouse. Death followed shortly afterwards, cause being manual strangulation. The uterus was removed post mortem.'

McKenzie, reading over his shoulder, pointed to a paragraph towards the bottom of the page.

'Look at the comment about the knife strokes. It sounds like they were cruder and more forcibly made than the cuts made to Mrs Forker.'

York picked up the cover letter that had accompanied the report. He started to nod.

'The doc mentions it here. He says the difference could indicate the killer's state of mind — maybe he was more angry or upset while he was doing it — or it could mean that he didn't have as much time and had to rush it.'

He set the letter aside and continued to flick through the report. The next page he stopped at revealed what they had long suspected. There, in black and white: tests had revealed the presence of HCG hormone in the dead woman's blood.

'So, she was definitely pregnant,' McKenzie said. 'I get that he removed her womb and foetus to prevent us from disproving his account of their relationship, but why remove Mrs Forker's kidney?'

'To confuse us by sending us on a wild goose chase looking for some deranged serial killer.' York closed the report and threw it down onto the desk.

'How did Robbie know she was pregnant if it wasn't his?'

'She could have told him when she was pleading for her life. Begged him to spare her for the sake of her unborn child.'

McKenzie's brow crimped.

'After going to all that trouble, it was pretty stupid of him to leave the body where he did. It was bound to point us in his direction.'

'Or his father's. If this is all the result of Robbie Skinner's fucked-up childhood, he could be trying to lay blame at his dad's door.'

'I guess we're going to have to let Marshall know about the pregnancy now.'

'That's my next job.' York gave a grimace. 'Can't say I'm looking forward to it.'

35.

McKenzie left York in his office. Returning to the main office, she made her way over to Wynchcombe.

'Spence...' He looked up from his computer. 'Alex says he asked you to look at the CCTV cameras between Skinner's Yard and their house on Monday.'

'Yep. All done.'

'And?'

'Robbie Skinner's white Escort van appears at various points between the abattoir and his house between 16:00 and 16:10. There was no sign of it at any other time during the day. But I did find this...' He passed her a copy of a photo showing a white Escort van.

She looked down at it, clocking that the registration number was different to Robbie Skinner's van. The timestamp in the corner showed 12:05 on Monday.

'This was coming from the direction of Skinner's yard to their house?' she asked.

'Yes. I know. What are the odds of someone driving the same type of crappy van down the same stretch of road we're interested in at the time we're interested in? Do you think Skinner could have put false plates on?'

'It's a possibility. If I was going to abduct and kill someone, I think I'd make some effort to cover my tracks.'

'I could do a trace on the plates, see if they're cloned?'

'Good idea. Let me know how you get on.'

With the need for evidence at the forefront of her mind, she went to Crawley next.

'Darren, did you manage to get anything out of the lab about the ropes I took from Robbie Skinner's van?'

'What's that?' He looked up at her, distracted.

'I left a note on your desk before I went into the interview. I stuck it on your keyboard so you wouldn't miss it.' Crawley's eyes flitted momentarily to his in-tray. There was the slip of paper with the request printed in her neat script.

'I was going to do it later.' He handed it to her. 'You can do it yourself, now you're free.'

She snatched the sheet out of his hand, stormed back to her desk and put a call through to the lab.

'You might be in luck. That's a priority case,' said the woman that answered. 'Bear with me while I go and check.' McKenzie heard the hollow click as the handset was put down. A minute later, 'Hi. Yeah. The report's been drafted. I just need to find the file. Let's see…' After a short pause, 'Right, here we go… It looks like traces of human skin cells were found, plus plenty of animal hair and skin cells believed to be ovine. That's sheep to you and me.'

'Can you tell how many different people have handled the rope?'

'We're still working on that.'

'What about the van that was brought in earlier today as part of the same investigation?'

'We're still working on that too. Are you after anything in particular?'

'I need to know whether one of our victims could have been held captive in it.'

'Hang on.' McKenzie tapped her pen on her pad as she waited. Shortly, the woman was back. 'Hi. So far, we've found traces of blood on the front offside wing, though that was sandwiched in between layers of rust where some of the paint had peeled off, which suggests it's been there some time. We've also picked up three different sets of prints on the inside. All three were inside the cabin, while two of the pairs were also found in the rear of the van. They've been lifted but we haven't had time to put them through the database yet. I could call you once we've run them for matches, if you like?'

'I'd appreciate that, thanks.'

As McKenzie replaced the handset, Wynchcombe waved her over.

'What've you got?' She pulled over a spare chair and sat down.

'The plates are a match for a white Escort van registered to a guy in Surrey. But get this… I gave him a ring to find out who was driving it on Monday and he said he sold it three weeks ago… for cash. I figured three weeks is a long time to take to register it, so I ran some checks.'

'And…?'

'Wednesday night there was a car fire in the middle of a patch of waste ground on the other side of Ashford. There was nothing left of the plates but the fire crew did manage to get the chassis number. It's a match to the Surrey guy's van.'

McKenzie blew out a long breath. Had Robbie bought the van to slip home undetected? He had a push bike… it would have been easy enough to stick it in the back, drive out to Ashford, torch the van and cycle home. So why wasn't she feeling like they'd struck gold?

'Did you get a description of the buyer?'

Wynchcombe reached for a small notepad.

'White, male, tallish, not fat, not thin. Wore blue jeans and a grey hoodie.'

'Hair…?'

'Short. He wasn't sure about the colour as they were wearing a black Nike baseball cap.'

'That narrows it down. Not.'

'I've put a request in for all the ANPR footage for that plate between when the van was sold and when it was torched. You never know, we might be able to get some images of whoever's driving it.'

'Good thinking.' Just then, McKenzie's landline started to ring. She hurried over to her desk and snatched up the phone.

'DC McKenzie.'

'Hi, it's Sophie from the crime scene team. You wanted to know if there were any matches to any of the prints we lifted from the van. You're in luck. We got matches for all three.' McKenzie felt her breath catch in her throat. Sophie went on, 'Prints on the driver's side and in the rear are a match to a Mr Robert Skinner; passenger side and rear matches to a Mrs Fern Marshall, and passenger side only is Mr Donald Skinner.'

'You found Fern Marshall's prints on the inside rear of the van?'

'Yes. Part of a palm print at the top corner of the right-hand-side door, unlike Robert Skinner's, which were all over the inside of the van.'

'Right. Okay, well, thanks for letting me know.'

McKenzie hung up and sat pondering this new development. Proof-positive Fern Marshall had been in Robbie Skinner's van. But in what capacity? Robbie had never said she hadn't been in it. Plus, if his version of events was true about rescuing the lambs, she could have left her print on the door when she helped him get them out of the van. And not forgetting her prints inside the cabin of the van. Perhaps he'd taken her somewhere on the promise of rescuing more lambs? If that was the case, where had he kept her in the intervening hours? The way it was going, the defence would be able make as much play on the evidence as the prosecution. Alex was not going to be happy.

She crossed the room to his office and peered through the glass dividing wall. Spotting him at his desk, she knocked and entered. Three steps in she froze. In the corner of the room, sitting in one of four low chairs was Karl Marshall. He uncrossed his legs and stood up.

'I'm sorry. Didn't realise you had company,' she said, turning to leave. 'I'll come back later.'

'No, please, stay.' It was Marshall who spoke. He cleared his throat. 'I came to apologise… for my behaviour. I shouldn't have followed you to that place and I shouldn't have interfered like I did. It was just when I saw him run, I suppose my instincts kicked in. I couldn't let him get away.'

'I had him on the ground, restrained. He was going nowhere,' McKenzie said.

Marshall looked down and nodded reluctantly.

'I realise that now. I'm very sorry.' He held his hand out. McKenzie reciprocated and found her hand gripped in a firm handshake. 'Thank you… for catching the bastard who killed my wife.'

York rose and moved to the door.

'As I said, we'll keep you informed as to how things progress. Don't forget to let us know when the funeral is.'

The two men stood at the threshold of the room and shook hands. York called DS Bells over and asked him to show Mr Marshall out. As soon as they were alone, he resumed his seat and turned to McKenzie.

'I take it you wanted something?'

'There are a couple of things I wanted to update you on.' She recounted the discovery of the white van bought and left in a burnt-out heap shortly after Fern Marshall's murder. She then went on to tell him about the fingerprints.

He leaned back in his chair.

'I agree with you about the burnt-out van — could be Robbie Skinner trying to cover his tracks. He could have slipped out from the yard, left his own van there for all to see, and taken the second van and grabbed Fern Marshall.'

'But why would he buy another van that looks exactly like his own, if he was trying to throw us off the scent?' McKenzie said. 'Also how do you explain how Mrs Marshall's fingerprints were found in his van on the passenger side?'

York's mouth twisted into a grimace.

'Maybe this second van has got nothing to do with the murders. As for the fingerprints — he could have given her a lift anytime. Sometimes the simplest explanations are the best.'

She made to leave but paused at the door.

'You changed your mind then, about telling Mr Marshall about the baby.'

'No. What makes you say that?'

'Only... well, he didn't seem very upset... for a man who's just learned he had an unborn child who was murdered at the same time as his wife.'

'He looked shocked enough when I told him. And then anger got the better of him and he started baying for Robbie Skinner's blood.'

'He had no idea then... about the pregnancy?'

'No.'

'Had they been trying for a baby?'

278

'I didn't ask. I thought it might be a little insensitive given I'd just broken the news that the foetus had been cut out of his dead wife, along with her womb.'

McKenzie felt her face begin to flush.

'You're right. Sorry.' After a moment's pause, she added, 'It's only … I can't help but wonder why she hadn't told him.'

'From what Marshall said it sounds like she might have been about to. She'd booked a table at Le Petit Cauldron for Saturday night. He said they always went there for special occasions.'

McKenzie recognised the name of the very expensive, very exclusive restaurant.

'Did he say what he thought the occasion was? If he didn't know about the baby.'

'The guy's wife's been murdered. He'd just found out she was pregnant. I didn't think it appropriate to quiz him over their dining habits.'

'I'm sorry. I just think it's odd she didn't tell him sooner. They're supposed to have this wonderful marriage, yet she's far enough gone to have had a scan and still hasn't told her husband. And don't you think it's weird that she wouldn't want to give him the news in a more private, intimate setting?'

'You can't project your own ideals and expectations onto everyone else, Cat. The Marshalls were obviously into their high-end lifestyle. She might have thought that slipping him a copy of the ultrasound across the table in a Michelin-starred restaurant would be more memorable.'

McKenzie took in the scowl that had settled on his face.

'You're right. I'm sorry. I think this case is just getting to me.'

'Try and stay objective. We've got a long way to go yet.' He turned in his seat to face his computer.

McKenzie took it as her cue to leave. Feeling despondent, she slumped at her desk, unsure what to do next. So they'd made an arrest. But the evidence didn't exactly finger Robbie Skinner as the murderer, and nor did her instincts.

Wynchcombe called to her, 'Cat…'

She looked over. 'Yeah?'

He beckoned her over and pointed to his screen with his pencil. On it was a grid of six images.

'These were taken on three separate dates.' He tapped one of them. 'Take a look at the guy driving.'

The image caught the driver's window at an obtuse angle, through which a dark figure could be seen. It was clearly a man but it was impossible to make out any facial features.

'That's not Robbie Skinner. He's the wrong shape.' Her gaze travelled across the other three shots. In the others the driver was wearing a long-peaked cap but the physique looked the same. '

Crawley appeared from behind them and leaned in, peering at the screen.

'What are you looking at?'

'CCTV images of a white van we think might have something to do with Mrs Marshall's murder,' Wynchcombe explained.

'Look at the driver,' McKenzie said.

'What about him?'

'Does that look like Robbie Skinner to you?'

He shrugged.

'Could be.'

'What about the hair? Robbie's hair is lighter than that.'

'Maybe he was wearing a wig,' Crawley said.

McKenzie screwed her face up.

'It doesn't look anything like Robbie Skinner.'

Crawley leaned in closer.

'You can't see his face in any of these shots.' He stood up, shaking his head. 'I can't believe you're actually looking for evidence he didn't do it. Course he fucking did it. Just because he's got one of those faces girls go for, all Brad Pitt like, you think he can't possibly be guilty.'

Wynchcombe looked up at him.

'I don't think it's him either. Does that make me a Brad Pitt fancying girl?'

'You said it,' Crawley said, but had the good grace to look sheepish at the same time.

McKenzie turned her attention back to the screen. A puzzled frown crumpled her brow.

'He definitely reminds me of someone though.'

36.

It was late afternoon when McKenzie got the call from the vet's saying that Harvey's ashes were ready for collection. It was almost a relief to have an excuse to leave the office. Her eyes were tired of scrutinising the images of the white van taken from the roadside cameras and she had the start of a headache brewing.

The receptionist said a few kind words as she handed over the precious package. McKenzie managed a grateful smile in reply. It would be good to have him home; to be able to finish saying her goodbyes, now she was better prepared for it.

She set the rainbow-patterned bag on the floor in the passenger footwell and slipped the car into reverse. In her rear-view mirror a large sign for Greengages Garden Centre on the industrial park opposite caught her eye. Seized with an idea, she drove the short distance to the store and hurried inside. Ten minutes later she was back on the road, a large, leafy shrub rustling in her ear as it lolled around in the rear footwell behind her. At home, she headed straight for the garden. By seven o'clock, with dirt under her nails and the trace of tears down her cheeks, she stood back and admired the amelanchier that stood in pride of place in the centre of the garden. The patterned bag and the small box it had contained lay on the floor nearby, their ashy contents buried deep in the ground, sustenance for the shrub.

'Goodnight, Harvey. Sweet dreams.'

She stood for a moment, her eyes roaming the ground in front of her, then picked up the packaging and made her way indoors, her footsteps ringing through the empty house. The quiet suddenly seemed unbearably loud. She peered into the fridge but her appetite had abandoned her. Instead, she poured herself a glass of white wine and ambled into the lounge. In the corner, the answer machine blinked red. Probably Phil. They still hadn't spoken since her *chat* with the lovely Lolly. She hit the playback button. Her mother's voice rang out. Reminding her, yet again, of the crematorium visit. Her heart sank and tears threatened to well up for a different reason this time. Perhaps she was destined to come second in people's lives: second to Pete, second to Lolly, second to Alex's wife...

Where had that come from? Wherever it was, it could go straight back there. But like a child who had spied their daddy stepping out of a Santa suit, somethings couldn't be undone. Her thoughts jumped back to the night Harvey died. When she'd really needed somebody, Alex had been there. Her emotions might have been raw and her perceptions blurred, but there was no denying it: the moment he'd moved in close had stirred a primitive longing inside her. What's more, she was sure he'd felt it too. Or had she misread the situation? Maybe he'd simply been about to put a comforting arm around her shoulder. But what about before... that time he'd punched her ex during a night out. He never had really explained what had happened, and she'd never pushed it. After it happened, she'd told herself it was because he was going through a rough time: his kid was sick, his wife upset. So upset — or jealous? — that for the best part of a year Alex had done everything he could to avoid being alone with her. The only reason he'd do that was if he was in love with his wife, wasn't it?

Maybe she should keep her focus on trying to figure out the psychology behind the players in the two murder cases rather than those in her own life. She took a sip of her chilled white wine and thought about Fern Marshall.

Had she really been a devoted wife, in love with her husband? Had she willingly relinquished her independence, as it appeared she had? Perhaps. McKenzie thought back to the photograph with the lamb on her lap, looking truly radiant, with its inscription on the back, 'Thank you for saving me'. Had Fern Marshall been the one doing the saving and who exactly had she saved? The one thing McKenzie was convinced of was that Karl Marshall had known nothing about that photo. What if the image of their perfect marriage was all in Marshall's imagination? What if she really had found solace in the arms of Robbie Skinner? What if everything Don Skinner hated about his son were all the things Fern Marshall had loved? Was that such a ridiculous proposition?

If it was true and she and Robbie really had been planning on running away together, Karl Marshall wouldn't have been the only man to have had his nose put out of joint. She couldn't see Don Skinner embracing the prospect of having to look after himself. But then Don Skinner had an alibi.... didn't he?

She thought about all the lies already unearthed that week. What if there was one more?

If you took away Skinner senior's alibi for Monday lunchtime, then anything was possible. What if he'd found the message from Fern to his son, suggesting a later meeting? What if he'd replied to it as Robbie, saying he couldn't reschedule, begging her to stick to their usual midday rendezvous. He could have driven to the house and intercepted her. She would have been like a rag doll in his meaty hands. Was it too much of an impossible ask to imagine him keeping her locked somewhere for the afternoon, while he thought about what to do with her, only to find her screaming down the phone for help when he slipped out to check on her? Was that what forced his hand and made him silence her forever? But the man couldn't have been in two places at once.

She thought about her conversation with Sean Campbell. He and Don Skinner went way back; the pair of them had both been out drinking the night Robbie's mother died. And what was it Robbie said about Don commanding loyalty from his associates? Perhaps it was time to question that loyalty.

Campbell answered on the second ring.

'Mr Campbell. It's DC McKenzie. My colleague and I spoke with you the other day.'

'You're the pretty one, yeah?' he said, with a soft slur. She heard him laugh at his own joke.

'Mr Campbell, I'm sorry to bother you again—'

'Don told me you were a pain in the arse. He wasn't wrong. What do you want now?'

'I wanted to check the times Mr Skinner was with you on Monday lunchtime. I wondered, if it was possible that he arrived later than you recalled, maybe closer to one o'clock?'

'If I said one o'clock, I meant one o'clock.'

'You didn't say one o'clock, you said just after twelve. I was asking—'

'Asking, shmasking. Don't you lot have better things to do?'

Suddenly she was listening to dead air. He'd put the phone down on her. She slumped back in her seat, wondering why she couldn't just take it at face value and accept Robbie Skinner was their man.

**

The next morning, it came as no surprise to McKenzie to learn that Don Skinner had been released, with Robbie remaining the only viable suspect. She hurried in to see York. After a night tossing and turning, she knew she needed to share her thoughts with him.

'I couldn't sleep last night, worrying that we've arrested the wrong guy.'

York raised an eyebrow.

'Go on.'

'I started by asking myself, why would Robbie Skinner remove Mrs Forker's kidney? It doesn't fit with who he is. And as for the idea of him taking Fern Marshall's womb and foetus to stop us proving the baby wasn't his, well... The whole idea that he's a demented serial killer, who collects organs as some sort of weird retribution for the fact his mother was killed and her organs donated just doesn't fit. Not least seeing as forensics suggests the kidney was fed to the dogs. I know you suggested he might have taken the kidney to give the impression of a serial killer, but we have to remember, the likely reason Mrs Forker was killed was to stop her revealing the identity of the man she saw on Tuesday morning. Why would seeing the public appeal have jogged her memory? If it was Robbie, I would have expected her to recognise him sooner. They were neighbours after all. And if it wasn't Robbie, someone went to an awful lot of trouble to make it look like it was. When she called me, Mrs Forker said—'

York's mobile started to ring. He picked it up and glanced at the display. He swiped the screen, rejecting the call.

'It's only Mel. I'll call her back when we've finished. Probably wants to change the kids' pick-up time or something. You were saying?'

'Mrs Forker... When she called and said she'd recognised the jogger she saw on Tuesday morning, what she said was...' She paused. Her mouth fell open. 'Oh my God.' She started to shake her head.

'What is it?'

'I need to go and think about it some more.' She rose from her seat.

'You do that. Let me know when you've figured whatever it is out.' He picked up his phone and hit redial. 'Mel, it's me. Sorry about that. I was in a meeting. What is it?'

McKenzie stood immobile, as another piece of the puzzle slotted into place.

York put his hand over the mouthpiece.

'Close the door on your way out.'

She walked trance-like to her desk. With every step, her thoughts came together to clothe the skeleton of her idea. Was it really possible?

A minute later she was talking on the phone to one of the force's forensic IT team.

'Sure, it's possible,' the young woman said. 'It's not even difficult.'

'For you maybe.' McKenzie reached for her pad and pen. 'Give me the Janet and John version.' Five minutes later, she ended the call and hurried over to Wynchcombe. 'Spence, you know the white van that got torched? Have you got details of which cameras clocked it between the date it was sold and when it was dumped? I know it was heading towards the Skinners' place around midday Monday, but I need to know where it had been before that.'

'No problem.' McKenzie returned to her desk and began to pore over an OS map. A couple of minutes later, Wynchcombe called to her, 'I just sent the details over.'

She opened the document and began to check its contents against the map. Soon her heart was banging in her chest at the realisation she might be right. She mapped out the movements on a print-out of the map. It might have looked like a dot-to-dot picture with half the dots missing, but what there was all fitted. She needed more. She thought about the route she now believed the van had taken. Most of it was given over to commercial premises — offices, warehouses and the like — which meant there was a good chance there would be private CCTV systems she could request access to. She opened Google maps, selected street view and started a virtual tour of the area. Shortly, spotting a refuse lorry she was seized with an idea. A few minutes later she was on the phone to the manager of the commercial waste collection company whose truck it was. After convincing them of her identity, they happily consented to letting her have the dashcam footage from the vehicle that had done the rounds the previous Monday. Half an hour later, after having seen what she'd least expected, she gave a sigh. The facts were the facts, but all the same, it was hard to believe. And if she was having a hard time believing it… it was a sure sign she needed more. A lot more.

She thought back to every conversation, every piece of evidence. Somewhere amongst it all, she would find the evidence they needed. First job was to go back and fill in the gaps. She picked up her phone and called the one person she knew would have answers.

Shortly, she ended the call and sat stony faced. Now she knew her suspicions were more than flights of fancy. Not only was her hypothesis possible, but it was looking increasingly probably. Yet still, it came down to the psychology… the why. Why had they done what they did? Without that everyone was going to have a hard time believing it. Perhaps the answer could be found in the past?

After a short trawl of the internet and a few quick calls, she picked the phone up one last time, for what turned out to be a conversation that made sense of it all. At last, she knew how it all fit together.

She looked over to Wynchcombe.

'Spence...'

He spun around in his seat.

'Yeah?'

'The guy that sold the van... I take it you asked him in to look at some mugshots?'

'Yes. Though I expect he'll drag his heels, seeing as he's got to come all the way over from Surrey.'

'Can you call him, put a bit of pressure on? If it's a problem, tell him we'll send someone over to get him. I'll go and get him myself if I have to.' Wynchcombe nodded and picked up the phone as she started across the room.

York was alone in his office. Spread across the surface of his desk were six blown-up images of a car. He stared down at them. The lab had done a good job. An excellent job, in fact. Better than expected. There was no mistaking the zoomed-in face or number plate. He blew out a sigh. A knock at the door tore his attention away. McKenzie peered in. He quickly gathered the photographs together, slipping them into his drawer and gestured for her to enter.

McKenzie came in, eyes alive with excitement.

'Have you got five minutes?'

'Sure.'

She perched on the edge of the seat opposite.

'This might sound crazy but what if we're wrong about the timing leading up to Fern Marshall's death? With things as they are, Robbie Skinner is the only person who could have done it, but if you challenge some of our assumptions, well... you get a very different set of possibilities.'

York frowned but said, 'Go on...'

For the next few minutes, in broad brush strokes, McKenzie painted a very different picture of how the two women's murders might have happened. When she finished, York steepled his fingers and pressed them to his lips. He sat like that for a while, before looking her in the eye.

'It is going to be tough proving it.'

'I think I know how we can do it. The first thing we need to do is—'

The phone started to ring. York answered it. As he sat listening, his eyes slowly grew wide.

'And you're sure it's hers... even from that small sample? Okay, thanks for letting me know.' He returned the handset, shaking his head. 'Well, well. Looks like Don Skinner's got some explaining to do.'

37.

York and McKenzie continued to work on their plan and by the time the afternoon briefing came around, it was as tight as Crawley's trousers. York handed the floor over to McKenzie, asking her to run through the latest hypothesis for the murders of Fern Marshall and Bridget Forker. She stepped forward and delivered her ideas, her excitement growing as each stage of her thinking slotted in like the cogs in a well-oiled murder machine.

'The phone call Mrs Forker made to me the night she died is the key,' she said. 'The actual transcript of the call has been printed and is on the board,' she pointed to one of five whiteboards lining the walls. 'Without trying to make any excuses, you can see the call was a little garbled, which is why I didn't pick up on what she meant at first. It was only after I—'

Crawley leaned in to DS Bells.

'I, I, I... What happened to "there's no I in team"?'

York shot him a sharp look. Crawley looked down and crossed his arms like a sullen schoolboy.

With the occasional adjunct from York, McKenzie went on to outline a plan that would set in train a course of events designed to give them the vital evidence they needed. With everyone briefed, the team broke up and started to put the plan into action.

The following morning, after a sleepless night, McKenzie entered the station pumped and ready to go. At 8:00 a.m. the custody suite called. Sean Campbell had arrived. She hurried downstairs to find him leaning against the wall, waiting for her.

'Mr Campbell, thank you for coming.'

He regarded her with watery, blood-shot eyes.

'Did I have a choice?'

She led him into an interview room. DI York was there already. Half an hour later they escorted Campbell to a holding cell and left him contemplating a charge of aiding and abetting.

'So far, so good,' she said, as she and York made their way back upstairs.

'Don't count your chickens. That was the easy bit.'

As they entered the office, York's phone could be heard ringing in his glass box. He rushed in and snatched it up. He listened for a minute then hung up. He gave McKenzie, who was waiting at the threshold, a thumbs-up, then picked up his mobile.

He eased back in his seat and waited. Shortly he sat upright and said, 'Spence, it's Alex. How far away are you? Oh, okay. Call me the second you get here.' He swivelled his chair around and said to McKenzie, 'Spence reckons he's a couple of minutes away. Given we need him for the next bit, I'll wait here until he's arrived, while you go down and stall.'

McKenzie jogged lightly down the stairs. At the bottom, she rounded the corner and passed through a pair of large glass sliding doors. She spotted Karl Marshall standing to the side of the reception desk, languidly scanning a public noticeboard. Just as she started towards him, the external door opened and she instinctively looked. There, clutching the elbow of a tall, leggy blonde, was Simon Parry. His face lit up on seeing her.

McKenzie stopped and looked at him, a confused frown on her brow.

'Mr Parry. What are you doing here?'

'What do you think? We've come to see you.'

'But… did someone call you and ask you to come this morning?'

Because they shouldn't have.

'No. We've just come to explain. This is Anika. The woman I was with on the Monday that Fern died.'

McKenzie cast a glance over to Karl Marshall, who still had his back to her.

'Mr Parry. I really don't have time to—'

Ignoring her, Parry turned to the blonde.

'Go on, tell her.'

'I'm Anika Mostue. You called me the other day, asked me if I was with Simon on Monday. I know I said I wasn't, but I lied.' Her eyes met McKenzie's fleetingly. 'I'm sorry. I didn't realise how serious it was.'

'That's okay Ms Mostue. Perhaps you can put that in an email and send it to me, only I'm—'

Parry pushed his fingers through his hair.

'We need to do this now. I can't have it dragged out any longer. Melissa's moved back in with her mum. Says she can't live with a suspected murderer.'

'I swear, he was with me all Monday afternoon, until early evening,' Ms Mostue said. 'I didn't tell you before because…' She shot Parry a dirty look. 'Simon didn't tell me he had a girlfriend until he was about to leave my hotel room, when I asked him if he wanted to go out sometime.'

McKenzie shot Parry a look of her own, then said, 'Look, it's fine. Now you've told me, you're okay to go.'

'That's it? Seriously?' Parry looked dumbfounded.

293

'Yes.' She flashed his companion a warm smile. 'And Ms Mostue, thank you for doing the decent thing. And I don't just mean talking to me today.'

With the unexpected visitors dispensed with, McKenzie started towards Karl Marshall.

He turned, alerted by the click of her heels on the tiled floor, and waited as she approached. No outstretched hand this time.

'Good morning, Mr Marshall. Thank you for coming. Have you signed in?'

He waved a visitor badge in her direction.

'What's happening? Detective York said something about new evidence.'

'That's right.'

'What is it?'

'I'd rather leave that to the DI to explain.'

'So where is he then?' Marshall snapped.

As she went to reply, the external door whooshed opened. McKenzie looked over as Wynchcombe ushered in a small, wiry man with stubby grey hair that stood up on his head like iron filings.

'Spence,' she said, nodding as Wynchcombe led the man towards the desk.

The man glanced over as he passed, then suddenly stopped walking.

'Hey...' he said, nudging Wynchcombe with an elbow. 'That's him.' He pointed towards Karl Marshall. 'That's the guy who bought my car.'

McKenzie looked at Marshall.

'This gentleman seems to know you.'

'He's mistaken.' He turned on his heel, presenting his back to Wynchcombe and the older man.

'That's definitely him,' the wiry man said, before stepping around Marshall to face him. 'Hey, you... don't you go ignoring me. You're the reason I've had to come all the way over here. On my day off, too.'

Marshall observed the man down the length of his nose.

'I'm sorry. I have no idea what you're talking about.'

'The hell you don't. Two bloody hours it took me to get here.' The man turned to Wynchcombe. 'I don't need to see any pictures. It's him. Now can I go?'

Marshall unclipped his visitor badge and offered it to McKenzie.

'Please tell DI York that I don't appreciate being kept waiting. I'm going to have to go. I've got a meeting at eleven.'

Just then the lift stopped with a ping. The doors opened and York stepped out. He looked at McKenzie, who nodded in reply.

'Mr Marshall, thank you for coming.'

'I'm sorry, but I'm going to have to go.'

York looked at him and frowned.

'You only just got here.'

Marshall roughly pulled up his cuff and looked at his Omega.

'I've actually been here for over five minutes.'

'You can't spare five minutes for the investigation into your wife's murder?'

He looked at York's unsmiling face and issued a sigh.

'Of course. So, what's so urgent that you needed me to come in?'

'We need to check your phone for details of the call from your wife. It shouldn't take long.'

Marshall reached into his pocket. He pulled out his phone but just as he was about to hand it over, his grip tightened around it and he pulled it back towards him.

'I don't understand. Check what exactly?'

'We need to confirm the time and duration of the call and the fact it came from your wife's mobile.'

'You can get all that information from the phone networks.'

'I prefer the old way of doing things. Like to see the evidence for myself. I read your LinkedIn profile earlier. Sounds like you're a real whizz when it comes to technology. You must think I'm a real luddite.'

Marshall's brow smoothed; an amused expression alighted on his face.

'Not at all. Besides, my LinkedIn profile might be a little exaggerated. I'm more involved in the sales and marketing side of things these days but it gives people confidence in the business if they think I'm tech savvy.' He unlocked his phone and handed it over. 'Here... if it helps.'

'Thank you. While that's being done, I've got a few more questions, if you don't mind.'

York passed the mobile to McKenzie and while he was ushering Marshall through to the interview rooms, McKenzie slipped through a door to the side of the reception. A solitary figure looked up.

'This is the phone we need examined,' McKenzie said, setting the mobile down on the table. She then reached into her jacket pocket and pulled out two more phones. 'These are the ones for the test. They're all unlocked.'

Leaving the forensic IT technician bent over her work, McKenzie joined York in the interview room; a small windowless box equipped with audio and video recording equipment. It was clean, as far as any communally used room could be, but that was about all in its favour.

'If it's okay with you, I'd like to record our conversation,' York said.

'Are you planning on arresting me?' Marshall asked. 'Because if you are, I want a lawyer.'

'Should we be?' York asked. When Marshall didn't reply he went on, 'At this stage, this is a voluntary interview, which you are free to leave at any point. However, you are perfectly entitled to request the attendance of your legal representative, if that's what you want.'

Marshall waved an impatient hand.

'Just get on with it.'

After setting the equipment to record and running through the formal introductions, York slid a photograph out of an envelope and set it on the table in front of Marshall.

'Do you recognise this man?'

Marshall looked down at the picture. He clenched his jaw.

'That's the bastard who killed my wife.' He pushed the photograph away so violently McKenzie only just managed to stop it from spinning off the table.

'Do you know his name?'

'Robbie Skinner,' he said, spitting the words out like an insult.

'How do you know his name?' York asked.

'What?'

'How do you know his name is Robbie Skinner?'

'I must have seen his picture on the news or something.'

'It hasn't been on the news.'

'In the papers then… from when there was that trouble at the sanctuary.'

'Mr Skinner wasn't involved in the disturbance at Freedom Farm.'

Marshall shrugged a shoulder.

'I don't know then. I've clearly forgotten.'

'Perhaps you know him from having seen him with your wife?'

'Don't be ridiculous.' He shook his head. 'Fern wouldn't have anything to do with the likes of him.'

'Fern and Robbie Skinner were at school together. Did you know that?'

Marshall opened his mouth, then closed it again. After a short pause he shook his head.

'I didn't know that, but I fail to see the relevance. I doubt Fern would have even remembered him.'

'According to Mr Skinner not only did your wife remember him, but when they met again recently, she was very keen to get to know him better.'

A brooding scowl darkened Marshall's face.

'The man is deranged. Nobody is going to believe that Fern was having an affair with him.'

'Who said anything about an affair?'

'I could tell that's where you were going. And I'm sorry to disappoint, but Fern wasn't having an affair... with anybody. We were happily married. We were about to have a baby for Christ sakes.'

'Were you?'

'You were the one who told me she was pregnant. So, what, now you expect me to prove I was the father, is that it? You know full well I can't, seeing how that bastard ripped the child out of her.'

'Removing the foetus doesn't actually prevent us from learning the identity of the father,' McKenzie said. 'I doubt many people realise it but foetal blood appears in the mother's bloodstream as early as seven weeks and remains there until well after the birth. The pathologist has in fact succeeded in obtaining a paternal DNA profile from Fern's blood.'

York set his elbows on the table and leaned forward.

'Do you still maintain you were the child's father?'

Marshall shrank back in his seat and let his gaze drop to the scarred table top. Shortly, he cleared his throat and gave them a doleful look.

'I don't know what to think any more. If I wasn't the father then I'm sorry Fern didn't feel our marriage was enough for her. It certainly was for me. And despite what you think, I never for a second suspected her of having an affair.'

'So you never fitted a tracking app on her phone?'

'I may have. I can't recall. I test all manner of devices. Part of our product development strategy depends on keeping abreast of the market.'

'I thought you were more sales and marketing these days.' When Marshall gave his best stony silence, York asked, 'What you were doing on Monday between midday and two o'clock?'

Holding York's gaze, Marshall replied, 'I was in a meeting.'

'Are you sure?'

'Yes.'

'We were told you left the office shortly before twelve to go for a run,' McKenzie said.

Marshall didn't react at first. Then his eyes tracked sideways and fixed her in his sights. He stared at her for a long moment, then said, 'Whoever told you that was mistaken.'

'Your PA doesn't seem the sort to make a mistake like that,' she replied.

'You've been checking up on me.'

'It's a murder investigation,' York said. 'We've been checking up on a lot of people. You were out of the office for almost two hours.'

'I forgot. I went out for a training session. I've got a marathon in a couple of months.'

'I understand the meeting you chaired Monday afternoon — the one you were in when the call came from your wife — had originally been scheduled to start at one. Why did you change the start time to four?'

'To accommodate people who couldn't make the earlier time.'

'According to your PA, you asked her to change it so you could fit your run in,' McKenzie said.

'Why the hell ask me if you already know the answer?' Marshall replied calmly. 'You do like wasting people's time, don't you detective?'

McKenzie ignored the slight and asked, 'Do you normally arrange your business affairs around your exercise plan?'

'Where on earth is this going?' The two detectives looked at him, saying nothing. Marshall eased back in his seat and let out an exasperated sigh. 'To answer your question, no I don't but I had meetings scheduled for the rest of the week. I knew if I didn't get out for a run then, I wouldn't get the chance any other day. As Monday's meeting was internal, it was easy enough to change the time, so I did… it's called management's prerogative.'

'Which route did you take on your run?' McKenzie asked.

'God, really?' Eventually Marshall said, 'I left the office, turned left down to the bridleway along the old train line, then I crossed to Green Lane, then went up as far as—'

'So you ran past your company's warehouse?'

'Yes. The path runs behind the boundary fence.'

'Do you have any staff based at the warehouse?'

'No. It's a storage facility, we use it to hold stock when we do a large fit-out.'

'Like computers, monitors, keyboards… that sort of thing?'

'And other hardware. Yes.'

'Generates a lot of waste, I imagine. Cardboard boxes and the like.'

Marshall rolled his eyes. 'Yes. What of it?'

'Only that it means you have a regular commercial waste collection, which happens to be on Monday mornings.'

Marshall shrugged.

'So?'

'We've been lucky enough to get the dashcam footage from the firm that does your collections.'

McKenzie tapped away on a laptop on the desk in front of her. She spun it around for Marshall to see. On the screen was the image of a large industrial waste bin.

'Eleven a.m. Monday morning. Notice what else is in the picture...' She pointed out a small triangle of white that could be seen jutting out from behind one of the bins. 'I'll run it forward a few frames. Keep watching.' Slowly, the camera advanced and the bonnet of a white van appeared, tucked in the corner behind the bins. 'Recognise it?'

Marshall's eyes flicked to the image and then away again.

'No.'

'You didn't notice it as you ran past?'

'No.'

'This van was seen parked near to where your wife's body was found, Monday lunchtime.'

'Really? Then why are you both sitting here with me and not out looking for whoever was driving it?'

'Because we know who was driving it.'

Marshall fixed her with his flint grey eyes.

'You've got evidence of who was driving it? Stand-up in court type of evidence?'

York raised a hand.

'We'll be okay in court, don't worry about that.'

Marshall went to say something, but a knock at the door caused him to pause. As York briefly explained the interruption for the benefit of the recording, McKenzie crossed to the door.

She stepped out of the room, before returning a moment later, carrying a clear plastic evidence bag containing a mobile phone, plus two other mobiles. She returned to her seat and set all three items down onto the table.

York turned back to Marshall, who was eyeing the row of phones suspiciously.

'What was I saying...? Ah yes. Evidence. That's what it always comes down to. You know, people are rarely clever enough to cover their tracks completely. People don't realise that the adrenalin rush that comes with committing a criminal act can make you overlook the silliest of things. We see it all the time.' York eased back in his seat.

'This is all very interesting but I see you've brought my phone back.' He gestured to the mobile in the evidence bag. 'So, if we're done here...?' He rose out of his seat.

York set out a hand.

'Please sit down, Mr Marshall. Just a few more questions.'

'Look. I've tried to be helpful. I've sat here, answered all your ridiculous questions, but I really must go. I have business to attend to.'

'What if I told you your wife didn't die at four o'clock?' York said. Marshall's head snapped up. 'What if I told you she was killed earlier, at lunchtime, while you were supposedly on your run?'

'I would say you were talking rubbish. My wife called me at four and presumably your so-called IT expert was able to confirm that — that was the whole point of checking my phone, wasn't it?'

'Not the *whole* point exactly,' York replied. 'Though you're right. We know you received a call from your wife's phone when you say you did. But whether it was your wife calling...' He let the comment hang in the air and picked up one of the unbagged phones. 'We're such slaves to technology, don't you think? Especially now they do so much more than just make and receive calls. I mean they can play music or track the whereabouts of loved ones. But most people set limits on their usage. For example, if I'm in a meeting, I switch my phone to silent. According to your PA, you usually do the same. I take it you must have just forgotten on Monday, eh?' Marshall said nothing. York returned the phone to the table. 'It must have been a terrible ordeal, having to listen to your wife crying out for help.' Marshall pinched his lips together and nodded. 'Do you remember whether she called your name or was it just a scream?'

'She…' He swallowed heavily. 'She cried my name, asked me to help her. I tried to get her to tell me more, but…' He buried his face in his hands and took a deep breath.

'Your PA couldn't recall hearing your name,' McKenzie said. 'The way she described it was more of a series of screams… like something from a horror movie, she said.'

Marshall fixed her with a hard stare.

'Why are you even bothering to ask me anything? Just ask Dawn. Seems she's got all the answers. Of course, she wasn't the one who actually took the call. I was. But why let a fact like that get in the way?'

His rant might have continued, only the phone York had returned to the table lit up, a number appearing on its screen. Three seconds later, the second unbagged phone lit up and started to emit an annoying jingle. Marshall stared at them both with an expression that was a cocktail of confusion and unease.

York reached for the ringing phone and swiped the screen, unleashing a nerve-jangling scream.

Marshall jumped out of his seat and took a few steps away from the table, staring at the phone with a maniacal expression.

'Make it stop!' he shouted.

York waited until the screams had stopped then ended the call with a single swipe of his finger.

Marshall took a deep breath and ran his perfectly manicured fingers through his hair. He approached his chair and pushed it underneath the table.

'I'm leaving.'

'Mr Marshall, please sit back down,' York instructed.

'You drag me in here under the pretence of a new development then force me to listen to some sick imitation of my wife's dying moments. You have totally overstepped the mark.'

'What you just heard was a recording,' York said. 'Not of your wife, but a different woman. Probably taken from a horror movie. But you'll know that better than us. We found it in a sound file on your mobile phone.' Marshall clenched and unclenched his jaw. York continued, 'What you've just witnessed was a rather crude experiment to test our hypothesis of how you killed your wife, who we know you attacked at lunchtime. Not at four o'clock, which is the time you intended it to look like. We know all about the elaborate set-up, the fact you used an auto-dial app on your wife's phone to make the call at four o'clock, at a time when you'd be safely alibied in a meeting. The app that *you* installed on her phone. You then answered your phone, which had a different app on it that triggered it to play the sound file of a woman screaming. Once the sound file got to the end, you then terminated the call and established yourself the perfect alibi.'

McKenzie took over, 'Or would have done, if you'd had the sense to get rid of your phone as well as your wife's. You of all people should realise it's impossible to completely remove all traces of an installed app.' She paused for a second, before delivering the final blow, 'Oh, and you forgot to delete the sound file. What you just heard was the exact recording you played in your meeting.'

Marshall regarded her coolly.

'You've proved nothing more than I'm a bit of geek who likes installing unusual technology on my phone and I've got a penchant for horror movies.' His lips curled into a sly smile as he shook his head. 'Your entire theory is based on supposition. So what if I've got an app that plays a sound file triggered by an incoming call? Fern would have needed to have had an auto-dialling app on her phone and I would have had to set it to go off at four, and you've no evidence any of that actually happened. Plus, you're forgetting that I had no idea where Fern was. As far as I aware, she was at home.'

'You knew exactly where she was,' York snapped. 'We know your wife had a second phone she used to communicate with Mr Skinner on — a phone she tried to keep hidden from you. Only, you found it and used it to send a message to Mr Skinner, rearranging their usual Monday rendezvous from lunchtime to four o'clock. Naturally, your wife, not being party to the deceit, went to the treehouse the same time as usual, only when she got there, it was you she found waiting, not Robbie.' York set his hands wide on the table in front of him and leaned forward. 'That's when you throttled her and threw her out of the treehouse, breaking both of her legs, before doing the most unspeakable act any man could ever do to a woman. And if that wasn't enough, you left her to rot in that stinking hellhole.' Despite York's voice brimming with anger, Marshall remained expressionless.

'You were seen near the Skinners' the morning after you killed your wife,' McKenzie said. 'A neighbour was walking her dogs when she saw you looking in the verge. No doubt you were looking for Fern's phone that you hid there after setting it to make that call at four. You left it near to the Skinners' place hoping it would lead us to Fern's body and implicate Robbie Skinner in the process.'

'Where is she then, this witness?' He shook his head and smiled. 'You'd have had me in a lineup if what you're saying is true.'

'You know exactly where she is. In the morgue, along with your wife. You found out she'd talked to us and figured the only way to save your skin was to kill her and set Robbie Skinner up even more... I mean who else would take the poor woman's kidney out and feed it to her dogs, other than some deranged slaughterman?'

'If the shoe fits,' Marshall said.

McKenzie shook her head. The man's audacity was astounding.

'What you might not realise is that the witness called me after the appeal aired. She told me you were the man she saw.'

Marshall gave a mocking laugh.

'Now you really must think I'm stupid. If that was the case, you would have hauled me in here days ago.'

'You're right, we would have done — should have done — only I made a mistake. I didn't *listen* to what she was saying,' McKenzie replied flatly, her guilt still bearing down heavily. 'But it's there. Clear as day, on my voicemail.'

York leaned back in his seat and crossed his arms. After a moment spent staring down the man sitting opposite, he said, 'So, Mr Marshall, we have a white van parked near to your workplace on Monday morning, which was later caught on camera approaching the place your wife was last seen alive; we have the van's previous owner who is prepared to swear under oath that you were the man he sold it to; we have you leaving the office at midday around the time your wife was last seen alive; and we have proof that it is possible for your wife's phone to have auto-dialled your number, which, when you answered it, could have played a pre-recorded sound file of a woman's screams, to give the impression you were busy in a meeting at the time of your wife's murder.'

'Sir, you forgot to mention the bank notes used to buy the car with,' McKenzie said, keeping her gaze on Marshall. 'I'm sure when they test them for prints, they'll find a match to Mr Marshall.'

Marshall rolled his eyes and waved a hand in the air.

'Blah, blah, blah. It's all circumstantial. If I had evidence my wife was having an affair, why didn't I just divorce her? That's what people do these days. Isn't it... Detective Inspector York? How is your wife, by the way?' One corner of his mouth twitched into a smile.

'You killed her because she was going to leave you,' McKenzie said. 'And you couldn't allow that. Not again.' Marshall glared at her: his pupils, two malignant pin-pricks, boring into her. She felt her flesh crawl but went on anyway, 'I spoke to your first wife on the phone yesterday. Sounds like she got out just in time.'

Marshall clenched his fist; knuckles shining white. He glanced down, seeming to notice and slipped his hands below the table top.

'The bitch is a liar. Whatever she told you, it's not true.'

McKenzie arched a narrow brow.

'Are you telling me she didn't run away with nothing but the clothes she was wearing and hole up in a women's refuge after years of having to deal with your controlling, abusive behaviour?'

Marshall slammed his hands onto the table top and stood up abruptly to tower over McKenzie. She quickly leaned back as York shot out of his seat. Marshall quickly held up his hands and sat back down.

He smoothed his hair down and, without missing a beat, said, 'Do I look like the sort of man who beats his wife?' Yet despite his words, his eyes glinted dangerously.

307

McKenzie resumed her previous posture, cleared her throat, and replied, 'Appearances can be deceptive… seeing that it turns out you are a man who knows exactly how and where to punch… or bite… or burn without leaving any obvious marks. Probably thanks to two years training in medical school. Your ex-wife was unable to furnish us with the reason you were thrown off the course but we will find out and I'm figuring what ever the reason, it's not going to cast you in a good light.'

Marshall launched himself across the table, reaching for McKenzie's throat. York, twice Marshall's size, threw himself at the other man, knocking him sideways. McKenzie shot over to the door and shouted for back up while the two men grappled on the floor. By the time she looked back, York had Marshall pinned down, face pressed into the dirty linoleum. She walked over, looked down at their murderer and read him his rights.

38.

'Aside from killing and butchering his wife and her baby, the lengths he went to to frame Robbie Skinner are unbelievable,' McKenzie said. They had just finished processing Karl Marshall, seeing him safely escorted to a cell, and were heading back towards the interview rooms.

'Retribution for stealing his wife,' York said.

'And poor Mrs Forker. Talk about being in the wrong place at the wrong time. What I don't get is, if he knew she'd seen him why didn't he kill her on Tuesday? Why wait till Wednesday?'

'Maybe it took him a while to find out where she lived? He could have hung around the area, waiting to see her out walking the dogs, and followed her home.'

'On a quiet country lane? She'd have spotted him. I wondered whether he wasn't going to do anything, thinking his disguise had worked, and then somehow later found out she'd seen him and couldn't risk her identifying him. Though I don't know how he could have found out. Not many people knew.'

York suddenly stopped walking. Shoulders slumped, he let out a long sigh.

McKenzie looked at him, surprised at his sudden change in mood.

'What is it?'

He shook his head.

'Just had a thought. And not a good one. It'll have to wait till later though. We need to get Skinner senior out of the way first.'

'About bloody time,' Don Skinner fumed. 'Over an hour I've been stuck here. This had better be good.'

His considerable girth filled the interview room, making the space feel cramped and claustrophobic. Mr Fray, his solicitor, sat primly on a chair at the corner of the table.

York quickly ran through the formalities.

'Mr Skinner, you have been arrested for murder. I understand the arresting officer read you your rights. Is that correct?'

'Yes, and I'll tell you what I told him… you can stick your arrest,' he said, his face as red as the meat he regularly set a cleaver to. 'My friend here…,' he jerked his head in Fray's direction, 'will be lodging my complaint and demand for compensation for false imprisonment faster than I can slaughter twenty head of cattle.' Spittle flew from his mouth and settled on his chin. He wiped it off while glowering at them.

'You seem very angry,' York said.

Skinner looked at his lawyer and jerked a thumb in York's direction.

'Is this guy for real?' He looked back at the detectives and said, 'How many times have I told you? I was someplace else when this woman I didn't even know got murdered, yet here I am again, in this shitty little room having to go over it all… again. I know my rights. You can't keep bringing me in like this.' He turned to his lawyer. 'Howard, for God's sake, say something.'

But it was York who spoke next, 'Mr Skinner, perhaps if you hadn't been so busy shouting the odds at the officers who brought you in, and listened for a change, you might have realised that this is nothing to do with the deaths of Fern Marshall or your neighbour, Mrs Forker. You have been arrested for the murder of Margaret Beech.' York fixed him with a penetrating stare and waited for the penny to drop.

'Margaret Beech...? My Margaret?' Confusion crowded Skinner's flabby features. 'That was years ago. You lot tried to stick me with that back then, but I had an alibi for that too.'

'Ah yes, the trusty Mr Campbell. The same friend who you were out with this week. We had a very interesting chat with Mr Campbell this morning. Likes a tipple, doesn't he? To the extent he admits to regularly—'

'I'm sorry to interrupt Detective, but could you get to the point?' the grey-haired Mr Fray said, pulling up the cuff of his shirt and looking pointedly at an expensive gold watch.

'Nearly there, Mr Fray. As I was saying, Mr Campbell told us how his memory lets him down after a heavy night's drinking. Has done for years, apparently. Anyway, it turns out he had a skinful on the night your ex-wife was killed. He told us that the pair of you spent several hours in the pub before going back to his house for a takeout curry and more drink. He admitted to us today that despite what he told detectives at the time, he actually had no recollection of what time you left his, having been far too drunk. He does remember, however, that you called him the following morning and gave him the news about your ex-wife and made some comment about it being lucky you'd been at his place until ten, otherwise you might have been in a lot of trouble. Being a good friend, he took your comment at face value, and told the investigating officers you were at his until ten o'clock on the night of the hit and run, putting you in the clear.'

'If he can't remember when I left, who's to say it wasn't at ten?' Skinner sneered then turned to his lawyer. 'They can't keep me here on the basis of *that,* can they?'

Mr Fray looked at York and arched a thin, grey eyebrow.

'My client has a point.'

'I would be inclined to agree with you, if that was the only evidence we had. It isn't. Traces of blood and DNA have been found on the white Escort van currently being used by your son. They are a match for your ex-wife, Mr Skinner. It appears the blood and tissue traces had been spray-painted over some years ago. Most likely at the same time a dent in the front right wing was hammered out. You happened to be the registered keeper of said van at the time your ex-wife was killed.'

'I don't believe you.' Though judging from the ashen colour of Don Skinner's face the reality of the situation was beginning to sink in.

'The science doesn't lie. Given you bought the van after your wife had left you, it's difficult to see how her blood could have got on it, other than at the time of her death, wouldn't you say?'

Skinner opened his mouth to speak, then closed it again. He leaned back in his seat and crossed his arms over his extensive chest.

'No comment.'

***

'All those years her blood was there, waiting for the paint to flake. Lucky for us he's a tight bastard and gave the van to Robbie, otherwise we'd never have known,' McKenzie said, hurrying to catch up with York as he took the steps two at a time. They alighted on the third floor and crossed to the serious crimes office door. 'So, that's it then. Now it's just a matter of dotting the Is and crossing the Ts for the CPS, I suppose. '

'Not quite. A couple of things still need sorting. Like how Marshall found out Mrs Forker had seen him, plus the parcel left on your doorstep.'

McKenzie grimaced at the memory of the head in the box.

'Presumably Don Skinner put it there. Some pathetic anti-authority gesture. Though how he got my address is a bit of a worry.'

'Don Skinner had nothing to do with it.'

'Who then?'

'Not yet. There are a few things I still need to organise. Why don't you grab yourself a cup of coffee and I'll see you in my office in, say, twenty minutes?' He set off, with long, loping strides, head bowed, looking inexplicably troubled.

Exactly twenty minutes later, McKenzie knocked at York's door. Half-way in, she realised he wasn't alone. Sitting in the far corner, partially obscured by the open door, was a slender woman with elfin features and long, dark hair. She looked up.

'I'm sorry. I didn't mean to interrupt,' McKenzie said.

'You're not. Come in. Take a seat.' He gestured to one of two chairs on the opposite side of the desk. 'This is Tania Finch, one of our HR officers. I've asked her to join us. Tania, this is Detective Constable Cat McKenzie.'

McKenzie felt her heart skip a beat and her throat go dry. Had she done something wrong? The only time she'd ever been in a room with a member of the human resources team was when she'd been taken off a case in which one of her relatives was a key suspect. She approached the desk with trepidation.

'We're just waiting for Darren,' York said as she sat down.

Three minutes later, they were still waiting. As York reached for his phone, Crawley's face appeared around the door.

'You wanted to see me, boss?'

'Darren. Come in. Take a seat.'

With his eyes darting between the two women, Crawley closed the door and took the empty chair next to McKenzie.

'I hear Marshall still hasn't fessed up. If you want, I don't mind trying. He might talk to me, seeing as me and him got on quite well.'

'Yes, I noticed you built up quite a rapport with him, didn't you?' York waited until Crawley nodded then asked, 'I take it he never said anything that with hindsight gave any indication he was our killer?'

'Not at all. Mostly he just asked questions.'

'After we filmed the public appeal, you showed him out, didn't you?'

'Yes.'

'Did he ask many questions then?'

'A few. He was upset about the lack of progress and wanted to know what we'd been doing.'

'What did you tell him?'

'I said we'd been talking to the Skinners and were following up with witnesses.'

'When you told him about Mrs Forker having seen a man looking in the verge near to the Skinners on Tuesday morning, did he react at all?'

'Not really. I think he just said he was pleased to hear we'd made some progress.'

McKenzie turned to Crawley, wide-eyed.

'It was you... You're the reason she's dead.'

'What?'

'You told him that she'd seen him.'

Crawley looked at York.

'I didn't say she'd seen him. I said she'd seen a man jogging. It was important to let him know we were on the case. I only did what anybody else would have done. He tricked us all. If it's anyone's fault the old woman's dead then it's hers.' He hooked a thumb in McKenzie's direction. The room fell quiet. Even the scratching of Miss Finch's pen stopped. York's eyes looked as black as a shark's. Crawley turned on McKenzie, 'If you'd traced the phone like he asked and arranged for the area to be searched, we'd have found the body sooner and there wouldn't have been an appeal and I wouldn't have had to talk to him at all.'

McKenzie shook her head.

'You told a key suspect that a witness had seen something and you're trying to blame me?'

'How was I supposed to know he was a murderer? He had a cast-iron alibi.'

Now it was York's turn to round on Crawley.

'You don't share case information with anybody. Ever. Whether they've got an alibi or not.'

'Family liaison officers are always telling people how the investigation is going.'

'It's one thing to say we're making progress, it's another thing entirely to give out witness details.'

Crawley bowed his head, suddenly looking sheepish.

'Sorry, sir. It won't happen again.' After a moment, he looked back across at York. 'Is it okay if I go now?'

'We're not done yet. Not by a long chalk.' York pulled a large brown envelope from out of a drawer. Wearing a sour expression, he placed six blown-up images onto the desk. He slid the first photo across the surface to Crawley. It showed a black BMW saloon heading away from the camera, its number plate clearly in shot. Crawley glanced at the other photos, which were all of a similar vein.

'I take it you recognise the car?' York said.

'It looks like mine, but...'

'But?'

Crawley declined to comment.

315

York spread the photos out, taking care to keep them in the same order.

'Note the date and time these were taken.'

Crawley barely glanced at the photos. A flush of colour had already begun to creep over his shirt collar.

'Where did you go between here and here?' York pointed to the third and fourth pictures, then looked Crawley in the eye.

McKenzie leaned over and studied the shots. The significance of the date and time dawned on her. She looked accusingly at Crawley, who was doing his best to avoid making eye contact with anyone.

'You? It was you who left that disgusting thing on my doorstep? Why? What on earth would make you do that?'

He shrank away from her.

'It was a joke.'

'You mutilate an innocent animal and leave its head in a box outside my house and you think that's funny?' she said, her voice an octave higher than normal.

'I didn't mutilate anything. I got the head from my uncle. I told you, he's a butcher.'

'I don't give a toss where you got it from, what possessed you to leave it outside my house?'

'Cat…' York set a hand out, gesturing for her to ease off, before turning to Crawley. 'Darren, what you did was unforgivable. Not only did it cause considerable distress to one of your fellow team members, it misdirected the investigation into the Skinners, wasted the time of the CSI service and, unless Cat gave you her address, means you accessed her personal details, which you are not authorised to do. I can't tell you how disappointed I am.' York started to gather up the photographs. 'Obviously, there will be a formal disciplinary hearing. In the meantime—'

Once again Crawley bowed his head.

'I'm sorry. I misjudged it.'

'I'm sorry too, Darren, but it's too late for apologies.'

'Are you sure?' Slowly Crawley looked up and addressing York directly, said, 'You know, if there's a formal investigation, I'd have no choice but to mention what I saw at Cat's house... or rather, *who* I saw.'

'You say that like there was something dodgy going on,' McKenzie said. Quickly adding, 'Which there wasn't, by the way,' for the benefit of the HR woman sitting quietly in the corner.

York's brow rolled like thunder.

'You know what, Darren? You have just made what is usually a difficult job that much easier.'

'You don't have a problem then, with everyone knowing you were round at Cat's house at ten o'clock at night?' He looked over to Miss Finch and nodded. 'It's true.'

York rose from his seat and leaned over the desk to tower above Crawley.

'You can tell as many people as you like, you little...' He stopped and clamped his jaw shut. Exhaling heavily, he sat back down. Speaking more calmly now, he said, 'I have no problem with anyone knowing I was at Cat's that evening. Her dog had died suddenly that afternoon and she was upset. I've always made it clear to my team that in return for their hard work and loyalty, they can always count on me when they need moral or emotional support. Now you, Darren, you have broken my trust, and as a result I don't feel able or willing to offer you any support, which is why I want you off the team.' He looked at the HR officer who had stopped writing. 'Miss Finch...'

The HR Officer cleared her throat and in a cool tone said, 'Mr Crawley, you are suspended until further notice. If you'd like to come with me and get your things.' She stood up and started for the door. 'You are required to leave all police issue equipment on your desk and I'll need your warrant card before you go.'

'Fine by me. I could do with a bit of paid leave,' Crawley said over his shoulder on his way out.

'What the hell just happened?' McKenzie said as soon and she and York were alone.

'At least the little shit didn't bother denying it.'

'How did you know it was him? The sheep's head, I mean.'

'Call it a gut feeling.'

'Seriously… gut feeling?'

'Years ago, there was a PC. A nice girl… well, woman, I suppose. Anyway, someone put a photograph of her naked on a noticeboard in her local supermarket. On close inspection it was obvious that her head had been photoshopped onto someone else's body, but to a casual glance it looked real enough. Understandably distressed, the PC reported it and got the pictures taken down. With no obvious enemies, we were in the dark as to who might have done it. And then we got lucky. The lab managed to pull a print from one of the drawing pins used to fix the photo onto the board. The print turned out to belong to one of her colleagues, a sergeant from the same station. Apparently, he'd tried to chat her up; told her he could put a good word in for her, help get her a promotion, if she went out with him. She gave him the brush-off; he took umbrage and that was the result.'

'That's an interesting story, but I still don't get why it made you think of Darren? I mean it's not like I ever gave him the brush off.' She thought fleetingly of the stupid conversation in her car that day, when Crawley had suggested getting her own back on Phil. But she'd never mentioned that to York.

'Because the copper in the previous case only happened to be Detective Sergeant Crawley.'

'Darren's dad?'

York nodded.

'The motive might not be the same. I expect Darren was pissed off at you for being on his case all the time. But whatever the reason, he obviously takes after his old man in coming up with quirky ways of getting his own back. What is it they say? The apple doesn't fall far from the tree.'

'Apart from Robbie Skinner, maybe,' McKenzie said.

'You know what else they say… there's always an exception to the rule.'

39.

In the weeks that followed, York and the team managed to find sufficient evidence to shore up the case against Karl Marshall for the murder of his wife and Mrs Forker.

'There's no such thing as a perfect marriage,' York said, as he and McKenzie emerged from yet another interview where Marshall had tried to convince them of his and Fern's undying love for each other, all while protesting his innocence.

'That's a bit cynical,' she replied, hurrying to keep pace.

'Not really. To make a marriage work you have to make too many compromises, so it'll never be perfect. Anyway, who wants perfect? A good relationship is one where you both feel able to challenge each other while keeping things in balance. Marshall's idea of perfect was like something from the Stepford Wives.'

York stopped at the door to the stairwell and held it open for her.

'Thanks.' She started up the stairs. 'You're right. All the way through this case I kept wondering whether Fern was happy having such little independence. I can see why she might have gone with Marshall in the first place, given she didn't have much at the time and he seemed to have everything to offer, but you can only pretend to be someone you're not for so long. She must have felt pretty trapped.'

'Hence the affair, I suppose.'

'No wonder she and Robbie were drawn to each other; both in the same boat. Poor bloke. First his mum and then Fern... and the baby. At least with his father out of the way, he's got a chance to start again and find some happiness.'

'Talking of starting again, how are you doing, now you're on your own?'

'By on my own, do you mean without Phil or Harvey?'

York shrugged.

'Either. Both.'

'I'm okay. Phil wasn't working out. I don't think either of us were happy. And as for Harvey, he'll always have a piece of my heart. But one thing I do know is, I can't stand going home to an empty house. So...' She smiled and her eyes twinkled. 'I've been in touch with the rescue centre that took Mrs Forker's dogs. It seems nobody's shown any interest in them — not surprising as there's three of them and they're not that young — so I said I'd be happy to give them a good home.'

'Three dogs? That's quite a commitment, isn't it?'

'I need the company and they're a lot less trouble than a bloke. Plus, my neighbour has said she's happy to pop in and see to them at lunchtimes, like she used to with Harvey.'

'Great news then, I guess.'

They alighted on the third floor and started down the corridor, which was empty apart from the two of them.

'What about you?' she asked. 'Are you and Mel still trying to work things out?' When York didn't reply, she said, 'Sorry, I didn't mean to pry.'

He gave her a sideways look.

'It's alright. It's only fair. I asked you about Phil. It's just... well, it's complicated. Always is, I suppose, when there are children involved. So, when do you pick the dogs up?'

'Not until the weekend.'

'Good. Then how about we nip out for a drink after work? Save you having to go home to an empty house.'

McKenzie's heart lurched in her chest. Did that mean she should or shouldn't go?

'We've got a lot of celebrating to do,' he said, with a lop-sided grin that made her stomach flip.

'Why not?' she said.

Why not indeed?

Before you go...

I hope you enjoyed reading Close to Death.

As so many readers rely on reviews to help them decide whether to try a new author, it would mean a great deal to me if you could spare five minutes and leave a review on Amazon or Goodreads.

If you'd like to know more about me and my work, check out my website www.susanhandley.co.uk or follow me on Twitter @shandleyauthor or Facebook @SusanHandleyAuthor

Acknowledgements

Back when Close to Death was still being fleshed out, two individuals were generous enough to bid for the chance to name a character. As a result, Sean Campbell is now immortalised in print as the trusty friend of Don Skinner, and Eileen Brown's mother, Bridget Forker will be remembered as the dog-walker who gave Cat McKenzie a lot to think about. Their bids were part of a charity auction run by the UK Crime Book Club, which raised funds for a very worthy cause; namely the Lighthouse School in Leeds for children with autism.

I must also give a shout-out to Julie Platt and Kath Middleton. Both have once again been a great help getting my scribblings fit for publication thanks to their impeccable sense of what makes good fiction, great grammar and an eye for a typo that any self-respecting author would kill for. I am immensely grateful for their time and invaluable feedback.

Finally, closer to home, I must also say a big thank-you to my wonderful husband, John, for his unstinting support, not to mention his patience and encouragement, as he has the thankless task of reviewing the first draft of everything I write. Ever the diplomat, his feedback helps me craft the best story I can.

Printed in Great Britain
by Amazon

80363083R00187